THE OFFICE RIVAL

KAT T. MASEN

Kat T. Masen

The Marriage Rival

Kat T. Masen

Copyright 2015 Kat T. Masen
All Rights Reserved

Editing by Nicki at Swish Design & Editing
Proofing by Kay at Swish Design & Editing
Cover design by Sarah from OPIUM HOUSE Creatives
Cover Image Copyright 2021
Second Edition 2020
All Rights Reserved

BLURB

Arrogant, cocky, immature—how many ways can I describe
my co-worker?
I should have called in sick that day and stuck to my rule of
keeping my personal life private.
But like always, he got to me and pushed all the wrong
buttons.
Then we made one mistake.
To prove just how much we hated each other...

Presley Malone knew her relationship with her fiancé had
run its course.
The second that ring came off her finger, she didn't expect
to be the pawn in an immature game played by her stuck-up
co-worker.

Haden Cooper enjoyed playing games, and when it came to
Presley Malone, it was all too easy. Miss Know-it-all, with
her over-the-top OCD, was soon going to get a taste of what
it was like to live on the edge.

But what starts as an innocent prank in the office soon becomes an unhealthy obsession.

NOTE TO READER

This book was previously published with the title #JERK
and now has a new cover in addition to being rewritten and
re-edited.

The truth is that Haden Cooper is still a *Jerk*.
So this is my warning to you... you'll hate him, probably
even cuss out loud, and vow *not* to finish the book.
But chances are, you'll fall in love with the Jerk.
And if you do, I promise you'll get your Happily Ever After.
You may just need to fasten your seatbelt first and hold on
for the ride.

PROLOGUE

Haden

The dictionary defines a jerk as a contemptibly foolish person.

That's being nice.

And nice isn't something I do.

Give me something in return, and *maybe* I can play nice. Like the time I sucked up to get that promotion with a made-up title, or when I befriended the local stoner and got an extra stash of weed. And we can't forget about last night with the promise of some sweet pussy, but what a disappointment that turned out to be.

I get what I want because I don't give a damn.

About anyone or anything.

I just want to have fun, but even now, that game is fast becoming old.

I am bored and need a new challenge—something to keep me occupied. And one day, it all just fell into place by accident, of course.

Our office is one giant playground. I dub myself the

school bully, and the Ice Queen is my target. It's her own fault, though. I've never met a woman so fucking uptight where you'd need a whole army to pull the giant stick out of her ass.

It is one juicy ass, though—perky, with that round bounce that you just know will make a terrific sound when you slap it with your palm.

But that is beside the point—way beside the point.

I don't like her stubbornness, nor her obsessive need to have everything clean and in order. I loathe the way she answers every question like a pompous know-it-all bitch. And that ridiculous skirt she always wears which makes her look like a schoolgirl. All right, perhaps there are benefits to that skirt if you picture her in eight-inch heels and a pair of garter belts peeking through, but it is not appropriate office attire.

What irks me most is the way she parades around the office with her nose stuck up in the air—Miss I'm-Too-Good-For-All-You-Juveniles-So-I'm-Going-To-Act-Like-A-Fucking-Grandma.

Yeah, she thinks she is fucking all that. I don't like *women* like her, especially when they parade that ring on their finger like some fucking accomplishment. The guy probably gave it to her because he had a small dick and knew he'd hit the jackpot. Yeah, well, I've got a big dick and probably could teach her a lesson or two.

Then it happened—the day that ring no longer taunted me.

The day the office gossip went into overdrive because Presley Malone was back to being single. The Ice Queen didn't even look sad. I don't even think she shed a tear, and probably Mr. Small Dick found some less-frigid pussy else-where and jumped ship. But a victory for every goddamn cock and balls in the office that went ape-shit fighting over who could get her in bed first.

It is exactly the challenge I need.

And I don't intend to play nice.

Nice is for chumps.

It wasn't a payback, and it wasn't vindictive.

It was clean, harmless fun.

Fuck that... it was *dirty* fun.

There is only one way to get her attention, just one way for her to finally notice I exist. I have to make her life in the office a living hell and push all the right fucking buttons. She is vying for a promotion, and perhaps—so am I. The same very role.

According to her, if it walks and talks like a jerk, then *I am* a jerk.

But I understand the meaning of 'jerk' a little differently—to be a selfish, manipulative, insensitive asshole luring her in by playing Mr. Nice Guy, only to give her false hope and leave her cursing the day I was born.

ONE

Presley

From a very early age, I knew I was different from the rest of the kids I hung around with. I may have only been seven years old, but my mother wasn't shy about telling me I was an old soul with the wisdom of an eighty-year-old. I didn't consider it a bad thing as my grammy was the most beautiful lady who ever existed, next to my mother, of course.

It was the mid-eighties, and the biggest thing to rock my world was the newly released Peaches 'n Cream Barbie. I still remember the epic moment when the box was placed in my hands and how incredibly beautiful she was, dressed in her flowing peach gown and shimmering bodice. Her hair was golden, perfectly styled, and adorning her neck was an exquisite diamond-like necklace fit for a princess. She deserved a special spot on my shelf, and Workout Barbie took a hit, moving out of center position.

My mother would often complain, "Presley, why don't you play with your dolls like other girls?" Well, dear

Mother, other girls had Barbies with godawful haircuts and missing shoes, and rings were a rare commodity.

I had to have everything perfect.

So, you can imagine my horror when I arrived at school the next day, and every girl with their new Peaches 'n Cream doll had short-cut bobs, mismatched shoes, and zero rings. I decided then that my Barbie deserved the best. So, I planned the most epic wedding event of all time.

Barbie was finally going to marry Ken.

I invited all my friends, and under the big oak tree in my backyard, they tied the knot on that sunny September day. The guests oohed and aahed. I overheard my friends commenting on how pristine my Barbie looked, 'fresh out of the box,' and then there was the groom. Ken looked ravishing with his light gray suit and pink pocket square to accentuate his tanned skin and plastic comb-over.

The thrill and excitement of this perfect day were forever engrained in my memory, and at the ripe old age of seven, I knew exactly what I wanted—I wanted to get married to my Mr. Right and live in our two-story dream house.

I had a plan.

The problem with plans is the second they fall apart, you have absolutely no idea how to cope.

Fast-forward twenty years, I was certain that Mr. Right just sat at my table. His name is Jason Hart—tall, handsome, with the deepest blue eyes—and if you stared long enough, it was like looking into the ocean.

We met at a mutual friend's wedding and were thrown together at the shameful singles' table in the back corner of the ballroom. All we needed was a neon sign flashing 'sad and pathetic single people looking for a good time.'

This time, however, the party was at our table. It was a

fun group—we were all in our mid-twenties, looking to get drunk on some free alcohol. Jason was seated directly opposite me, and it was impossible to ignore his flirtatious smile. My ovaries were having a celebration, the party was on, drinks were served, and damn, we would make very cute babies together.

Lucky for me, Jason turned out to be the sweetest guy you could possibly know. It was the perfect story to pass on to our grandkids—met at a wedding, love at first sight, and who could forget the moment I caught the bouquet? Okay, so maybe I was pushing fate by stepping on another woman's foot to dive for the bouquet but so what, bouquet-catching should be declared a sport—it's every woman for herself out there.

The moment Jason grabbed my hand and asked me to dance, I thought, *Yes, he is Mr. Right. He is my Ken, minus the plastic comb-over, of course, and together, we could live happily ever after in our dream house.*

We went through the relationship milestones—moving in together after a year, joining our bank accounts to save for our first apartment, and last year on our fifth anniversary, he popped the big question, and obviously, I said yes.

My parents loved him, and his parents loved me. It was just one perfect moment after another, and to curb my OCD, which had intensified over the years, it was all going according to plan. Until the day I had lunch with my mother and mother-in-law.

We spent hours going through magazines, interviewing wedding coordinators, immersing ourselves in various fabrics, and all the while, alarm bells were ringing in my head. Miss Plan-Out-Her-Whole-Life had absolutely no clue what she wanted. Every magazine page thrown in front of me was showing a blushing bride staring lovingly into her groom's eyes. I couldn't remember the last time Jason and I looked at each other with such love. We were comfortable, but comfortable wasn't perfect. I loved him, it was impossible not to love him, but there was this tiny bug crawling within my gut telling me something wasn't right. I prayed every night that this mysterious bug would grow into a beautiful butterfly and remind me what we were all about.

Yeah, that butterfly never showed up, and that bug had sunken its teeth in even further.

We both were stuck in routine—working late, ordering takeout almost every night, sex on Fridays, and the Saturday trip to the laundromat. The spark which had ignited that day at the wedding had died down to a dwindling fire.

I craved more. Not being sure of what that was, I tried spicing things up by cooking in some nights, a quick rendezvous to The Hamptons for Valentine's Day. Maybe I should have fought harder for us, but we both agreed our perfect relationship had run its course.

"It isn't working out, Jase. It's just... I can't explain it," I spoke solemnly.

Sitting on our sofa dressed in a neatly pressed tux having just returned from a wedding, he leaned back and rubbed his face vigorously with his hands. I, on the other hand, didn't want to cry. This shouldn't be about emotions. Rather, it should be a rational decision between two adults.

"Are we doing the right thing, Jase?"

His voice croaked, but quick to compose himself, he smiled and, as always, managed to say the right words. "We're just so comfortable. I didn't..." he paused then said, "... never mind."

"No, tell me, you didn't what?"

He hesitated at first, then opened up, attempting to relay his emotions. "I didn't think we'd fall into this rut so quickly. Couples get married all the time, and then the relationship becomes a routine."

Remaining quiet, I gave myself a moment to get my words right. "You expect raw and wild sex at random moments, dinners at fancy restaurants, making out at the movies, but it's not like that."

He chuckled heartily. "Presley Malone, I'll sure miss your ways. I hope the next relationship I have won't shoot me for placing my black socks in the same row as my white."

Ouch, that stung a little.

Brush it off, you wanted this. Yes, you loved him dearly, you're just not in love with him anymore. You knew it wasn't right, you knew you wanted more. More what, though?

"But this is so calm. Aren't breakups supposed to be full of tears and throwing bags of clothes out the window?" I asked.

"Yeah, maybe, but we're beyond that. I'll always love you, Pres. But this... this is the best for us. We owe it to each other," he reaffirmed.

He was right. We had given each other five great memorable years. I couldn't have asked for a better person to have shared that with, and now we both needed to see what else is out there in the world.

I wasn't sure if it was proper breakup protocol to hug it out, but I leaned in anyway, and for the very last time, I held on to Jason. His embrace was warm and familiar, and I knew that no matter what happened to me, wherever I go or whatever I do, I have a friend in Jason Hart.

We called off the wedding and parted ways.

Single. Again. At thirty-fricken-two.

Marriage, three kids, and that damn dream house just flew out the window.

What terrified me most was maybe it wasn't in the grand plan for Presley Malone. Maybe fate and the universe got together and said, "Hey, Miss Plan-It-Out needs to learn a lesson in life. Let's screw her sideways and see how she copes."

The problem wasn't fate or the universe—it was the biggest jerk of all time.

My office rival.

And unfortunately, now, I am bound to him.

Forever.

TWO

I am running a marathon and beside me, others speed past threatening to reach the finish line before I do. The adrenaline is kicking in, and just at that point when my legs are about to give out and refuse to carry me any further, the black and white checkered flag comes into sight, waving proudly.

The end is within reach, only a few more minutes, and you'll cross the finish line and crown first place. My heart is thumping loud, ready to burst out of my chest and collapse onto the ground. The sweat beads are forming and dripping down my face. The time clicks over to thirty minutes, and like a strike of glory, I hit stop.

My marathon is actually me running on the treadmill. My lungs hurt so much that I am this close to calling the cute personal trainer over to resuscitate me.

Okay, so I'm being a drama queen.

It's way too early in the morning for this, and let's not forget to highlight the fact that I am a gym virgin. I don't mind a brisk walk or run in the park once in a while, but the gym and I, we're complete strangers.

Since my ex-fiancé, Jason, moved out last week, I have come here almost every day hoping to relieve the anxiety and tension consuming me. It's not like we ended on bad terms. In fact, it was the best breakup you could have asked for—no tears, finances were divided evenly, and we decided to put the apartment on the market and split our profit. I couldn't have planned a more amicable breakup.

The problem here is that it is going way too smoothly, and I can sense something looming on the horizon. No matter what I do I can't shake it off, and so here I am today, sore and working out like I'm about to enter a real marathon.

Maybe I'm telling a little white lie. Yes, there is no doubt my anxiety is stemming from the fact I feel I have no sense of order in my life, but for the most part, I find the gym surprisingly entertaining.

I have absolutely no life right now, and I'm one step away from joining a pottery class.

The treadmill has become my newfound friend. The running becomes mundane at times, which is why I zone out and pretend to run a marathon or watch others around me in amusement.

Take last week, for example—a man fell off the treadmill as a ridiculously made-up gym bunny walked past.

In my first week, I learned a few things—some treat the gym like a sport, dressed head to toe in spandex, often a little too tight around the groin, and the wannabe Arnies huddle in the weights area, grunting and throwing around the barbells as if they were inflatable balloons. You can smell the steroids and testosterone a mile away.

There are some cute men in the Zumba class, but I suspect those men are eyeing the cute Zumba teacher and his perfectly sculpted ass. Boy, does he know how to shake his bonbon.

Today's entertainment consists of two ladies attempting to do yoga on the mats in front of me. I grab my towel and wipe myself down before I sit on the floor beside them. One of the women, Trina, works at a marketing firm on level ten. We run into each other often and got to talking one day. She's a nice enough girl, a little naïve, which is expected since she's in her early twenties.

"Be honest, I'm hot, right?" Trina asks, looking at the woman beside us. "Oh, Presley, this is Sarah, she works on six."

I smile at Sarah, and she smiles in return. We then look at each other awkwardly, questioning if we should answer Trina. Perhaps it's a rhetorical question.

Sarah screws her face into a grimace, yet indulges Trina with a response. "Look, Trina, of course you're hot. Get over him. Sounds like a douche to me."

"But... but we had a connection," she confesses innocently.

Sarah snorts. "The only connection you had was when he stuck his pecker in your bird hole. A dime a dozen, Trina. Let it go."

In my uncomfortable pose, I try my hardest not to laugh at Sarah's comment, but I do and attempt to cover it up by leaning forward and stretching my legs to the point they scream in agony.

"It isn't just about sex, we flirted for weeks. He even mentioned something about visiting his mom."

"Oh, the mom card. That's pretty serious," I admit.

Trina nods in agreement, looking heartbroken.

With a hint of sarcasm, Sarah asks, "Uh-huh and remind me again what happened?"

"He left in the middle of the night without saying goodbye and has avoided me ever since," Trina mumbles.

"Okay, so put your big-girl panties on and forget about him!"

This time, I agree with Sarah. Only a loser would do that, and the worst part is, this is what I had to look forward to being single.

"I have to agree with Sarah. He doesn't seem worth it. You're young, beautiful, and surely can find better fish in the sea."

"But he's the prime catch," she pouts.

Sarah butts in, "And tell Presley who paid for dinner that night, the taxi ride back to the hotel, *and* the hotel room?"

Trina appears to be agitated at Sarah's blast of information.

"It was a misunderstanding."

"Right, as was the accidental text he sent to you instead of another woman about how he was going to screw her brains out the night after he left you?"

Ouch.

"Trina, do yourself a favor and seriously grab another fishing rod because he's so not worth your time." With my water bottle and towel in hand, I stand to head on out. "Listen, ladies, I have to get to work. Sarah, don't let her go anywhere near this douchebag."

Sarah salutes me. "Once a douche, always a douche."

After showering at the gym, I dress in my new designer white blouse for the very first time. It took me *forever* to save up for it. In fact, I have several bank accounts I coordinate with my paycheck, and finally, my 'special' account had enough money to purchase this gorgeous blouse. It taunted me for weeks in that boutique window. I am so in love with it that I spend minutes staring at the mirror, eyeing myself from every angle. To complete the outfit, I'm wearing my vintage gray pleated skirt which kind of looks like those skirts we used to wear in school, but it's my absolute favorite piece.

With my black pumps on, I shove my gym gear into my bag and quickly apply some makeup. If I'm on the market, I need to take better care of myself. Then it dawns on me how unfamiliar it is to be alone, and the thought of finding someone new fills me with fear. Thank the Lord I'm not Trina, though, and being thirty-two should make me wise enough to avoid the douchebags who lurk in the city.

My hair is always quick to misbehave, so I run some product through it and let it out. I may control and plan everything in my life, but my hair will forever be untamed. Bouncing curls may be ideal to some, but I call it a walking disaster.

It's just before nine when I make my way into the office. Honestly, there is nothing more enjoyable than sitting in a quiet office before all the mayhem begins.

I have been working at Lantern Publishing for almost ten years, starting as a junior and working my way toward my goal of Editor-in-Chief. It's not as big as other publishing houses, but we retain good staff, and together, we work well.

At times, my job is repetitive, reading manuscript after manuscript with no end in sight. Occasionally, that golden egg hatches, and there is nothing more exciting than holding the next bestseller in your hands.

After working long hours last week, I feel confident

pitching a new manuscript to my co-editors in a few hours. My presentation is ready to go, and I have prepared myself for the usual questions or negative comments that might arise.

My steaming hot tea sits on my coaster beside my computer monitor. Allowing it to cool down, I arrange my pens in order from shortest to longest and place my Post-it notepad in exact alignment with the pens. I glance over at the clock, and the second it flicks to nine, I turn my computer on and start scouring through my emails.

The noise starts to invade the office floor as colleagues drag themselves in, fleeing to their cubicles as they talk above the partitions. I try my best to avoid the distraction, but office gossip is difficult to ignore, especially when the office tramp, Dee, starts talking about her Saturday night. Talk about loose lips, and I don't mean the ones on her face.

I reach for my mug and throw the tea bag into the trash, pulling the mug toward my lips. I allow the steam to linger when all of a sudden, my seat jerks forward, and part of my tea lands on my keyboard and blouse.

"What the f—"

"Office 101, no cussing in the workplace," he interrupts.

The hot liquid scalds my skin, and I turn to see who knocked into me so carelessly.

I grit my teeth to control my temper. My vision is all red with his face as a target.

The fucking asshole.

Haden Cooper—my office rival.

Do not encourage childish behavior. I'm not giving him anything to work with.

Grabbing some tissues, I attempt to wipe my blouse. The brown stain seeps through the loose white fabric. *Just great*. Months of saving for the ridiculously expensive blouse only for it to be ruined with a tea stain.

His hands land firmly on my seat, and he swivels me around until we are facing each other. I am ready to blow and give it to him but am distracted as he grabs some tissues and attempts to wipe down my blouse.

"Um, excuse me? Get your filthy hands off me." I push his hands away, his widening smirk indicating how much he's enjoying this.

"Sorry about that, you're a little wet and stained."

"Well, no shit. The next time you want to play dodgem cars with your office chair, have some respect for your colleagues around you," I huff.

"Aww, what's wrong, Miss Malone? Sounds to me like someone woke up on the wrong side of the bed."

I stop wiping my blouse, abruptly moving my head until my eyes meet his. Never having paid this much attention to him before, I stare directly into the hazel eyes that sit behind his thick, black-rimmed glasses. Tiny freckles are scattered across his nose, and his annoying smirk is accentuated as his lips purse together. For some reason, my focus turns to his eyebrows, perfectly sculpted on his freshly tanned face. Such a metrosexual. I wouldn't be surprised if he hit the tanning salon along with a hot wax afterward.

The nerve of this fucking asshole to do this today, a Monday morning for Christ's sake, when I have a presentation to do in one hour. And my poor, poor blouse. I had high hopes that it would keep me smiling throughout the whole presentation ordeal.

I no longer care what comes out of my mouth.

Haden Cooper needs a lesson in manners, and I am just about to give it to him when he pulls my chair closer to him, catching me off guard with a devilish grin.

"You know, if you woke up with me, you'd always be on the right side of the bed."

These young guys are their cheesy lines. It's almost laughable.

"Haden, thanks for nothing. Now get out of my way."

I spend close to an hour in the bathroom cleaning my blouse while standing in my bra, trying to dry off under the hand dryer. My heels tap impatiently against the floor tiles. *Argh!* The nerve of him. And to make it worse, what kind of a line was that?

I replay the words in my head, ignoring the lingering sound of his voice. So what if he sounded sexy? He's just playing his usual games. Lately, he's been really getting on my nerves with the extra unwanted attention he gives me.

Thankfully, I borrow a blazer from a fellow employee and button it to cover the stains. Providing the room stays at the same temperature, I can manage.

The boardroom is filling with colleagues, and I prepare my materials, ready to stand at the front of the table. Having done this a dozen times, it has become second nature. Halfway through my presentation, the air becomes stifling hot, and my armpits start to stick to the blazer. *Did someone turn up the heat in here.* It'll be all right as long as I don't sweat where anyone else can see.

As I look at others seated around the table, some are peeling their jackets off while others use a piece of paper to fan their face. My eyes scan the table for the remote to the air conditioning unit but can't spot it for the life of me.

There are a million questions asked, and normally I enjoy answering, but today I am a bitch in heat and ready to tear that smug look off Haden's face. It's clear this presentation won't end as quickly as I want it to, so I take the jacket off and watch as everyone stares at my stained blouse with curiosity.

"Enough with the staring, a moron spilled tea all over me this morning."

"Sounds to me like you need to pay more attention to those around you." Haden snickers.

I shoot him a death stare, ready to tear into him again. No one dares to question me further, so I carry on and wrap up as quickly as possible.

Making my way back to my desk, I slam my notebook and pen down, nearly missing the showdown that's happening beside me.

"I know you don't want me to come up here, but you've been avoiding me."

As the familiar voice continues, I lean my head slightly to see Trina at Haden's desk.

Why am I not at all surprised that the douche is none other than Haden. Of course, he would do something like this. Young, irresponsible—thinks with his dick and not his head.

The voices become muffled until Trina storms off, visibly in tears. I give it a few moments before standing to confront him. He is leaning casually over Dee's partition, and from what I can see, she is flashing some major leg. You've got to be kidding me. Even though it's none of my business, I head over to where he's standing.

"Wow, it's like you have no moral conscience whatsoever."

"What's your problem now, Malone?"

"You just don't care about anyone but yourself. I mean look at me, you don't care that you've ruined a brand-new blouse that cost me a hell of a lot of money. Then you embarrass me in front of everyone in that presentation. And to top that off, you treat Trina like last night's takeout box."

Dee is shocked at my outburst and carefully pulls her skirt down to cover herself up. Haden is livid, and I swear if you look closely, you can see steam coming out of his ears. His eyes have narrowed behind his glasses, and to control himself, he runs his hands through his dirty-blond hair.

"Some mouth on you, Malone. You better watch your back. Human Resources would deem that as harassment."

"Harassment? I'm the victim here. Not you!" I storm off, having spent enough time and energy on him that I forgot all about my best friend, Vicky. She is sitting on my desk when I return, all smiles and giggles, having returned from Paris only yesterday.

"Ah... Mademoiselle Malone," she says in a thick, but fake, French accent.

Defeated, I slump in my chair. "Tell me about Paris in your normal voice, please?"

She sits on the corner of my desk, crossing her legs appropriately. Vicky and I met a couple of years back through mutual friends. At the time, she was having an affair with the biggest loser to walk this earth—a married man with three kids. It ended badly, so from that day on, Vicky vowed to never get into a serious relationship again and is happy to play the field.

"The shopping was fantastic, totally maxed my credit card. The sightseeing was awesome and the men... Pres, like seriously, the French men know how to make you scream so loud, I swear the people at the top of the Eiffel Tower could hear us."

"A one-time type of thing?"

"You know me, Pres. I like my men foreign. Keeps the fantasy alive."

"But aren't you worried about what could happen after?"

"Like what? I'm always protected, you've got to make sure both of you understand it's a no-strings-attached kinda night. Anyway, I met this guy, Jean-Phillipe, and he's been texting me all day."

Distracted by her phone, she types something ridiculously fast into it, then places it on the table.

"So, are you going to finally tell me what happened with Jason?"

"We broke it off. I'm fine, really," I lie, convincingly.

"We so need to get you drunk and in someone's bed, pronto."

"Wait, Vicky, that's awful. I'm not like that. Plus, I'd never do that to Jason."

"How do you know he hasn't done it already? Where did he stay last night?" she is quick to interrogate.

"At a friend's house. And besides, Jason isn't like that."

The thought of Jason being with another woman pulls on the jealous strings I thought laid dormant. I am not that type of girl, and I strongly believe Jason wouldn't so heartlessly jump into the next bed that came along. He is a better man than that.

"Pres, look... I'm not trying to be insensitive. Jason is a guy. Just don't be surprised if he has moved on," she says, this time in a softer tone.

I'm not a big crier, and the thought of crying at work is embarrassing. I can control my emotions, even if Vicky is staring at me like I'm an orphaned child with no shoes on my feet.

"We only broke up last week. His stuff is still in our apartment," I croak.

"Yeah, well, trust me, they only need a minute of being released from the ball and chain."

"I'm not a ball and chain."

"Well, you're not exactly a spontaneous let's-push-everything-off-the-table-and-fuck-like-wild- animals kinda gal either now, are you?"

She has a point, and I can't imagine anything worse. What a mess that would make. And my pens? No, don't go there.

I move my mouse to start up my computer when I notice some excess tea on my desk. Letting out a huff, I grab another tissue to wipe it down. This day needs to be over so I can crawl into bed and forget the world exists. Vicky raises her eyebrow at me, and I unbutton the blazer that I had placed back on, revealing the stained blouse.

Unable to control herself, she laughs out loud, resting her hand on my shoulder with a sympathetic look.

"On the bus ride over here?"

"Nope, just an asshole who's now trying to get into Dee's pants."

"Haden? How can someone so hot be such a royal pain in the ass?"

"Hot? I can't see past the arrogance and petulant behavior. He's like a goddam box of mixed chocolates... you don't know what you're going to get next."

"Dee told me he wanted a threesome on Saturday night. Tried to get with her and her sister."

"Are you joking? How inappropriate."

"Yeah, maybe, but Dee sure looks happy today."

Just when I thought my opinion of him couldn't get any lower, I am proven wrong.

Vicky's phone vibrates on my desk, and immediately

she picks it up with an amused smile and shoves it in my face.

"What am I looking at?"

She points to the message from Jean-Phillipe—it's hot, heavy, and wow, can this man talk dirty!

"What's with all the hashtags?" I ask.

"Oh, it's this thing we do. You know, rather than typing sentences together, we just hashtag a word or a string of words which kind of means the same thing."

Right, I am so out of the loop. Is this how you communicate today with potential lovers? All in hashtags? What happened to old-fashioned flirting? You know, some playful face-to-face banter and a hey-how-about-a-nightcap-at-my-apartment type of wink at the end?

"So, tell me, Vicky, what would you type to describe how much of an asshole Haden is?"

She places her index finger on the corner of her mouth, then as if a light bulb goes off in her head, she says, "Worst day ever #RuinedBlouse #Jerk."

I smile instantly. "You summed it up perfectly."

THREE

Whoever invented the saying 'time flies when you're having fun' had obviously never been knee-deep in manuscripts requiring immediate attention. Thursday rolled around quickly, and being the busiest day in the office, one person is always nominated to do the lunch run. With deadlines hovering over my head like a gray cloud, I quickly passed the buck to someone else.

Deep into the second chapter of an erotic thriller, I feel the presence of someone beside me. The charcoal gray pants are a dead giveaway, and inadvertently, I groan, granting myself some patience to deal with him today. Why the hell won't he leave me alone? I've met my share of annoying human beings, but Haden Cooper takes the cake.

"I'm taking orders," he huffs in annoyance.

I give him my full attention and decide to have a little fun with him. After all, he did ruin a blouse that even the dry cleaners declared to be a write-off. Yes, I will have fun. Serves him right for being such a jerk.

"At my beck and call? Well, I'll have the roast chicken on rye, lettuce, tomato, and no mayo. I repeat... no mayo."

He stares back at me without writing down my order.

"You might want to write it down."

"I have a good memory."

A loose laugh escapes me. "That's funny, I bet Trina down on ten would beg to differ."

His eyes twitch, caught in an awkward moment. I want to see what pathetic excuse he has for this.

"Who?"

"Really, Haden? I don't know how men can just screw around with strangers and not even take a moment to remember someone's name," I rant.

He leans on my desk and rubs the slight stubble on his chin. "You seem awfully interested in my sex life, Presley Malone. Is there something I'm missing here?"

"What?" I shoot back, almost a little too nervous. "Please, I wouldn't touch you with a ten-foot pole. No, make it a twenty-foot pole with an extension. God, you're so insensitive. You don't care about anyone's feelings and have zero respect in the workplace."

"Anything else?"

"You're a jerk."

He leans into me, invading my personal space. "Her name is Trina Flower. I didn't call her back because after the one time we had sex, she cried and said she loved me. There's nothing wrong with sleeping around if it's mutually agreed. Maybe you need to try it sometime." He raises the finger that once held my engagement ring. "And since there's no longer a ring on this finger, maybe that's just what you need."

The fucking nerve! To blatantly come out and suggest such a thing. The vein in my forehead is surely going to burst, and my hands are itching to smack that smirk off his face.

"How dare you say that? You don't know me, and I'm certainly glad you don't. Don't you have lunch to collect?"

He stands up straight, and I relish in the thought of him leaving me alone, the whole conversation disappearing along with him. Why does everyone assume that because Jason and I broke up, we would drown ourselves in meaningless sex with strangers? I am not that person. Before Jason came along, I had slept with three men, and each time I had been dating them for at least seven weeks before I jumped into the sack. It is my rule, and I strongly believe it gives me sufficient time to get to know the person I will be intimate with. And anyway, the mere thought of another man touching me right now makes my skin crawl. I still have a tan line on my finger from where my engagement ring once sat.

Surely, there has to be some rule to follow for breakups. For example, one year of a relationship equals one month before dating, two years equals two months, and so if that is the correct equation, five months is officially my back-on-the-market-and-ready-to-date timeline. I know if I run this past Vicky, she will give me a lecture about how my hymen could grow back, and I would be re-virginized or some bullshit like that.

An hour later, the Jerk returns, throwing a brown paper bag onto my desk before walking away. I pull it toward me as he laughs along with Dee at her desk. Not wanting to eavesdrop because I don't give a shit, I open my sandwich and see mayonnaise spread all over it. I stomp my feet under my desk. I am allergic to mayonnaise. Scooping my sandwich into my hand, I follow his voice until I am standing at Dee's desk, interrupting their flirtatious encounter once again.

"I said no mayo." I shove the sandwich in front of his chest.

Haden pushes it back toward me. "Sorry, princess, I've got the memory of a goldfish apparently. I'm sure you can handle a little mayo. The extra calories won't harm your precious diet."

"It's not about being on a diet. God, Haden, you're a jerk, you know that?"

"Apparently so," he responds, amused.

"I can't even... just stay away from me."

I throw the sandwich into the trash and storm off back to my desk.

By three o'clock, I'm starving. My stomach is making a symphony of noises that sound like a bunch of angry lions. The vending machine provides comfort, but a bag of crisps and a chocolate bar are a far cry from lunch.

I immerse myself in my work until the office starts to clear out for the evening. Knowing I'm going home to an empty apartment makes it hard to leave. For the past week, I have purposely stayed late until that nagging voice inside my head reminds me it was my decision. I chose to let go of a perfectly good man for reasons that still haunt me. Being alone is something I have to get used to, but after five years of having a man beside me every night, sleeping alone has become tough, and insomnia has reared its ugly head.

Tonight, I want to curl up with a good book and visit my fictional boyfriends. The kind of men that drive you crazy yet you can't stop thinking about them when you're nursing the book hangover from hell. It's why our romance sector is our strongest performer.

I pack my things, and just as my monitor shuts down, there is muffled chatter coming from Dee's desk. I make my way toward the lift, happy to put this awful day behind me. Entering the lift, I hit the button to take me to the ground level when a pair of hands push the door open. I look up and see Haden's arm draped over Dee's shoulder. As the doors close, I move as much as I can to the corner and count down the seconds until we hit the lobby. Her lighthearted giggles and a possible pinch on the ass as he whispers something in her ear are highly inappropriate in this confined space.

When the lobby greets us, I have already made my way to the front of the elevator, ready to flee this nauseating display of affection which I'm sure is for my benefit—well, on his part, anyway.

"Have a good night, Miss Malone," he mutters under his breath.

I ignore him, walking as fast as I can and exiting the building into the cool night.

It doesn't take me long to get home, even after I stop off to grab some Chinese takeout. As I open the door to my apartment, I quickly notice that Jason's things are gone. Throwing my purse onto the sofa, I walk around and focus in on the empty mantelpiece where his precious baseball trophies once sat. Even the groove in our sofa has disappeared. The more I walk around, the deeper my heart sinks into my chest. By the time I reach the bedroom, my tears are splattering down my face, and I'm leaning against the wall, then my body slumps to the floor.

It's like he's been erased. Not a single trace of him is left in our apartment, and never did I expect how painful it would be. I had been through relationships before Jason but none so meaningful, and usually, the guy cheated on me or was such a douche that breaking up was an easy and logical decision.

Lost in a pool of tears, it's obvious that I am in denial

thinking I can walk away from a relationship with a man of five years who had only ever treated me with love and respect.

But what am I supposed to do now? The temptation to grab my phone and call him is difficult to overcome. *I am stronger than this.* I've spent enough of my life watching people go through the same thing. Why can't I forget and move on? Sometimes, I wish Jason would have hurt me. Perhaps that would make this easier. Taint his perfect image so our love could never be repaired.

At some point during the night, I peel myself off the floor, ignoring the cold Chinese box that sits on the table. I take a long, hot shower to erase the day from hell and climb into bed with a bowl of ice cream. Having not eaten lunch and skipped dinner, ice cream is the only thing that sounds good right now.

I stare at my phone once again and contemplate texting Jason. It could be an innocent text, a 'Hey, how are you' and not an I-think-we-made-a-huge-mistake kind of text. Just as I type my opening line, a notification flashes on the top of my screen, and I exit out of the current message.

The text is from 'unknown,' but I read it anyway.

Unknown: *I was a little distracted this afternoon with my extracurricular activities so I forgot to tell you that you have a presentation at nine sharp. Have your manuscript review ready.*

This has to be a joke, right? And who the fuck is this? Seconds later, it dawns on me which jerk would send me a text this late. I am emotionally drained, and the last thing I want to do is climb out of bed and prepare a presentation. My fingers, however, are typing at record speed, almost spitting back at him.

Me: *You've got to be kidding me? It's late and how on earth do you think I can do that between now and 9 am?*

I wait for his response, praying I can just shut my eyes and pretend today never happened. In my dreams, Jason is also lying beside me, massaging my shoulders and reassuring me that everything will turn out just fine. My happy bubble bursts as another text appears.

Haden: *How would I know? I'm just a Jerk, right?*

The nerve of him. Reluctantly, I get out of bed and walk into the kitchen. Sitting at the table, I open my laptop and make myself a cup of coffee. Who the hell drinks coffee just before midnight. Time is lost on me until a constant beep startles me, forcing my eyes to open, only to wake up with my head lying on the table. Shit! I must have fallen asleep. I flick the mouse on my laptop, and thankfully, the final page I wrote appears. Quick to hit save, I glance at the time. I have less than twenty minutes to get out of here.

My OCD is causing a mental breakdown. Being disorganized is foreign to me, and all of a sudden, I'm panicked and showering in record speed. With no time to iron, I grab the only dress that is dry-cleaned from my closet and quickly put it on. No time for makeup or my hair to be styled, I rush out the door armed with my purse, laptop, and a bruised apple from my kitchen.

The bus is heaving as usual, and at each stop, I balance myself and poorly attempt getting some mascara and lipstick on. My hair doesn't cooperate, so I shove it up into the neatest bun I can manage while I'm wedged between a man who has a serious case of body odor and a woman who stinks like garlic.

I rush into the building with only minutes to spare, dumping everything on my desk and racing to the board-room with my USB stick. Surprisingly, it is empty when I look around. The owner of our publishing company, Mr. Sadler, strolls in and takes a seat at his usual spot. Great, the Jerk didn't tell me Mr. Sadler would be sitting in on this presentation. There had been talk of late of an upcoming restructure which could land me a promotion, something I am yet to discuss with him. And there had also been a rumor floating around that Haden is to be promoted to the same role. Why on Earth would he get a promotion given the guy barely clocked in. If he wants to rival me for that position, he has no clue who he is messing with. My career is the only thing I have going for me right now.

"Good morning, Miss Malone," he greets me with a genuine smile.

"Good morning, Mr. Sadler. Will it just be yourself today?"

The second I ask the question, the Jerk strolls in casually, taking a seat beside Mr. Sadler. Unlike Mr. Sadler, who came with a notebook and pen, Haden is empty-handed, staring directly at me with a pompous grin.

"It'll just be us, Miss Malone."

To this day, I have no idea what exactly Haden's role is in this publishing firm. Mr. Sadler is a kind man and definitely sees the good in people. He is a great boss, but occasionally I have to question his decisions—like hiring Haden. I am fairly certain Haden is sleeping with some head honcho, given his half-assed attempt to get any work done, plus his timekeeping is nonexistent.

I clear my throat and begin presenting the latest manuscript I have been reading which is well received by my co-editors. Somewhere during my introduction of the characters, Mr. Sadler's phone vibrates, and he excuses himself to take the call. *Great.* If Haden leaves this room alive, it'll be a fucking miracle.

"So, let me get this straight," Haden questions, leaning back into his chair like an arrogant asshole. "The main character, Violet, is a sex addict and somehow meets this twenty-five-year-old virgin who she falls in love with? How is that even possible?"

"It's fiction," I seethe. "Anything is possible, Mr. Cooper."

"Yeah, but give your readers some credit, Malone. A twenty-five-year-old virgin?"

"He was raised by a religious group who believed sex before marriage was a sin. His character moves to the big city, and he runs into this woman at his local grocery store. How is that unbelievable? And I'm fairly certain that the last time you checked, you were missing a vagina and therefore have no clue what women want."

"Quite snappy this morning, Malone. Something keep you up?"

I am ready to pounce on him when Mr. Sadler pops back in and asks me to resume. I do so without looking at the Jerk, and by the end, Mr. Sadler is pleased and asks to see a final presentation by the end of the month.

He leaves the room, and I pack up my materials in silence.

"Perhaps next time, you prepare in advance. Doesn't hurt to plan ahead," he tells me. "You should try it sometime."

"Perhaps next time, you stop being an ass and tell me in advance that I need to prepare a presentation. I don't appreciate being told late at night. Some of us use the night hours to sleep, not whore it around the city."

"You can sleep when you're dead, Malone. I had you pegged for being a little bit more adventurous."

I almost drop my items in a blind rage. "You don't know me," I grit through my teeth. "So whatever game you're playing, leave me the hell alone. You've got your toys to play with. In fact, she's probably waiting for you now."

Leaning against the wall, he crosses his arms as his lips turn upward, forming an annoying smile with a hidden agenda. "Ouch! Jealousy is an ugly trait on you."

"Jealousy?" I laugh. "I know what it's like to be with a real man, so don't for a second think you're worth my time."

"So, tell me then, Presley, if you know what it's like to be with a real man, why did you break it off with him?"

He catches me off guard. "Excuse me? How did you know I broke it off?"

"Office gossip. Helps that I'm sleeping with her."

I am at a loss for words. The subject of Jason and I no longer being together is still very raw, especially in my current state of mind with lack of sleep and no morning coffee.

It overwhelms me.

He isn't worth a single second more, so I walk past him. Ignorance is bliss.

For the rest of the day, he is smart enough to avoid me. It

doesn't stop him from canoodling with Dee, and because I am exhausted, my hearing is impaired, and I accidentally find myself asleep for a few minutes at my desk.

"Pres... Presley." A hand shakes my shoulder.

Dazed, I focus in on Vicky's face. "Did I fall asleep?" I mumble.

Vicky laughs, handing me a cup of coffee. "Uh, yeah. Rough night?"

"Yeah."

"You know what you need? A girls' night out. Drinks, dancing, and some good, clean fun."

"Clean fun?"

"Well, I could have said dirty fun but one step at a time, honey."

"Thanks, Vicky, but I just want to head home and—"

"And what? Wallow in self-pity and cry yourself to sleep?"

"No," I lie. "I'm exhausted. Maybe next weekend?"

She raises her eyebrows at me. "Okay, next weekend, but call me if you change your mind."

With only an hour left, I speed-read through some work, and the second it turns to five, I'm packed up and ready to go home. It has been a long time since I have felt so drained, and boy does it take me back to my early twenties when I would party all night.

I enter the already-cramped elevator and squish myself against the wall. Just when it's apparent we've maxed the people in it, another body mashes against mine. I look up to be met by the Jerk's reflection. Ignoring him wouldn't be difficult, but the more people who enter the elevator, the more appropriate he feels it is to practically rub his body against mine.

Act cool, pretend you're not bothered one bit, and

totally ignore how good he smells. So what if every woman in the office think's he is hot? I didn't understand why I am the only one who loathes him.

Check, check, and fucking check!

It may seem silly, but holding my breath helps, even though I look like a complete idiot. Thankfully, I find myself distracted by the buzz of my phone. It's a message from my hairdresser, Chantelle.

Chantelle: *Pres, what's going on? I saw Jason today at a restaurant.*

There is an attachment, and I open it to be met with a photograph of Jase locking lips with another woman. I stare in disbelief. This cannot be him, and to try and prove myself wrong, I zoom in on the picture

It's him, all right.

My hands start to shake, and the confined space in the elevator starts to claw at me. Suddenly, I feel like I'm suffocating, my body overheating as a result of the jealousy boiling up inside me. If I cried, here, now, everyone would see how pathetic I am.

"Nice picture. You stalking other couples?"

"It's my fiancé," I say without thinking.

I quickly put the phone back into my bag, praying for the elevator to hit the ground floor. Staring at the numbers, the second the door opens, I am out of there so fast I give myself whiplash, desperately trying to escape the sound of my name being called behind me.

The tight grip on my arm startles me, and on first instinct, I wrestle my arm out of his grip.

"Hey. Jesus, Malone, would you just stop for a second?"

I turn to face him, and surprisingly, he looks concerned.

"What, Haden? You want to point out how funny that picture is? Or how I mustn't be any good at sex which is why he strayed?"

"Calm down, will you?"

"I'm sorry. Someone sent me a photo of my fiancé practically fucking another woman a week after we broke up. Excuse me for thinking that the word calm does not belong in my vocabulary right now."

"Ex, Presley. *Ex-fiancé.* Plus, he wasn't fucking her. Woman, you need a reality check. Men don't huddle with their pals eating bowls of ice cream as they watch *The Notebook.* They go find some new pussy and fuck it like a jackrabbit."

He said what?

A thousand shades of red are flashing before me, and for a split second, I wonder what it's like to do time in jail for murdering someone with your bare hands. The nerve of the guy. The worst part is, I'm scared there is some truth to it, and the ass is me, living in a world of denial. Stop telling yourself Jason is, *was,* the perfect guy.

"Wouldn't hurt you to follow in his footsteps," the Jerk chides.

I lift my hand to strike him, but he catches me just in time, strengthening his grip on my wrist. "Don't even think about it."

"I tell you what, you leave me the fuck alone, and I promise I won't smash that pretty-boy face of yours," I fire back.

"Pretty? C'mon, Pres, you can do better than that."

"I'm not your friend, so cut the nickname bullshit.

Honestly, Haden, let me go. Despite what Jason's done, I need to go home."

He lets me go, and defeated, I straighten my arm.

"I'm not surprised he strayed. You need to pull that stick out of your ass and put something else in there instead, Ice Queen."

What did he just call me? I'd heard a rumor that someone in the office had dubbed me Ice Queen, but it never occurred to me it was him. I let out a fake laugh as I watch his cocky grin quickly disappear.

"It will be a cold day in hell before you're attached to the end of any stick coming near me."

He closes the gap between our bodies. I never paid attention to how tall he is until he stands head to head, facing me. Running his finger along my chin, he leans in and whispers in the softest voice, "Frigid little Presley couldn't please her man. Small Dick probably got fed up with you."

And with that, there is no holding back. I step away to gain some distance and swing my fist in his face to connect with his jaw.

Bam.

Game over.

FOUR

I run so fast from him, still reeling from the fact I had punched him in the mouth. The adrenaline is coursing through my veins at a rapid rate, and when I make it home, I slam the door hard, terrified yet somehow exhilarated from the excitement of it all. Collapsing onto my bed, my knuckles begin to throb in pain. Seeking comfort in an ice pack and a bottle of red will do the trick.

What was I thinking?

Somehow, I allowed the anger and uncertainty to build up, so it was only a matter of time before I flew off the handle. How stupid was I to think Jason would sit around and not look for another woman? The hurt and jealousy are so much more painful than I anticipated, to the point that I was driven to punch Haden after his tactless comment.

Does he have a point, though? No, the Jerk is clutching straws and has no sense of decency. He has it in for me, God knows why, and the bottom line is I have to watch my back. The cunning bastard is probably used to getting his way no matter who he steps on. I bet he is vying for a promotion, trying to take me out of the running. Well, take that, asshole! I doubt he'll be able to get laid with a face like that, especially when he admits a woman hit him.

Nothing sounds more appealing than a quiet night in, but Vicky rushes over the second I call her to tell her what happened. Before I know it, the bottle of wine is empty, and Vicky will be my savior tonight.

"Pres, what were you thinking?"

"I wasn't, that's the big problem. I don't think about consequences anymore." I shake my head at myself, staring at the wall, trying to figure out where the Presley Malone I've known my whole life has disappeared to. "When I was with Jason, everything was so easy. I didn't have to think. We had a routine, and life was simple."

"How boring. Be honest for a split second. Wasn't this a tad bit exciting?"

Vicky is my best friend. I can't lie to her face. "Even if it was, I can't go around punching every man in the city. I'll end up in jail and fed to the lesbians."

"Nothing wrong with that." Vicky winks.

That catches my attention, but I'm not going to delve into Vicky's wild sexual history—not tonight anyway. Plus, I will probably need more than a night.

"I'm going to end up an old lady surrounded by cats." I nestle my head against her arm. "Promise me you'll stop me when there are too many cats?"

Vicky chuckles. "Honey, the only pussy you have is the one currently filling up with cobwebs. I'm glad you decided to go out tonight, although you may need to sober up a little, or we won't be able to get in anywhere."

"I'm fineee," I slur.

"I'll whip up something to eat. Go have a shower, and by then, you will be fineee," Vicky mimics.

Two hours later, I am fed and dressed, and we are

standing at the bar ordering shots. Vicky's omelet had some magic ingredient to sober me up enough I was able to put on a tight red dress and apply some makeup without looking like a circus freak. Vicky looks gorgeous dressed in a short white number enhancing her olive skin. Being tall, she doesn't need pumps, and when she wears them, she is a goddess on legs with curves in all the right places. Men are naturally drawn to her which makes me feel like the third wheel.

"Slippery nipples?" she asks.

"What the hell, Vicky?"

She laughs, placing her arm around me. "It's a drink."

"Oh."

The bartender, cute as he may be, serves us drinks but does not stick around to chat. A little bummed, I swivel my chair to be faced by a tall man dressed in a fitted white shirt and black denim jeans. He is very broad, and with a sly grin, he flashes his pearly whites. Wow, they are white! I mean, it's dark in here, and those bad boys are glowing enough that you can make out the footprints on the floor.

Remember what your mother once told you—it's rude to stare.

He introduces himself as Ian, a gym junkie from California. As Vicky turns to face us, she almost falls off her chair whispering in my ear, "He'd make your beaver glow with the amount of bleach he's sporting."

I look at her, confused. Then the penny drops. Vicky apologizes to Ian, then drags me to the dance floor to save me.

"You're welcome," she yells over the music.

"What was wrong with him?"

"Oh, honey, you got to up the ante now. Jason was great and a real looker, but hey, you could have done better."

Offended, I stop dancing and stare at my friend. "What do you mean I could have done better?"

Vicky continues to sway her body, oblivious that her comment struck a nerve.

"Jason is everything you wanted on paper, but he wasn't the guy for you. You need someone who will challenge you, and most importantly, make your toes curl in the bedroom."

"Jason was great. Maybe I'm the problem, I'm the one who didn't challenge him, and maybe I'm the dud in the bedroom."

Vicky stops dancing mid-song, and her green eyes appear agitated. Her long golden-brown locks stop swaying and rest nicely against her chest. With no warning, she latches onto my arm and drags me back to the bar. She motions for the bartender ordering two rounds of shots. Without saying a word just yet, she waits until the glasses are placed before us, then turns to face me with a stern look on her face.

"Now, you listen to me, Presley Malone. I never, *ever*, want you to say you're the problem. Any fucking guy in this club would be lucky to have you. And don't you dare let that stupid photo of Jason make you feel any less. You understand?"

I nod like a child being scolded, then Vicky gives me a tight embrace, reassuring me that we are going to have the greatest night. She slides the shots closer to me, and I down them in one go each.

We giggle uncontrollably as the alcohol sets in until Vicky abandons me to use the restroom, claiming she has some tampon emergency that has dampened her chances of hooking up.

I sway to the music, the band playing a recent pop song, and all the while, I am forgetting that Jason ever existed, and I'm feeling as free as a bird. Vicky's right, Jason was great on paper. He was your typical six-foot, blond hair, blue-eyed hottie. He had a great job, great family, and loved his sports. In the bedroom, he was great. Well, great compared to what I had experienced in the past. He knew how to make me come, but even then, it was routine. Kind of like playing a piano—once you know the notes, you can play with your eyes closed.

When I think back to the last year of having sex, it was dull—same old positions, me on top, and once in a while, he would take me from behind. Foreplay was ancient history. The reality was we were both busy, knew how to get each other off, and did it within five minutes.

I was equally to blame.

The question now weighing heavily on my mind is, is it possible to have a relationship with someone and still keep those butterflies and foreplay alive? I need someone who can crawl under my skin and plant that seed of lust where all I care about is our bodies banging together in perfect harmony.

You're horny and need to get laid.

Oh, and tequila, please stop talking now.

The night was not meant to be spent thinking about Jason, so I divert my eyes to a group of people in their mid to late twenties huddled in the corner. The guy with the jet-black hair is smoking hot, and even in my intoxicated state, I am not immune to getting down and dirty.

He is wearing only a khaki wife-beater, and every inch of his arms are covered in tattoos and boy, oh boy, does he have a set of arms. The way he is standing against the wall shows off his tall muscular build. C'mon, would I really screw a guy I didn't know? Probably not. God only knows where he has been. For all I know, he could be part of some underground drug ring willing to kidnap me and hold me ransom.

I am happily sipping away at my drink when Vicky returns, and I'm quick to point out Mr. Smokin' Hot. Of course, she agrees he is one fine specimen, but her enthusiasm is short-lived when she abandons me for some dude wearing a bowtie. Way to go, Vicky, you sure know how to pick them. She promises to return in a few minutes. Yeah, whatever. She's totally broken the girl code.

Keeping myself entertained, I continue to watch Mr. Smokin' Hot and happen to catch a glimpse of the female beside him. She is wearing the tackiest gold dress that drops low, exposing her very fake, ample bosom. On closer inspection, the lady beside her looks strikingly similar, and as I focus in, I realize they are twins, and one of them is Dee Simmons from work. Totally explains the skankiness I was smelling in here. Honestly, her sister looks no better. Why, oh why, are the hot men attracted to such tramps? He just lost five points on my scale of one to ten—ten being the kind of man I could see myself bending my five-month rule for.

Just when I am about to turn away, bored by the sleaziness, a very dark and mysterious guy beside him catches my attention. Perhaps all is not lost. So I prepare my flirtatious smile only for my stomach to do a backflip as I realize it's none other than the Jerk himself.

Oh shit.

I swivel back around, almost causing myself whiplash, and pretend to be waiting for the bartender, praying to the Lord he didn't notice me. Vicky is standing at the opposite side of the bar. Amid the heavy noise, I attempt to gain her attention, so she can ditch bowtie dude, and we can blow this pop stand before the angry wolf hunts me down.

No such luck, of course. I pull my hair forward to

remain inconspicuous and strategically cover my eyes. The bartender is looking at me like I'm some crazed weirdo, so I slip him a twenty and order another drink. He appears again moments later with some hard liquor, and I down it in one go, much to his amusement.

The room is spinning, flashing colors and lights blurring as they speed past me. Everyone at the bar looks distorted which only adds to the hilarity, and so I find myself laughing at absolutely nothing. I am definitely not in the mood for another confrontation, but given that minutes have passed, I assume he has the sense to stay away from me. An unfamiliar cold hand is placed on my shoulder, and I jump and turn to be met by Haden.

Oh fuck. Here we go. No good can come of this.

Looking supremely pissed off, his lip is swollen from the smack in the face, and there is a slight cut on his cheek from the costume ring I was wearing at the time. Behind his glasses, his eyes have narrowed, and beneath his lips I see a puff of air followed by a grunt. He looks different from his usual self, and I figure it's because he's wearing tight black jeans and a denim, collared shirt rather than his corporate attire.

Gee, he smells nice, and look at the way his forearms flex when he is angry.

My shoulders begin to move up and down, and I start to laugh again, unable to control myself.

"You think this is funny?"

I don't, but it is. God knows my sense of humor was swept away with my will to live the past couple of days. Is it so wrong that I am getting off on his pure hatred for me right now? The way his brows furrow and the death stare that follows makes it all the funnier.

"You got punched in the face by a girl." I chuckle. "It's kinda funny."

The bartender overhears me, and with a grin, he pours me another drink.

What a swell fella.

I give him my best wink.

"Shouldn't you stop drinking now?" Haden growls, holding back the glass from my lips.

"What are you, my dad? I'm thirty fucking two. I can do whatever the hell I want. Presley Malone is wearing her big-girl panties," I slur, followed by more laughter.

I could swear, even in my intoxicated state, that he is smirking, and his eyes have wandered down my body. Maybe I need to stop drinking. My imagination is off with the fairies. It was only minutes ago you thought he was mysteriously handsome.

"Jesus, would you stop? You'll end up taking some idiot home at the rate you're going."

"Wait a minute. Weren't you the one who told me that I needed to pull the stick out of my ass and replace it with something else?"

He remains silent, and I laugh in his face, ending our argument. Grabbing his arm, I hop off the stool and push him aside to head to the dance floor. Sober, there would be no chance in hell I would dance by myself, but what won't kill me will make me stronger. That, and I want to escape him.

The dance floor is stifling hot, and bodies are squished together forcing me to bump butts with a cougar beside me. She has to be at least fifty, dressed in the tightest leather pants I have ever seen, trying to tongue-wrestle a guy young enough to be her son. God help me, I don't want to be single at fifty. *What if I have to wear tight leather pants.* This image is depressing, and all of a sudden, my self-esteem has sailed away until Mr. Smokin' Hot is dancing in front of me. I am pulled out of my mini-funk so fast, my confidence returning. Just for a split second, the idea of having this gorgeous man inside me is sending signals to all the right places.

I move in a little closer, and he leans in to whisper. "You're gorgeous. What's your name?"

"Presley," I respond in my seductive, yet intoxicated voice.

The heat is radiating off his body, and the closer I move in, the more excited I feel. He wraps his arms around my waist, and just before our bodies connect, I am pulled into a different direction, and the distance between us grows. Moments later, I am in the alleyway, and Haden is standing in front of me, eyes wide and nostrils flaring.

"What the hell just happened?"

"I don't get you," he yells.

"What?" I am still looking at the door, confused and trying to understand what the hell just happened.

"You act all Miss Perfect, and then you're on the dance floor like a tramp."

"What did you just call me?"

He almost looks apologetic, but verbal diarrhea is hard to control, I should know. The bubbles of anger are simmering at the surface, and I clench my fists, controlling my behavior as much as I possibly can. I'm not going to rule out the idea of smacking that pretty face of his again.

"God, you think it's okay to punch people in the face?"

"You think it's okay to bring someone down when they are already on the ground barely able to walk? The shit you said hurt, okay? I've been single for two minutes, and I see my ex-fiancé with another woman. This is the guy I was going to spend the rest of my life with. I love him. I didn't just forget what love is even if I called it quits."

"Why did you call it quits?" he demands, yelling.

"Because I wanted more, okay? I don't know what the hell that is, and maybe I'm stupid for thinking that life isn't about being comfortable. I want excitement, kinda like punching you in the face." The laughter escapes me again, and my fists relax, moving toward my stomach to control the stitch forming from the uncontrollable giggles.

"And you still think that's funny?"

I bet it hurt. The swollen lip looks terrible on him, and all I want to do is make it worse.

I have my devil suit on, pitchfork standing proud, and I play nasty.

I move my body forward and smash my lips onto his.

Oh shit.

Now it's officially game over.

FIVE

Sometimes, in our wildest dreams, something extraordinary happens. A moment where you pinch yourself because you're certain it's just a dream, only to find out it is, in fact, reality.

When I was eight, my mom dragged me to a shopping mall where the cast of *Dallas* was appearing. Never had I seen my mom so excited to meet a bunch of old folks who were royalty in the soap opera world. My dad found it both hilarious and pathetic but gave her some extra spending money to buy a new dress, should she be lucky enough to get a photograph.

I never forgot the moment when one of the lead actors asked a question to the crowd, picked my mom to answer, then welcomed her up onto the stage. Every woman in that overcrowded shopping mall was green with envy. On the car ride home and for days following, it was all she could talk about. Her wildest dream came true, and maybe, one day, if I am fortunate enough, it could happen to me.

I wasn't aspiring to meet the cast of *Dallas,* but I had

high hopes that the cast of *Friends* would make it out to Virginia. It never happened, of course.

Making out with Haden Cooper—the biggest jerk to walk the planet—is not my wildest dream. Yet everything about what is happening between us in this dark and secluded alleyway is the wildest thing to happen to me. Dreams and reality become a hazy fog. *What the hell am I doing?* Purposefully, I move my hands toward my thigh, pinching myself in hopes that it's all a dream, but low and behold, each pinch only causes me to scowl as his lips press hard against mine.

It was supposed to cause him pain. So why the hell is he kissing me back?

I try to pull away, but he has my body pinned against the dirty brick wall, and my head is telling me to kick the Jerk in the balls.

What the fuck is that thing my body is doing? Thinking about all the places where he could stick that tongue of his.

I bite his lip with slight force, coercing him to pull away, but his body is pressed hard against mine, and like ice, my body is melting under his touch. I know this is wrong, yet something is happening that excites me in a way I have never experienced. I loathe him. He is annoying, and his sole purpose on this earth is to push my buttons.

And he happens to be pushing the right ones.

His tongue is circling mine at a slow yet intense pace, teasing it enough to make me moan. I am unable to pull away now and surprise even myself with my hands moving to his hair, tugging it until he grunts in my mouth. These sounds are foreign, and the excitement is overwhelming.

I know I have too much pride to allow this to happen, and slowly coming to my senses, I make a proper attempt at moving my mouth away from his and using my upper body to twist out of his grip. Of course, it is fruitless, and with a forceful body slam, his groin presses against me so hard that I feel it throbbing, exciting me further.

Pulling away, his warm breath smothers the air between our faces. "This," he says, with a low rumbling growl, "is payback for smashing my face."

This beautiful yet damaged face is only inches away from mine and so close that I can count the tiny freckles along the bridge of his nose. His lashes are long and curl just above his hazel eyes. Even as we stand in the dark, and I am heavily intoxicated, the color of his eyes has this shimmery light speckle that I never noticed before. Well, why would you notice? You're too busy telling him to shove it where the sun don't shine. So, no point giving him a bigger head, excuse the pun, and telling him how pretty he is. Give it back—jerk style.

"You deserved it," I tell him, catching my breath in between his ravenous kisses.

"Then you, Malone... deserve this."

Against the wall in the dark and dirty alley, he pulls my dress above my thigh, scratching my skin as he clasps his grip firmly on my ass. I beg myself to stop this madness, but the desire has driven me into such a blissful paradise that my body is in full control, not my head. His kisses are heavy against my neck as I arch to the right, giving him free rein to my sensitive spot. My body is sinking further, my pumps barely able to hold myself up with my legs quivering in anticipation.

It's the alcohol making me want him.

It's a rebound.

You want to forget Jason was with another woman.

You're an idiot and will regret this.

What was that last part my brain was saying?

The frenzy in his touch drives me to move my hands inside his shirt, and his body, cool as steel, is sculpted with lean muscle. I want him inside me. The thought is dangerously exciting and very off-limits. I feel the ache inside me, hungry for him to fill me and take me to places that previously only existed in my wildest imagination, one that never involved him.

"You're such a fucking tease, Malone. You know that?"

"I don't tease, you're just greedy and can't help yourself."

"Maybe you're right," he tells me, running his teeth along my lobe.

I can't even hold a conversation here, not when his hands move into my dress and are squeezing my breasts in a desperate plea. His constant rub against my nipples is driving me insane, and I am this close to stripping in the cool night air, so he can suck on them like the hungry beast he is.

I lose my train of thought and giggle. Fueled by the alcohol, I struggle to stop making my skin feeling so highly sensitive with every flick of his tongue. He lets me go, and my laughter stops. He produces a silver foil packet, and my body tenses immediately. Is this really happening? There is no turning back.

Back away right now, Presley!

My pathetic pleas are soon forgotten as he slams his lips against mine while fiddling with his belt buckle.

He is off-limits.

Think of the consequences. The office will go into gossip overdrive if this ever leaked.

You're giving him what he wants.

Unless, of course, you make this about what *you* want.

What the hell do I want?

I want to be lost in a moment, drowning in ecstasy, reminded why I gave up everything I had worked so hard for, and roll around in the green, green grass that is supposed to be on the other side.

But reality knocks me out cold, and in the distance, the noise of the night traffic becomes apparent. Even then, the tearing of the packet is the only sound I focus on.

I can tell him to stop.

You don't want him to stop, just admit it.

"Relax, I'll make you forget he ever existed."

He enters me as I fight for air. His entire cock is buried inside, leaving me breathless as my body adjusts to his size. I close my eyes, focusing on the sensations rather than making eye contact with him. A part of me knows I will regret this once I'm sober.

Something feels different—odd, yet arousing. He takes his time, easing in and out, but even then, I sense his struggle. He wants it rough. He wants to fuck me like a jackrabbit. Wasn't that what he said? Knowing that he is desperate to unleash his savage desire, I open my eyes and focus on his face. His eyes have met mine, and something odd passes between us. It's a silent agreement that this is a one-time release, a tension fuck, and both of us have our reasons for doing it.

He wants me to forget Jason.

And all I'm thinking is Jason who?

With my face in his hands, he thrusts inside me in sync with the roll of his tongue as I moan helplessly into his mouth, unfamiliar with the pressure down below. It climbs so fast I feel possessed in my own skin.

"Is this more?" he grunts in my ear, plunging deeper into me. The jagged edge of the brick wall is scratching my skin.

I'm barely able to string a sentence together. "More what?"

He slows down, easing in and out at a teasing pace. "You wanted more, is this the more you wanted?"

I have no idea what he is talking about due to the bottle of wine, and God knows how many other drinks I had at the bar. It clicks a few moments later, and like my conscience has been freed from wearing handcuffs, there is a moment of clarity, and all I can see is Jason's face.

"I can't... I can't do this," I mumble.

Haden stops, and under his glasses, his eyes are raging in a fury.

"You will do this. You know how much shit you give me in the office? You're begging for me to fuck you hard. This is what you need, Presley. You need to be fucked so hard that you will never forget this moment."

His stern voice, almost demanding, turns any fear I had into raw, heated, unadulterated excitement. I do the most unexpected thing, dropping to my knees and ripping the condom off so his cock is bare in front of me.

Sweet Jesus! The silver barbell is shining so bright, pierced directly into the tip of his cock. I have never seen one, let alone been fucked by one, which explains why it feels so different.

"Like what you see?"

It's not a question, rather the cocky bastard thinking he is some sex god because I can't stop staring at it. I'm drunk, I know, but fuck me dead, his cock is so full and large. No fucking wonder you were screaming in pleasure.

I take it in my mouth, slowly then forcefully, and watch him crumble. The moans escape his mouth are hidden pleas begging me to take him in further. The second his tip hits the back of my throat, I use my hands to control the speed, all the while stroking him.

He is completely losing control.

Serves him right.

His hands move to the back of my head. With his fingers running through my hair, he moans loudly, and in a sudden move, he pushes me away, turning me around to face the brick wall.

"Fucking tease. Now it's payback."

Another foil packet rips, and he re-enters me in just one short breath.

There is no holding back as he slams inside me—this time, his thrusts are hard and fast without any delicacy. I beg him to fuck me harder, surprised by my own words, and he obeys with a brush against my clit that throws my body into a complete meltdown.

"I feel you. You want to come, Presley?"

I nod, not sure if words come out of my mouth.

He gives a final thrust with the loudest groan, and just when I'm about to see stars, on the brink of orgasmic paradise, he pulls out of me, and my buzz is gone.

What the fuck?

I don't turn around instantly, allowing my brain to catch up with reality. My heart is thumping like a jackhammer, my breathing out of control as my lungs struggle to coordinate with my brain.

Did he just...

The sound of his zipper being pulled up alarms me, followed by a gentle kiss on my bare shoulder. Without seeing his face, his breath lingers against my ear as he whispers, "Now you know how it feels."

And then, it clicks. As I turn around, I instinctively

cover my breasts with my hands and attempt to adjust my dress.

He walks toward the motorcycle parked beside the door and climbs on. With his helmet in his hand, he blows me a kiss, then places his helmet on and jumps on the accelerator. He rides off with a rev of the engine, leaving me alone in the alley.

I watch him drive off, all the while thinking this is some fucking horrid nightmare.

Did he just fuck me then leave me hanging without a happy ending?

I stomp my feet in frustration, screaming out into the air, "*You fucking JERK!*"

What have I just done?

I don't have a second to think any longer, vomiting profusely onto the ground before I'm rescued by a worried Vicky and taken home.

SIX

I spend the weekend in hangover hell, dressed permanently in my sweatpants that have a huge hole in the crotch which I only noticed *after* I came home from the grocery store. To make matters worse, I happen to be wearing my big-girl panties, which are often referred to as 'Menstrual cycle couture' because I was fresh out of clean, sexy ones and had zip energy to do laundry. They are unflattering, have some weird cat pattern on them, and I could swear the old man in the cereal aisle spotted my Kitty peeking out from the hole.

Cats—it's an omen.

When you spend most of the weekend making friends with the basin, you vow never to touch an ounce of alcohol again. This is why drinking and being single is a deadly combination. Tequila was to blame. It always is. Nothing ever good comes from doing tequila shots.

Friday night is a huge blur, but I know one thing—I screwed the Jerk in the back of the alley.

Now my life is officially over.

There haven't been many moments in my life where I prayed a genie would appear and grant me three wishes, but right now, I'm on my knees begging for a magical wish to erase what happened.

The details of our 'fling' are a little hazy, and when I say hazy, I mean I don't remember anything apart from him driving off on his motorcycle without finishing our rendezvous and me vomiting like the exorcist with Vicky trying to salvage my hair.

When I spot the red mark on my neck, a memory of him biting my flesh like a deprived vampire flashes before me, and I shrivel up in embarrassment. I used almost a whole tube of toothpaste to keep the redness down. It takes me back to high school when I looked like a leper dating this jock, Calvin. I was forced to wear scarves during the summer and pulled it off as some new fashion trend. My mother was *so* gullible.

Vicky apologized a million times for having to visit her parents on Sunday, leaving me to fend for myself and come up with a solution. I figured I'd take the mature approach and ignore him. Then I realized that won't work, and the only way to face my demons is to confront him head-on. I've even gone to lengths preparing a speech. I've devised a plan of attack, and after I finish my laundry, the old Presley's slowly making her way back from her 'girls gone wild vacation.'

This, in turn, causes me a sleepless night and being exhausted when I wake the next morning. I decide I need to burn the excess energy and pent-up frustration by doing some major cardio at the gym. Trina arrives with Sarah again, and with a quick smile, I pretend to be busy on the treadmill with my headphones, hoping to avoid a conversation. If they catch wind of this, it will make me look just as pathetic as Trina.

With my music on shuffle, I purposely skip past the ballads and settle for some heavy metal as I push myself to ridiculous speeds, almost falling off the machine. Zoning out of my surroundings, the memory of the way he entered me and how my body reacted comes back to me, and a throb between my legs grows. For a split second, I close my eyes, and it's like a movie replaying in my head.

Bits and pieces.

Piercings.

Wait! Piercings?

"Hey, Presley! You look lost with the fairies. Anything wrong?"

Trina is standing in front of my machine, and it's a given that I cannot avoid her.

"Just a lot on my mind. You know, work stuff," I lie.

"I understand. So, listen... about the other day... I've decided to speak to Haden one more time, and if that's it, well... you're right, I have to let it go."

His name alone causes my head to contract into a massive migraine.

"Are you sure, Trina? Jerks like him ain't worth your time. Besides, you know Allan at the front desk? He asked me about you."

Her eyes light up immediately. "Allan, with the bulging arms?"

I nod. "Seems the shy type. Maybe just ease yourself in with light conversation."

She pats my shoulder, thanking me, and is already at the front desk by the time I have a chance to take a breath. I hate lying, but she's so young and needs to stay away from the Jerk. Yeah, where was that rational thinking on Friday night.

I wipe my face and step off the treadmill with unsteady legs, barely able to hold myself up. Leaning on the machine to catch my balance, I glance toward the exit and see the Jerk with Mr. Smokin' Hot beside him. Oh, hell no, it's a double whammy. There is only one exit unless, of course, I exit through the fire door which, in turn, would cause alarm and force everyone to look at me. I would make such a shit fugitive. I procrastinate way too much.

Yeah, except for Friday night.

There you go again.

My brain is working a million miles a minute considering every possible way to avoid him. I change my mind. I'm not mature, and seeing his face makes me want to slap it repeatedly then shove it between my legs so I can get my happy ending.

I'm pathetic. There are no other words to describe me right now.

This reminds me of a recurring dream I have about being naked. Usually, I'm on my way to work riding the bus completely naked. No one is directly looking at me, but for some reason, I can't find any clothes, and nobody will lend me anything. It's embarrassing and leaves me feeling exposed and ashamed. The similarities to that dream are uncanny. And even though I'm fully dressed, all eyes are on me, judging me on what happened with the Jerk. Or so I think.

Trina is busily flirting with Allan, Sarah is in the Zumba class eyeing the cute gay guy next to her, and so I am officially on my own without any friend to save me. Pulling my phone out of my pocket, I send an SOS text to Vicky.

. . .

Me: *At the gym. The Jerk is here. HELP!!!*

I wait impatiently, but she doesn't respond, and I am running out of time. I need to get to the change rooms which are located next to where Haden is standing. He hasn't noticed me yet, so I watch him from the corner of my eye.

He is laughing, and it's only now I notice he isn't wearing his glasses. He looks completely different, dressed in black shorts with a tight gray tank top that shows off his biceps. Oh, wow.

Okay, pep-talk time. Don't you dare drool over a jerk who sweet-talked you into the alley and left you high and dry—or more appropriately—low and wet. You didn't finish college to end up following a guy like a pathetic puppy dog. Yes, he is extremely good-looking. Yes, his hair looks like it belongs in a shampoo commercial, and yes, maybe his body is as irresistible as the new salted caramel sweets they keep showing on television.

I don't know whether I'm hungry, horny, or need to buy new shampoo. One thing's for sure, Mr. Smokin' Hot beside him is walking my way.

"Hey, gorgeous girl from Friday night."

His smile is endearing, and shyness overcomes me. Perhaps being covered in sweat without any makeup is a surefire way to lower my confidence.

"Hey, gorgeous guy from Friday night," I repeat back.

"You train here?"

"I wouldn't call it training. Just trying to let off some steam."

"How have I not seen you here before?"

I shuffle awkwardly. "Okay, you busted me. Until last week, I was a gym virgin."

He laughs softly. "I'm Marcus, by the way."

"Presley." I extend my hand, and he shakes it, lingering while he studies my face. His eyes are light green and brighten when he smiles. His dimples are set deep, and boy, is he cute. His jet-black hair is short, recently grown out from what I assume was a shaved head. He is also wearing a tank, and I have to stop my hands from reaching out to squeeze his arms.

"So, you know Haden from work?"

I nod and see Haden talking to some chick at the front with his eyes directly on me. His stare is penetrating, piercing me like a superhero trying to destroy his enemy. What the hell is his problem? He appears to be agitated; lips pressed flat with his arms crossed in front of his chest. His angered expression leaves me baffled, surely I should be the one angry after what *he* did.

Suddenly, I'm self-conscious. Then I realize I'm not the moron who left someone to die in a dark alley. Okay, maybe not die, but the Jerk infuriates me with his egotistical I-think-I'm-all-that persona.

Who in their mind leaves a woman mid-orgasm? An asshole, that's who.

"How do you know him?" I focus back on Marcus.

"He's my cousin. Our dads are brothers." His tone softens, then, as if shaken, he smiles again and changes subjects.

Weird, but I don't want to get into it. Cousins? Why is the universe punishing me. Marcus is so sexy, and he seems interested. What's the worst that could happen? I tilt my head to the side, smiling at Marcus to show him I'm enjoying his company.

"So, any chance of grabbing a bite to eat sometime?"

My gaze is drawn to his lips, and unable to ignore his dimples which appeared every time he smiled. In some sort of trance, I try to string a sentence together. "I'd like that."

Marcus passes me his phone, and I store my number. We talk for a few more minutes before he tells me he needs to leave for work. Saying goodbye, I make my way over to the lockers and grab my stuff to head to the change room. Confident that I have avoided Haden this morning, I shower and dress, then leave the gym to head into the office.

It's Monday, and I drown myself in my work until our editors' meeting in an hour. I don't have anything to present today and am happy to listen to what other manuscripts will be put on the table, anything to take my mind off the weekend. Dee is standing up front, and as everyone enters the room, I take a seat at the furthest spot from Haden.

From across the room, he is staring at me again, making me feel even more self-conscious. Normally, one would think I had spinach in my teeth or a milk mustache with this much attention. What I would give to have a milk mustache right now. He's probably thinking about how I got down on my knees and sucked him off.

Oh, dear God, another new memory.

My cheeks flush instantly, so I bow my head to avoid anyone noticing, my shoulders curling over my chest. I can blame many things for contributing to the night, but nothing will change the fact that I didn't stop him.

Dee commences her presentation, introducing a new erotic male-on-male romance. The heterosexual men in the room cringe. Clive, our resident fairy, is all over it.

"Totally love it, Dee. There's a demand for gay romance. Women love it." Clive claps his hands in utter delight.

"C'mon, Clive. How could women love it?" Haden questions, rudely. "I won't argue about demand. Figures show there need to be more books in this genre, but I don't get why women want to read about two guys' dicks slapping each other."

There are a few snickers, again from the men, but of course, the Jerk starts a heated debate. One that could have been easily avoided if he kept that mouth of his shut.

"Haden, get your pretty little head out of the lady garden. Women want to see lust and desire. They want to see acts that are unattainable."

Clive has a good point, but I don't want to admit it out loud. Vicky once showed me some random clip of two guys, and it was steamy, hot, and very taboo. There was something about it that intrigued me, not that I wanted to tell this to Jason at the time.

"Let the women in the room speak up, Clive," Haden urges him.

There is silence until my name is called. All eyes are on me and the Jerk—who once again has put me on the spot.

If he wants to play dirty, he is messing with the wrong woman. I need to show him that the other night meant absolutely nothing. It did not affect me whatsoever to the point that I have moved on. I'm not Trina, nor Dee, chasing and begging for him to pay attention.

"Clive has a point. There's something arousing about the image of two men. The sexual desire is, um... let's say, raw and uninhibited. And many homosexual men have very appealing bodies."

He looks amused, leaning back into his chair like an arrogant prick. He is no longer wearing his gym outfit, and I try not to stare at how sexy he looks in his crisp white shirt rolled up at the sleeves. All of this is a decoy which I need to ignore if I know what's good for me.

"Can't a man and woman have the same sexual desires toward each other?" he asks, mocking my point with a slight sneer.

"Probably. Depends on whether the guy's a jerk or not," I shoot back. "It all boils down to the build-up. From what Dee has summarized, the two men are sexually charged after years of denying their sexuality. Women love a good lead-up. It makes for a heated explosion. Excuse the pun."

Everyone laughs, and I find my confidence in the ultimate stare-off, not backing down. He doesn't back off either until Dee moves on, and the subject changes.

Focusing on a presentation proves difficult when you know someone is staring at you. Occasionally, I turn to look at Clive sitting next to Haden, and my heart skips a beat when the Jerk's eyes lock onto mine. Pressing my lips together, I cross my legs and tighten my thighs to ignore the forbidden throb between my legs. My body is betraying me, something it hasn't done in a long while.

After another hour spent talking about other projects, we filter out of the room. Clive has not stopped talking, having only just returned from a European vacation.

"We haven't done lunch in ages. You free today, Pres?"

"Sure, Clive. Plus, we need to catch up on your vacay."

He flashes me a wink and starts to ramble on about some Contiki tour until Haden interrupts us.

"Can I please speak to you?" His tone is demanding enough that even Clive raises his eyebrows.

Great, just fucking great. I knew there was no way to avoid it. I tell Clive I'll catch up with him at lunch and wait until everyone leaves the room.

"What?" I finally say.

"What? Is this the game we're playing?" he asks, extremely frustrated, running his hand through his hair again.

Don't look at his hair. *Repeat.* Do not look at his hair.

"Ignorance is bliss. What else do you want me to say?"

"You don't want to do the woman thing, drag what happened out, and talk about emotions and bullshit?"

"Nope. I'd rather not."

My choice to remain tight-lipped is increasing his anger, and I'm getting off on it. With a burst of confidence, my steady gait appears to annoy him further.

"I don't get you. You had no problem talking about your ex." The way he says the word 'ex' sounds like he's swallowing poison.

"Well, I'm done talking."

His eyes focus on my lips. I sense he is biting his tongue, and in a matter of seconds, he will explode.

"Why were you talking to Marcus?"

"Your cousin? Because it's polite when someone introduces himself." I almost laugh at the question.

"Is something going on between you two?"

"It's none of your business, Jerk. You keep reminding me I have an ex, which makes me single, right? So the last time I checked, I'm not bound to anyone."

"So that's it? You don't want anything more to do with me?"

"That's it," I repeat, staring him directly in the eyes.

"You're fine to sweep this under the rug and forget that it ever happened?"

"Consider it swept, vacuumed, and in the trash taken away. Are we done now?"

"Apparently so."

~

Lunch with Clive couldn't have rolled around fast enough. Haden had gone back to his desk, and I was happy to put my head down and forget about our argument. Except, I couldn't. Why was he so interested in my conversation with Marcus? He acted almost—don't say it, Presley—jealous.

Okay, rewind. Haden has never shown interest in me before Friday night. He has been working at the company for close to twelve months now, and apart from the annoying pranks, not once has he shown any interest in my personal life, including my dating status.

The same goes for me. All I know is he is a manwhore who somehow attracts women into his manwhore lair where he screws them without a name to the face. I never really took the time to notice him, being so caught up in my work and relationship with Jason.

I'm fairly certain I'm overthinking things. He made it clear we were to forget Friday night happened. Surely, he is happy-dancing deep down inside that I am not calling and telling him that I love him.

And with all that said and done, it's evident we both made a huge error in judgment. A mistake never to be repeated, and therefore, we move on because it's all in the past.

Clive takes my mind off things at lunch, re-enacting every scenario from his almost *National Lampoon's European Vacation*. All he is missing is Clark Griswold and a redhead named Rusty. We are sitting in a nearby café, having just ordered, when Dee walks in. She spots us immediately, and without using her manners and asking politely, takes a seat in the empty chair at our table.

Dee is the kind of woman who keeps the cosmetic

industry booming. Her bleached blonde hair against her fake spray-on tan does nothing for her. She reminds me a lot of a Playboy bunny, an extremely flat-chested one. Beneath the layers of makeup she wears is no doubt a pretty woman. If only she didn't make herself look like a Barbie doll.

"Your pitch was a winner. You've got that one in the bag," Clive tells her with a mouthful of salad.

"Haden raised some good points, though," she mumbles, a little disheartened.

"He has no clue, Dee," I remind her.

"He does. No offense, Clive, but women don't want to read about men getting hot and heavy. They want alpha billionaires breaking their virginity."

"Why are you letting him sway you? Yeah, I get that you're sleeping with him, but honestly, Dee, stand up to him."

Shit, did I say that out loud?

"What? First of all, Presley, I haven't slept with him. Fooled around, yes," she snarls.

"Ooh, catty." Clive raises his hand and makes a claw.

"I'm sorry, Dee. I shouldn't have assumed that because I see you both tongue-wrestling at every opportunity, you have actually slept together."

My tone is off. Snarky. Catty, as Clive just put it. Gee, someone would think I was jealous. Again, with that word.

"Everything but." She winks this time.

"Ooh, a wink? Do tell!" Clive's enthusiasm prompts Dee to fess up.

"He's pierced."

I choke on the cherry tomato that I'm swallowing that instant. Clive is patting me on the back repeatedly as I try to calm myself, gulping a whole heap of water.

"You all right there, cowgirl?" Clive asks.

I nod, bright red with embarrassment.

"I know, it's taboo, right? I mean it is pierced right on the tip. I can't wait to see what it feels like inside."

Clive laughs. "Why don't you just tell him you want to do the horizontal tango?"

"Because, Clive, I have, and he says soon. Lord knows what he's waiting for. We've kinda been fooling around for weeks but he always appears distracted.

I'm not a gossiper, but I am desperate to get answers, so I bring it up. "What about Trina?"

"The chick who cried after they had sex. Apparently, he was off his face that night. They were flirting for weeks."

What the hell does this all mean? He flirts with Trina, then fucks her when drunk or drugged. He hasn't sealed the deal with Dee, but he screws me in the alleyway without any thought.

Do not read any more into this. It means nothing, and even if it were something, I don't think of him that way. It was just a mistake. A big, fat huge mistake that should be listed in the *Guinness Book of Records* as the worst mistake ever. Haden's reputation with women is enough for me to forget all about him. I wanted a rebound, and that's what I got.

My thoughts are like poison, slowly seeping through my veins until I am consumed wholly by thoughts of the evil one. I need to stop this madness now. With Clive and Dee busy discussing genital piercings, I take out my phone and find Marcus' number. I am straight to the point, asking him to meet up for lunch tomorrow. He responds immediately, naming a place and time.

Whatever Haden's problem is with Marcus and me being friends, he will have to overcome it. A week into being single, and already there is drama. This is not what I had in mind when I broke up with Jason.

Marcus is sweet, friendly, and hopefully, drama-free. And to top it off, it feels good to sweep Friday night's regrets under the rug.

Just like I had said—swept, vacuumed, and in the trash the Jerk goes.

SEVEN

The next day, Marcus shows up at the office, midday on the dot. Since the last time I saw him, just short of twenty-four hours ago, I had forgotten how good-looking he is. Wearing a black-striped business shirt paired with charcoal pants, his tattooed arms are completely covered, and one would think he was some corporate mogul.

But I know how deliciously dangerous he is underneath.

He sits casually on my desk, and we briefly chat while I gather my purse, ready to head out for lunch. With him so close to me, my senses have picked up that he's wearing the same cologne Jason once wore. I'm trying my damnedest to remember my reasons for wanting more than Jason, scared to admit even to myself that it may have been a huge mistake on my behalf. Yes, I got that all from a bottle of Hugo Boss.

I stand up, straightening my dress when the Jerk invades my cubicle. Today, he is not wearing a tie, exposing his smooth, tanned skin. Dropping my gaze, a sudden flush of warmth spread's throughout me.

"Fancy seeing you here, *cousin*." Haden has stretched his arms wide, blocking our exit.

"Well, if you see a gorgeous woman like Presley, you ask her out," Marcus responds with a cocky grin.

The two of them watch each other intently, but I swear at this moment they are having a full-on conversation in their heads. I'm certain it involves boxing gloves and Brad Pitt standing in the corner of the ring saying, "Welcome to Fight Club."

Haden stands firmly with his arms crossed. "She just broke up with the love of her life."

"Uh, wait a minute. Now you've got my back?" I laugh in his face, infuriating him even further.

Knowing that I am playing with fire, I grab onto his forearm to move him out of the way.

Ignore it's hard. Damn! his muscles are hard. Jesus Presley, jump ship now.

In front of me are two younger men vying for my attention. Never had I thought I would be in this situation. Perhaps, I have done this all wrong. My interests in men should expand to the older generation. But then I think of my Dad, and unwillingly—I cringe at the thought.

"I believe Dee requires your attention." Leaning in further, I whisper in Haden's ear, "Not sure why you're holding back from her since you had no problem unleashing on me."

Pulling myself back, his head draws back quickly, eye's wide with raised brows.

My work here is officially done.

The look on his face—priceless.

I have never felt so empowered.

Marcus grabs my hand, and I allow him to do so, watching Haden divert his eyes from this intimate gesture.

Against the partition, Haden's knuckles are stark white as he restrains himself. I have no idea what his problem is apart from the obvious male ego and pride bullshit.

I'm not a prize, and this isn't a competition.

We aren't even dating, and we both agreed it was a sweep-it-under-the rug type of fuck.

Raising my head to meet his eyes, I give him my most evil grin. "See ya later, *Jerk.*"

Marcus and I sit in the booth near the entrance, lucky to get a seat at a popular diner. The burgers here are delicious, and so is Marcus. I have no idea how old he is, and given that it's rude to ask, I settle for assuming he's in his twenties. God, when did I become such a cougar. Guys in their twenties have this wicked aura around them. At least that's what Vicky tells me. I can see it, though. They tend to care a hell of a lot more about their appearance, obsessed with working on their physique. They often dress in all designer labels, and even when they dress down, they rock a pair of jeans and a tee like a model on a runway.

Then, there's the hair.

Marcus has beautiful jet-black hair.

Although it's short, you can tell it's silky smooth. If he grew it out, he would look like Cleopatra, and I would happily feed him grapes from a golden plate.

While the waiter serves us our meals, my phone vibrates. Expecting a much-needed text from Vicky, I'm surprised to see it's from the Jerk instead, and immediately roll my eyes before even opening the message.

. . .

Haden: *What do you mean unleash on you? Are we talking about this now?*

I should respond with something witty, but Marcus has focused his attention on me. So I throw my phone into my purse and dive into my meal. He has quite an appetite on him, almost polishing off the burger in a second.

"I could do another," he says with a satisfied smile.

"Why not? You only live once. There's always the gym..." I trail off.

"So, tell me, why are you a gym virgin, and why the sudden urge to work out? You look amazing, hot, sexy, just in case no one has ever told you that." He smirks.

"Nice flirting." I laugh in return, relaxing us both. "Long, long story. Maybe another time."

"I've got time."

"Super long."

"Hmm... okay, sixty seconds. Ten questions, I get to ask you anything, and that'll satisfy my curiosity."

"Huh?"

He looks at his watch. "Time starts now. Who did you last date?"

What was the rule of the game? He taps on his watch, so I answer quickly.

"Date? I was engaged to a guy named Jason."

"Why did you guys break it off?"

"It wasn't right," I stutter nervously.

He raises his eyebrows but does not pry any further.

"Where did you grow up?"

"Virginia."

"Siblings?"

"An older sister, Gemma."

"Favorite band?"

"Band? Bon Jovi."

"Nice," he adds. "Favorite song?"

"'In These Arms' ... Bon Jovi."

"Favorite movie?"

"*Father of the Bride.*"

He pauses, then follows with a short chuckle. "I love that movie, too."

"Really?" I laugh out loud.

"Favorite food?"

"Nachos."

"Ultimate holiday destination?"

"Australia," I answer with a smile.

"Why did Haden take you outside on Friday night?"

The question, a giant curveball, stuns me. Mentally, I try to calculate how many questions he has asked me, but all I think about is some excuse that will satisfy him without having to let the cat out of the bag.

"How many questions is that? I think your time is up."

"I'm sure you can answer the last one." His stern tone catches me off guard.

I could tell him the truth. Besides, if this goes any further, I can't hide something like that from him. What are the chances of this going further? He is young, I am older. The best we could achieve is copious amounts of hot sex.

"We argued earlier that day. Frankly, your cousin is a jerk."

He appears fixated on my movement, and I give him nothing to see how uncomfortable I am with this conversation.

"I think I'll order that second burger."

"Don't I get to ask you the lightning round of questions?"

"The next date you can." He winks.

"Oh, there's going to be a next date?" I ask coyly.

"Why wouldn't there be?" He angles his face closer to mine, and with his lips slightly parted, I follow his lead until our lips brush together. The butterflies have crept their way into my stomach, causing some major excitement, but soon the grim reaper follows—guilt. I don't know who or what I am feeling guilty about—my second attempt at playing the field since Jason and I broke up only two weeks ago, or the fact that he's the Jerk's cousin.

Don't answer that.

"Marcus?" I say softly as we both move away. "I just broke up with my fiancé. I'm slowly adjusting to life being single again."

"I'm not asking you to marry me, Presley. We can have fun together."

Fun. That either means hanging out at the amusement park or tied to the bed with a gag ball and chains.

We finish lunch and head back to the office. Marcus insists on taking me back to my desk. I put my purse away, and before I know it, he leans in to gently kiss my lips again. In the background, I hear a throat being cleared. It's Dee, and she is standing with an overly thrilled Clive.

"Listen, I better go. Call me tonight, okay?"

I nod, and when he turns the corner, I think all is sweet until the whispers become louder, and the three of us are standing there trying to eavesdrop.

"Just like when we were kids," the Jerk says.

"You said I had free rein," Marcus responds, frustrated.

"When did I ever say that?" he bites back.

"Friday night. Though you never explained why you pulled her away from the dance floor. C'mon, Haden, you're fucking the blonde. What do you care?"

Silence falls between us all. Dee looks hurt, but that soon turns to anger. She glares at me like this is all my fault.

"You're right, I am fucking the blonde. So why should I care about Malone? She's all yours, *bud*."

It's my turn to be crestfallen. I'm not angry or upset with Marcus. They have some bro code going on, and he clearly has been given the green light.

Yet, I am not a possession.

I don't belong to Haden but hearing him admit he doesn't care for me, not even one minuscule of a feeling after he had his way, is enough to eat away at me.

I cannot fall for him.

I cannot even *want* him in any way.

Praying for a miracle is my only

EIGHT

With the Jerk away in London, I slowly piece my life back together again. Jason still hasn't contacted me, yet every week a realtor shows prospective buyers around. I am not in a financial position to buy him out, so I settle for apartment hunting in a more affordable neighborhood. Nevertheless, I started packing my belongings and getting rid of items I no longer need like my MC Hammer pants from the nineties. There's nostalgia, and then there is just plain hoarding. Hammer pants fall into the hoarding category though my mother would argue that in a heartbeart.

As Marcus promised, we had fun. Fun is hitting the clubs, late-night dinners, and of course, hot sex with a confirmed twenty-seven-year-old. He didn't tell me directly, but when he took a shower at my place, I 'stumbled' upon his license. On a drunk bender one night, he asked my age. I wasn't going to lie, and when I asked him if he had a problem with that, he replied by taking me back to his place and making me come on his roommate's expensive leather sofa.

He told me only after that his roommate is his cousin, Haden.

From that moment, we only ever have sex at my place.

The Jerk virtually disappeared, and occasionally, Mr. Sadler would send out a group email in which Haden would respond. That was it in terms of contact. He never once tried to text or send me anything work-related, so it was easy to assume that the drunken night in the alley was all in the past and could easily be forgotten.

Marcus is fun, he makes me forget the stresses of everyday life, including my bad bout with the flu a couple of weeks back. I am not sure I saw it going anywhere, I simply enjoy his company, and for once in my life, I am happy to go with the flow. Very un-Presley like.

Then it all went pear-shaped—he said he loved me.

It happened last week at the Bon Jovi concert. The third beer of the night and halfway through 'Bed of Roses,' he pulls me into an embrace and whispers into my ear, "I think I love you, Presley Malone."

My instant reaction was to dry heave, which ultimately had me running for the bathroom, so I could projectile vomit my fears into the dirty toilet. How do you tell someone, "Oh, hey, thanks for saying I love you, but I don't feel the same way? However, it's nice to know you care."

I remember walking back to him and the puppy-dog look on his face when he saw me. It was the look of being in love. I simply smiled, told him thank you, and changed the subject by telling him that I wasn't feeling too great. He didn't seem to think there was an issue, so after the final song, we made our way home, and I pulled out the 'Period' card. He understood and left me alone.

It wasn't a complete lie. I was almost due, and this

month I was predicting a bitch of a cycle since the past three months had been light.

That bitch never came, and the emergency sirens were ringing, sending Vicky to the rescue.

It happened too fast. Starting off with a joke, then an impromptu trip to the drug store which lead to the moment of disabelief.

"It's blue."

Frozen on the spot, I stare at the little blue line and its evil twin. My skin tingles in discomfort as my chest tightens, restricting my ability to breathe so effortlessly.

This cannot be happening.

I am not irresponsible!

I got straight-A's in sex education class. I paid close attention to that condom being placed on the banana. In fact, I even took notes.

"No shit, but are there two lines?" Vicky is panicked, walking back and forth in the confined bathroom, or what I like to call my personal hell.

Without saying a word, I hand it over, wrong end first as Vicky snatches it away from me.

"Oh gross, I'm touching your pee." It falls to the floor, not that it matters—the damage is done.

"Is it Marcus'?"

Mental calculations of who you were sleeping with at a specific time scream 'slut' like nothing else. With Marcus, I stuck to my five-month-rule, minus four months, two weeks, and four days. Turns out the older you get, the shorter the timespan.

"Okay, let's take it into the living room with some Chinese takeout and get to the bottom of this," Vicky reassures me.

An hour later, the Chinese delivery guy has delivered

our food, and Vicky is wearing her Sherlock Holmes' cap and glasses. When it comes to sticky situations, Vicky Flinders is the person you want by your side. Despite nausea sitting in the pit of my stomach, I shove food into my mouth, not allowing myself any air to breathe.

"When did you last get your period?"

"Like, a month ago? It was an odd color and lighter than usual."

"You can still get your period while you're pregnant."

"Marcus and I only started sleeping together not long ago, and to be honest, he has an obsession with blowjobs, so we don't really have intercourse as much as you might think," I mumble, in confusion.

"Okay, that's a lot of information for me to take in. What is it with men and blowjobs? You know, it could be Haden's or Jason's—"

"Wh... why would it be Haden's?" The anxiety is curling in my stomach at the mention of his name. I hadn't even thought of him being part of this equation. My immediate thoughts went to Marcus. Even Jason seemed so far-fetched. Yet it would be my preferred option if given a choice. I am barely containing my tears, choking them back trying to figure out what the hell I'm going to do.

"Uh, because he stuck his GI Joe in your Polly Pocket?"

I almost choke on my eggroll. "You're getting cruder with age."

"I prefer the term 'wiser,'" she corrects me. "So?"

"Look, Vicks, he wore a condom... I think." God, I sound like a whore. "But if I didn't come, then he probably didn't."

Vicky spits out her drink all over my coffee table. Disgusted, I quickly grab some paper towels to wipe it down, mumbling under my breath at her disregard for a sanitary environment though it should be the least of my problems.

"You can't be that gullible. If I know Haden, the jerk blew his load and left you hanging, wanting more."

"I don't know," I barely admit. "As for Jason, we hadn't had sex since his trip back from Chicago. That was so long ago. Surely, if it were his, I'd be showing right now."

My mind is reeling with all this information, all the while reminding me how unbelievably stupid and irresponsible I am. I take a step back and ponder the scientific side of things, but Vicky interrupts my thoughts.

"So that was like..." Counting her fingers, Vicky does the math that my brain refuses to compute. "That was like five months ago, right? And you fucked Haden four months ago? So, it's simple, you get your blood test done and see how far along you are. Then you'll know who the baby daddy is."

Oh, dear God, *baby daddy*. This is not supposed to be how I bring a child into this world. I should be married, or at least living with the man. Love should have been the reason for this lifechanging moment—not some careless rendezvous fueled by desire.

"Vicky, it has to be Marcus' baby. I'm not ready for this, plus he's so young and not ready to be a father. How can this happen?" I yell in frustration.

"Well, you weren't exactly being responsible."

"I was on the goddamn pill back then! Besides, we always use condoms."

"Oh," Vicky mouths. "Well, it says on the warning label that the pill is only ninety-nine percent effective and condoms can break. Maybe you're one of those super fertile women, and Marcus has super sperm, and together it can break through anything."

"This isn't a joke. I can't be that one percent, Vicky."

"Someone has to be," she points out. "Why would you stop the pill?"

"I don't know, I didn't see the point since I wasn't in a relationship anymore," I sulk, burying my face into my hands. "I have no idea who I am anymore. I got so caught up in having fun and didn't think it would be a big deal since we used protection anyway."

I sink into the sofa, smothering myself with cushions and praying they would turn into monsters and suffocate me to death. Instead, I sit here feeling like a cheap hooker from some reality TV show. How could I not know who the father is of the baby I'm carrying? This isn't how I was raised or who I am. I know better than this.

"It's okay to cry, Pres." Vicky rubs my shoulder.

My hands are shaking. "I don't want to cry. I'm so angry at myself. How could I be so irresponsible? I planned to have kids with the right man when we were married. I didn't sign up for being a single mother. What will my parents think? What will everyone think?"

"It doesn't matter what everyone thinks, Pres. This is your life, not theirs." She continues, "As for your parents... they'll get over the initial shock, and I'm sure they'll be excited to have a grandbaby. It's not like Gemma is popping one out any time soon, you know, eating pussy and all."

"Vicky!"

"What? It's true. You'll look back at this moment one day and be thankful you're blessed with a child. Think about all those women trying their asses off... well, not their asses, but you know what I mean."

"So, in the meantime, can I wish I could climb into a time machine and stay celibate?"

"Yes, but first you need to find out who the baby daddy

is. Then you can revert to OCD Presley and plan your life away."

Stupid doctor's office with its sterile walls that make you feel like you're in a nuthouse.

It took me a week to find the courage to make an appointment and have my blood taken. In that week, I avoided Marcus at all costs with every believable excuse I could muster. He understood but warned me that if he hadn't fucked me by Saturday, I was in major trouble.

What does a pregnant woman say to that? I had no response but to send him a smiley face.

"Miss Malone, I have your results here."

Dr. Taylor procrastinates in the most annoying way possible. He's pushing close to a hundred— okay, exaggerating a little—and even the way he writes everything on paper versus using a computer bugs me.

Hormones—blame the hormones.

"You're definitely pregnant, and the blood work shows you're about four months along."

The lump in my throat is the size of the planet, Jupiter. My chest tightens, constricting my ability to breathe, and my eyes start to twitch followed by the room spinning. Dr. Taylor is concerned, calling my name in the distance. I focus on his face, mumbling the question that is bursting to come out.

"So, when you say four months, I fell pregnant around..."

"March," he confirms.

Fuck!

Fuck!

Fuck!

This. Cannot. Be. Happening.

"But it was only one time," I beg, almost in tears. "I was on the pill back then, and we used condoms."

"Miss Malone, I always advise my patients that the pill is only ninety-nine percent effective. You did the right thing using a condom, but even condoms aren't one hundred percent."

"Why does everyone say that?" I raise my voice. "I can't be pregnant! If nothing's one hundred percent, then why are people having sex?"

"Abstinence is your one hundred percent," he reminds me.

What a stupid remark. No one is going to abstain from having sex.

"I was with the same man before that for five years. I was on the pill, but that's it. How come I didn't fall pregnant with him?"

"It could be several things. Perhaps you weren't actually having intercourse during ovulation, but most likely you've found a male partner with strong sperm that's extremely compatible with your eggs."

Dr. Taylor retrieves a pamphlet from his desk, sliding it in front of me. The front has a picture of a woman, and clearly printed are the words, *What You Need to Know About Abortions.*

A sudden reflex, and I slide it back to him. "I can't do that."

"I understand. It's an option, one we don't encourage, but sometimes it helps to know your options. You don't have long, though, if that's the option you want to take."

"I'm thirty-two, Dr. Taylor. I have a secure job, money saved, and my own place. Well, kind of. I didn't plan this,

I'm not sure the father will take this well nor will he be present in the child's life, but I do know one thing for sure..." I say without taking a breath, "... I was raised in a religious family. My sister is a lesbian, but my family accepted her choices. My parents will be disappointed in me, but I know deep down inside, this has to be counted as a blessing."

At that moment, I realize this is not a therapy session, and I'm not quite sure why I brought up that my sister is a lesbian. Then it dawns on me that I need validation. I can't be a single mom without the support of my family. Gemma was eighteen when she told my parents she wasn't interested in men. At first, my mom cried for a whole week and even tried bringing nice boys home. Of course, it didn't work. Gemma was not switching teams. My parents eventually accepted her decision, and now they are persuading Gemma and her partner, Mel, to get married.

If they accepted homosexuality, they can accept I'm going to be a single mom.

"So, I take it you're not in a relationship with the father?"

"Three words for you, Doc. One. Night. Stand."

I see pity or maybe even a little bit of judgment in his eyes. He carries on about prenatal appointments, supplements, and other things that are flying in one ear and out the other. In my head, I only see the look on the Jerk's face when I tell him.

Or maybe I don't tell him?

No. No, I have to tell him.

Then there is Marcus.

This is too much to think about, so I opt for a quick escape, head to the nearest supermarket, and fill my cart full of chocolate. The checkout lady is definitely judging me, and I am quick to ease her curiosity.

"I just found out I'm knocked up after a one-night stand. I work in the same office as him, plus he's a jerk."

"You eat that chocolate, girl, and you enjoy it," she tells me, even discounting my total at the end.

It's a long walk back to my apartment, and as soon as I open the door, the boxes packed against the wall remind me of what's to come.

How can I have a baby when I soon will have no place to live?

How can I continue working, and who would take care of the baby?

The questions keep flooding my brain until I'm forced to sit down with a migraine of epic proportions.

I fall asleep, and when I wake up, it's dark outside.

My phone lights the room, and I pick it up to read the text.

Marcus: *Raincheck tomorrow night, babe. Haden's back in town and boy does he have a surprise.*

The phone slips out of my hand and onto the floor.

Running fast to the bathroom, I vomit profusely into the toilet. My unruly hair is mangled in my face, forcing me to turn the shower on. As the steam fills the bathroom, I undress and stare at my naked body in the mirror. My stomach still looks flat, and even as I turn to the side, nothing appears to be different. My breasts, however, they look like giant balloons. How did I not notice this before? There is a swell just underneath my nipples. When I touch them, my body jolts at the unpleasant tingle that follows. Even the color looks slightly different, darker.

The steam soon covers the mirror. I climb into the shower and allow the hot water to wash my worries away.

I have to be the adult here. He deserves to know the truth, even if he doesn't want anything to do with us.

Us.

I will tell him in person.

Tomorrow.

No, maybe Monday.

Or maybe I'll wait until I'm showing, and he works it out for himself.

Yep, I'm screwed any way you look at it.

NINE

"So, I Facebook stalked him."

I'm dazed and confused, primarily from the lack of sleep all weekend. Leaving Dr. Taylor's office that day confirmed I am fifteen weeks along, pregnant by a man I despise. A stranger, in fact.

I spent the weekend panicking, planning, more panicking, and eating way too much chocolate. It isn't the next five months I have to worry about, it is the rest of my life.

Am I even mother material? When I was fifteen, I changed my cousin's diaper and got shit all over her face. The little brat wouldn't keep still. Then, when I realized there was shit on the blanket, I threw it in the trash and told my auntie we left it at the park.

I'm going to be a terrible mother.

Vicky is sitting on my desk, cross-legged and shoving her phone in my face. I push it away in dismay, not wanting to deal with anything and trying my best to ignore the dry heaving. It's Monday morning, and the office buzz is that Haden is officially back in town. Even Dee looks nervous, although I don't know why since she has moved on with someone old enough to be her dad.

"You don't look well," Vicky sympathizes, handing me a bottle of water.

"Would you feel well if the man whose life you're going to turn upside down is just about to walk through that door?"

"You have a point. So, don't you want to know more about him?"

"I don't think now's the time."

Vicky ignores me. "He's into extreme sports."

"Aren't most guys?" I place my head down on my desk, resting my eyes for a brief moment.

"He loves animals. Has two dogs, Marley and Max. They're Yorkshire Terriers."

"Really? That's kind of... feminine," I mumble into my arm.

Vicky laughs, agreeing. "His favorite TV show is *Top Gear*."

"Such a guy show."

"Oh, and he plays the guitar."

I raise my head slowly, blinking at the bright fluorescent lights. "Hmm... kinda hot."

I cover my mouth immediately as if I were caught saying a naughty word. Vicky laughs but stops as soon as we hear the muffled voices. I try to shoo her away, turning around, so I am facing the computer and pretending that the words on my screen make sense when in reality, my nervous system has gone into meltdown mode.

"Hey, babe!"

Marcus turns my chair back around and plants a juicy kiss on my lips. Without seeming too obvious, I pull away

from him and flash a fake smile, a sign of endearment to
cover my nerves.

He slides his hand around the back of my neck and
pulls me in again. This is not appropriate work behavior, so
I gently scold him. He appears annoyed, but I ignore his
childish behavior.

The Jerk is standing beside him.

My eyes are heavily studying the pile in the carpet and
slowly but steadily move up and trace his shoes. They are
shiny black with a slight point. His pants are navy, tailored
to enhance his lean physique. Making sure my eyes avoid
his crotch, I slowly scan the buttons on his shirt until I have
no choice but to acknowledge his face. My eyes linger on his
lips. They are full and deliciously pink, parted slightly to
reveal his straight teeth. Just do it, just look at his goddamn
eyes because everyone is staring at you.

One, two, three, and there they are. Haden is watching,
and his simple stare has shot right through me, sitting in the
pit of my stomach. Maybe it's the four months apart, a new
hairstyle, or new clothes, but something about him is different. He looks well, sexy.

He is going to be your baby daddy.

You have to live the rest of your life around this man.

He has no fucking clue I am the devil in disguise
right now.

So why is he looking at me with an odd, yet familiar
stare?

There is a woman, or rather, a girl beside him. Standing
only just to his shoulders, she smiles kindly and introduces
herself as Eloise. She has perfect blonde tresses sitting on
her couture dress. With her ruby red lipstick and long dark
eyelashes, she is quite a stunning girl.

"Eloise is Haden's fiancée," Marcus gloat's.

Vicky moves her head in a not-so-subtle way toward me, watching my reaction and yelling with her eyes, "OMG, what the fuck?"

The shock and enormity of the situation are constricting my vocal cords, forcing me to reach out my hand and congratulate them. I manage to mumble something congratulatory, and when Haden's hand touches mine, I don't want to let go.

He watches our hands touch and holds on for a second before I pull away. Behind his glasses, his eyes fall upon me in silence until Vicky opens her mouth, breaking his gaze.

"So, you got engaged in London?"

"Paris, actually. Haden popped the question, and I said yes!" She flashes her ring, which I pretend to be interested in. There is something about princess cuts and Harry Winston in the same sentence. *Wow, I had no idea he had money since he bummed around so much.* Okay, that is not the issue at hand. What the hell is happening here? I mean, did fate just leave another pile of dog shit on my porch or what.

He. Is. Engaged.

You. Are. Carrying. His. Baby.

Everything that could possibly have gone wrong, has gone wrong.

Words are being exchanged around me, yet I'm deaf, falling into a dark hole and wishing I could rewind to the days when my biggest problem was Jason putting his white socks in with the pile of black ones.

"So, we should double date sometime," Marcus insists.

"Triple date. Find me a man, Marcus," Vicky adds.

"Hard to find you a man when you've slept with the whole city."

A mini argument starts, and I turn to face my computer,

fairly certain the contents of my stomach will soon end up all over my keyboard. I have been fortunate enough to avoid morning sickness, but I definitely know things are changing —including my appetite. I excuse myself and rush to the restroom.

Vicky follows straight after me. "You okay? Well, I know you're not."

"I can't do this, Vicky." I pace up and down the small restroom, then rush to the stall to vomit profusely. Vicky is holding my hair, rubbing my back until I flush the toilet and pull myself up.

Back at the basin, I repeatedly splash my face with cold water.

"You can do it because you have to," she reminds me, gently.

"Vicky, he's getting married. Four months is a short time to meet someone and get engaged, but fuck, I can't ruin his life."

"You're not ruining it! You have a baby inside you. That's a blessing."

"Then why do I feel like it's the worst thing that could happen to me?"

"Because you're scared, Pres. My mom was sixteen when she had me. Then eighteen when she had my brother. That's scary. You're thirty-two. You can handle this."

"So even if I can handle it, I'm not sure he can."

"He has time to get used to the idea. The baby isn't coming out now. You're only four months along. Still another five months. Plenty of time," Vicky reassures me.

I don't feel reassured. I know Haden well enough to know this is not in his plan. It wasn't in my plan either. But I know what I have to do. Haden would see this as the monumental fuck-up that ruined his life.

Marcus is still lingering around my cubicle when I return. He doesn't seem worried that I disappeared, and instead, makes plans for lunch.

"I won't be able to go out today. I've got a lot of work to do."

"It can wait," he states.

"No, it can't." My patience is wearing thin, and I just want to be alone for a minute to process my thoughts. "It's probably best you just go for now."

"What's going on with you?" He raises his tone.

"Marcus." I turn to face him. "I'm at work. I need this job to earn money. We can talk about things later."

I turn back around, ignoring the fact that he is still standing there.

"Okay, I'll call you tonight. I love you." With a solemn goodbye, he leaves my cubicle, and finally, I have the peace I deserve.

Later that afternoon, Mr. Sadler calls me into his office to discuss the manuscript I have been working on for months.

"Good afternoon, Presley," he greets me.

"Good afternoon, Mr. Sadler."

Taking a seat at the table, he finishes an email he is typing, then turns to face me. Beside his phone is a picture of his wife. She is a pretty lady, and the one time I met her at a work function, she was very nice. There are only pictures of her and who I assume is his daughter. He once told me she lived in Korea with her husband.

"I called you in today to briefly discuss the manuscript you've been working on. You've got the green light to go ahead with that one."

"Oh, wow! Thank you. That's fantastic news."

"There's just one—"

The Jerk walks into the room without even knocking. Mr. Sadler's face softens, and he motions for Haden to sit down. Taking a seat beside me, he leans back and crosses his legs accordingly, making me wonder how he managed that without squashing his masculine parts.

"So, as I was saying before Haden joined us, please go ahead with the manuscript for *Fallen Baby*. I'd like you to collaborate with Haden on releasing it before the holiday season."

What the...

"But... but I don't understand why we need to work on this project together. Besides, I thought he was busy with that sci-fi series he picked up in London?"

My panicked tone amuses Haden, and he cocks his head with a sly grin. From the corner of my eye, I can see that he is studying my body and, paranoid, I rest my hands on my stomach to cover the small bump that has grown overnight. Or so I think.

"Haden has been quite efficient, and that's already at the printers ready to go. Both of you have strong opinions, and together, I believe you will make a great team."

A great team? A great team was Regis and Kelly, Sonny and Cher, not Haden and Presley! And why is Haden not objecting to any of this, sitting here so quiet without an opinion.

"So that's settled? Okay. I need to head out. Please feel free to use my office if you need to brainstorm." Mr. Sadler is out of there fast, leaving my mouth gaping, staring in shock at the door.

"Why didn't you say something?" I snap.

"What do you want me to say? I already had the same

argument when he originally asked me," he responds, too casually for my liking.

"We can't work together."

"Why not? We're both professionals, Malone."

"Because it's awkward."

"Maybe for you. I've swept it under the rug as you suggested."

"What?" I shake my head, trying to process the enormity of another pile of shit added to my overgrowing doorstep. Working with him would mean I would have to talk to him, interact outside of working hours, and maintain a composed and professional relationship. There is no way in hell this will work, and even if I give it my best, his cocky attitude will only cause another fight between us. This all seems too much and makes me tired just thinking about it.

He opens his mouth to say something, but I interrupt him, noticing the time on the wall.

"I have to go."

I stand up and walk toward the door without saying goodbye.

"We're supposed to be discussing work. You can't just leave," he hisses.

"I have somewhere I need to be. I'll be back later."

He doesn't seem pleased with my answer. "Where?"

It's not the moment to tell him that I'm off to my sixteen-week scan. This lying is so draining, so I do the next best thing—I put on my bitch panties and unleash.

"None of your business, Jerk!"

I storm out of the room, then out of the building, hailing a taxi as I rush to my appointment.

Flustered, I barely make the appointment, and the receptionist ushers me to the room quickly. I'm instructed to undress and lie on the bed. As I settle in, the sonographer arrives and briefly explains what she'll be doing today since it's my first time.

Everything is going according to plan. The baby measures right, things and bits are in the correct positions. Not much to report, apart from the lack of emotion I feel. I always envisioned it differently. I'd be holding my husband's hand as we both cry at the sound of the heartbeat. Instead, I squirm uncomfortably from the gallon of water I am forced to drink while staring at a screen and pretending to know what I'm looking at, not to mention the copious amounts of warm lube spread all over me.

When she is finished, she gives me a picture of the baby.

I stare at it the entire taxi ride back to the office. Because I haven't felt the baby move, and the fact that I'm still in utter shock about being pregnant, the so-called attachment I'm supposed to feel is missing. According to a pregnancy book I picked up over the weekend, many women have already bonded with their baby at this point, and there's some bullshit about how it forms part of the mother-child bond after birth.

Great, my kid is going to hate me.

Back in the office, I drop my purse to the floor beneath my desk and make my way to one of the spare boardrooms, counting down the minutes until it's time to go home, something I rarely do.

"Oi!" Clive scans the area and pulls me aside. "What's the gossip with Haden getting engaged?"

"I know just as much as you... I think. Why? What do you know?" I pry.

"Dee is throwing a temper tantrum. I think she was hoping to pick up from where they left off."

"But Dee has Big Daddy now."

"Big Daddy has a big wife that caught wind of Dee."

"No!" I gasp. "Listen, I have to get to a meeting, but I want full details tomorrow. I swear, Clive, you really should work for the *Inquirer*."

"I know, my talents are beyond wasted here."

Upon entering the room, I see Haden sitting at the table with his laptop and coffee. He doesn't make eye contact with me and seems engrossed in whatever's on his screen. Probably porn.

"Make this quick," I complain. "I want to go home."

"You're the one pushing for this erotic make-believe story, not me."

"What's your problem with it? Obviously, Mr. Sadler has no issue, and neither does everyone else," I point out in a huff.

"There's fantasy, and then there is plain ridiculous. Men aren't virgins at twenty-five."

"Clearly, you weren't. Did you even read the story? He came from a strict Catholic upbringing. His mother had cancer from when he was eighteen to twenty-four. When she died, he wanted to honor her wishes."

"I did read it, it's just difficult for me to compute, but hey, I'm not a horny old woman reading erotic fantasies to escape my failing marriage."

"You don't need to be an old woman to enjoy these types of books. I was in a happy relationship and read books in this genre. It was fun, even gave me ideas."

Crap, I've said too much.

Haden shifts uncomfortably. "Right, when you were with Jasper."

"Jason," I correct him.

"Whatever," he mutters under his breath.

This is heading to an uncomfortable place, yet his snide comment irks me.

"Do you have a problem with Jason?"

"I don't know your ex-fiancé. Except for when you constantly mention him."

"I don't constantly mention him," I answer defensively.

"Right." He laughs. "It's obvious you're not over him."

"Of course, I'm not. I was with him for five years. I'm not that heartless. I'd like to think I'll always love him, just not in a way that would end happily ever after as soul mates."

"You read too much trash."

It's my turn to laugh. "You don't believe in love? You're engaged. Talk about the pot calling the kettle black."

"Yes... I am."

He doesn't reveal anything else, and I'm dying to ask how a man who is pushing twenty-six—thank you, Vicky, for the Facebook stalking—pops the question to a girl he has known less than four months.

Maybe she is knocked-up! Oh, this could be even worse than I thought.

"We should get back to work," I huff.

"So, chapter five. Crystal is a single mother with a five-year-old son forced to work as an escort to put food on the table. I'm worried that those feminist groups are going to bully the author. We don't need bad publicity."

"I agree. Perhaps the author needs to reword a few lines just to give a little more background as to how she was forced to become an escort."

We talk more and jot down notes, ready for our meeting with the author tomorrow. For the majority of our meeting, we don't argue. But of course, all good things must come to an end.

"I have to admit, this single-mom stuff is tough on this character. Glad I ain't a woman."

I swallow the massive lump restricting my ability to breathe and fumble with the button on my blouse. *This is your opening—go ahead, do it!* Yet, I continue sitting in silence, chickening out once again. I am such a coward.

"Life hands you lemons, you gotta make lemonade somehow."

"If life hands you lemons, you grab some tequila and have a party." He smirks.

"See, that's the difference between you and me. Tequila and partying are a thing of the past. When you grow up one day, you'll realize it isn't worth all the hangovers."

He leans in, too close for my comfort. "Funny, Malone, you seemed to enjoy tequila and partying that night at the bar."

"And that's exactly why you shouldn't drink. You always regret your actions the next day," I say, staring at him.

He appears offended, pulling back immediately. Straightening his tie and adjusting his glasses, he clears his throat. "You're such a bitch sometimes, Malone."

"Just like you are a jerk... all the time."

Shutting down his laptop, he storms out of the room without a word while I breathe a sigh of relief.

This is too hard.

It isn't worth forming a friendship when he will soon hate me and wish I never existed.

TEN

Avoiding Marcus is harder than I anticipated. The rational part of my brain knows it is best that I tell Haden before Marcus. It seems like the right thing to do, but Marcus is desperate, horny, and not afraid of letting me know that. I can't pull the *period* card out because he gives me alternatives, and seriously what is it with young guys and their desire for anal activities? Nevertheless, I manage to avoid any physical activity with Marcus knowing it's for the best.

My clothing has started to feel restrictive, and I am fairly certain I can see a small bump, still small enough to pass it off as bloating. I can't button my pants, so I stick to wearing skirts and loose-fitting blouses. On top of the stress of telling Haden and Marcus, I have my parents to deal with.

To soften the blow, telling my sister, Gemma, gives me a taste of what is about to come. She is over the moon and wants all the juicy tidbits about baby daddy. Then came a whole speech about how much she was going to spoil her niece or nephew. We talked about the right way to tell Mom and Dad, and agree it is best over the phone followed by a visit.

My nerves are shot to hell about making that phone call, but I can't hide it forever. Plus, I really need my mom and her parental advice right now.

As predicted, my parents were deeply disappointed, especially because they loved Jason so much and spent an hour telling me that I should have fallen pregnant with him. It isn't a rewind-and-let's-try-again situation. The damage is done. Mom, of course, is extra disappointed Haden is younger than me as it is frowned upon in her generation for a woman to marry a younger man. That lecture took another hour. By the end of the phone call, I am emotionally spent. As soon as we hang up, my mom calls me right back and starts panicking.

"Are you taking your prenatal vitamins?"

"Make sure you don't eat blue cheese and cold meats."

"Don't sleep on your stomach. You might squash the baby."

I could have listened all day to her. There is nothing more comforting at that moment than some motherly advice. I told her I will clear my schedule next month and fly to Virginia to spend a few days with them before I get too big. She seems more at ease by the end and even gloats about being a grandmother and knitting booties.

With that now ticked off my list, I know I have no choice but to tell Haden.

The perfect opportunity presents itself on Friday night, a week later. I suggested we work on finalizing some details on *Fallen Baby* and asked Haden to come to my apartment. Hoping he doesn't get the wrong idea, I ordered a ton of takeout remembering the old the-way-to-a-man's-heart-is-through-his-stomach saying. Not that I want to get to his heart, I just want to remain alive by the end of the conversation.

He turns up at seven on the dot, dressed in light jeans and a white tee. The Chucks on his feet make me think he will not be going out clubbing, especially since he is also wearing a baseball cap. I blame the hormones again for noticing how delicious he looks. I don't bother to dress up. I'm wearing a loose-fitting tank top and drawstring shorts. It's pretty much the only thing that fits right now, plus it is scorching hot outside. Being pregnant in the summer has not made me a happy camper.

Walking barefoot back to my sofa, I ask him to take a seat before offering him a drink.

"Nice place you got here. You moving?" he asks, spotting the bare walls and stacked boxes.

"Yeah, soon. This was ours, but we decided to sell. Had a few offers, and I think we're closing soon."

"Ours?"

"Jason's and mine. We bought it two years ago."

"Right. Have you found a place?"

"I've been to inspect a few. Not much in my price range. I wish I could afford to buy this place, but a part of me thinks it'll be good to move on."

That seems to be the extent of our forced conversation, so I grab my laptop and go through my bullet points, all the while finding the courage to start the inevitable. Throughout the conversation, my head is repeating what I'm about to say over and over again until the point when he waits for me to respond, and I have no idea what he's just asked.

"I'm sorry, what was the question?"

"You seem distracted. I asked if the author plans a sequel."

"Uh... not at this stage."

"All right," he says, crossing his arms. "I'll bite. Why are you acting weird?"

"Weird? Okay..." I take a long breath. "This... is very... I need to ask you a question."

He sits back into the sofa. With a composed yet undermining stare, he waits patiently if not eagerly for me to speak. I've become a little distracted, imagining myself sitting on top of him, riding his beautiful pierced dick, and then, fuck these damn hormones! Focus!

"That night in the alley—"

"You said we weren't to talk about that," he is quick to remind me.

"I know I said that, but I have to ask you something, and I don't want you reading more into it."

"What are you going on about, Malone?"

Here goes, my eggs all in one basket—literally.

"Did you..." *God, how do I ask this?* "Did you... you know, finish?"

"Finish?"

"Finish... do the deed. Shoot your load."

There is a wicked grin on his face and rubbing his barely-existent beard in an annoying yet smoldering manner, he has me stumbling on my thoughts.

"Let me get this straight, Malone. You're asking me if I came?"

Sitting cross-legged on the sofa, I feel so juvenile, nodding to suppress the sheer embarrassment.

"I'm curious as to why you're only asking me this now?"

"Because I just need to know."

With his arm draped along the back of the sofa, he inches closer, intimidating me with a persistent stare. He doesn't realize I'm in the prime of the pregnancy, loaded with hormones, ready to pounce and beg him to fuck me because I am so damn horny I can't even think straight.

"It's a personal question, and you're demanding an answer without explaining why you need to know."

"Cut the bullshit, Jerk. We passed personal when you decided to screw me in the alley."

"You cut the bullshit, Malone. Why do you wanna know?"

"I'm pregnant," I blurt out without thinking, without any emotion.

There.

Done.

Phew.

I release a breath, finally able to breathe a little.

It's not just one ball of tumbleweed, but a whole colony that rolls past as the silence falls over the room. I don't dare look at him, his heavy breathing enough of an indication that he's about to have a stroke.

"Why weren't you on the fucking pill, Malone?" he demands, raising his voice and catching me off guard while jumping off the sofa.

"I was on the pill! Why would you come inside me and assume that?"

He is pacing the floor, his hat thrown onto the table as he runs his fingers through his hair in utter despair. His eyes are wild with panic, and he looks ready to smash the first thing in sight.

I'm right.

He does it moments later, and the porcelain lucky elephant that Gemma gave me is splattered on the floor.

Okay, don't go ape-shit on him. The elephant is replaceable. Have some compassion for the Jerk, you've just delivered the most lifechanging news. He needs to process.

"I put a fucking condom on! You pulled it off. Then we used another one."

"What do you want me to say? Scientifically, we beat the odds, and I don't know what the hell happened or how," I yell back in frustration.

"How could this happen, then? And how can you assume it's mine? Who knows who you were doing? Marcus... it's got to belong to Marcus."

He didn't just go there. Yep, he did.

Unleash the hounds.

Quick to my feet, I'm eye to eye with him, matching his stance. Even though he towers over me while I'm barefoot, he doesn't intimidate me one bit. My arms are straight, hands locked into fists, ready to tear into him.

"I'm *not* that person. Blood tests and ultrasounds confirmed how far along I am. I can't even... you know what?" I say, barely able to control my anger. "You can walk away now. Forget I told you this. You're young, got your whole life ahead of you. I can raise this baby. I don't need someone in my life thinking I'm a whore."

"I didn't... look, I'm sorry. It's just—"

"Too late for apologies, Jerk."

Silence, again.

This time, he sits back on the sofa and bends over with his face between his legs. His arms are resting on his knees, but they appear to be shaking. Neither of us saying a word, the silence continues as the clock ticks over.

"I'm engaged," he mumbles, his words barely audible. "To Eloise."

"Yes, you are. I don't want anything from you."

Still, without knowing what the hell happened in London, the name and sentiment strike a nerve with me, almost like a how-dare-I-ruin-things-for-him attitude. It dawns on me that he doesn't even take a moment to ask me how I'm doing, whether I've had morning sickness, or anything about the baby. It's all about him, and why did I expect anything different from Haden Cooper?

I should have just kept this a secret and moved away, and life could continue for him. Except you want the best for your unborn child, and having a father around who is a positive male role model is supposed to be a good thing. I wouldn't go as far as saying the Jerk could be a positive role model, though.

Again, I shouldn't have breathed a word.

"Marcus. Does he know?"

"No... I thought you needed to know first. I'll tell him tomorrow."

"I want to be there when you tell him," he responds, threatening me as he struggles to compose his anger.

"Wha... why? I don't want to deal with your ego bullshit," I inform him. "I'll just tell him, and it's over."

I want him to leave.

I want to climb under my covers and cry myself to sleep.

I'm scared, frightened, and unsure of how I am going to raise this baby alone.

Somewhere deep down inside, I wish he would have stepped up and taken responsibility for his actions. But true to form, he grabs his phone and wallet from the table and without making eye contact he says, "I have to go."

There are no more words, and the second he is gone, I begin to cry myself to sleep.

ELEVEN

One thing that doesn't surprise me about Marcus' kitchen is that it is a complete and utter mess. It's midday Saturday, and the place looks like a tornado just blew through. My OCD is having a heart attack, desperate to grab some disinfectant and scrub the place clean, but this isn't the purpose of my visit. Although I am wondering if it would be highly inappropriate to offer to clean his apartment after I tell him I'm pregnant with his cousin's baby.

A late-night drunken call from Marcus alerted me to the welcome-back party being held for the Jerk and what's her face. *Okay, that's mean. She's got a face, a pretty one at that, so no need to get on that jealous horse, Presley.*

According to Marcus, Haden never showed. Eloise was worried but somehow got over it and partied hard with the rest of them. Of course, I know why he didn't turn up. He was probably smashing up the city, picturing my face on every pole.

So here I am, sitting in front of the countertop as Marcus sits beside me looking like death. Dark circles surround his dull green eyes, and his skin looks pale and sickly. Even though we are indoors, he is wearing his hoodie with the hood covering his head. The sun filtering through the small window appears to irritate him, and he squints his eyes involuntarily, curling his body like a nocturnal animal.

The giant curveball to this mad situation—I didn't expect the Jerk to be here as well.

He turned up only moments ago and sent Eloise on a mission to get everyone coffee from the café a couple of blocks away. She doesn't appear as wasted as the rest of them and still looks stunning after a night of partying. A mini-argument erupts after she blatantly refuses to be his coffee monkey, but he manages to convince her somehow.

Haden stands against the sink, and just as I predicted, his right hand is wrapped in bandages. I probably should ask if he is okay, but that would mean I care, which I don't.

He is purposefully avoiding eye contact with me and is clearly still very pissed off, insinuating that this is all *my* fault. Well, it takes two to tango, buddy, and one selfish dick to blow his load.

Earlier, I asked for a glass of water, but after witnessing how dirty the kitchen is, I leave my untouched glass sitting on the countertop. I am parched but can't be bothered to rinse the glass out. Marcus interrupts my thoughts, questioning why the three of us are standing in the kitchen.

So, I start with the beginning—what happened that night in the alley. Throughout my recollection of the events, I honestly have to pinch myself. Here I am standing with a guy I was fooling around with and a guy who is be my child's father.

The reality of the situation is that I barely know them, have no clue when their birthdays are, let alone their favorite colors. Okay, favorite color is lame, but I cannot feel any more like a stranger in this confined room. I have a better relationship with the man who owns the local laundromat, and that's saying a lot.

"You're pregnant with Haden's baby?" Marcus laughs, shaking his head in disbelief. "Honestly, what a sick joke you guys came up with."

"It's true. Why would I lie about this? But we aren't together. It's not like we were seeing each other," I tell him in my defense.

"You're not together. You're with me," he responds bitterly, spitting out his words in haste.

Clearly, I am stupid to think that being pregnant with his cousin's baby is not an automatic breakup. Not being accustomed to this possessive side of him, I choose my words carefully, not wanting to rub salt into his very open wound.

"Marcus. We had our fun, but the reality is, I'm going to be a mother. My priority is raising this baby."

Haden crosses his arms in silence, waiting for a reaction. I look in his direction, goading some sort of help from him to save me from this uncomfortable situation. Nothing, of course, even when Marcus reaches for the bottle of bourbon from the cupboard and drinks it straight from the bottle.

He wipes his mouth with the back of his hand. "Why the fuck did you both tell me nothing went on?"

I glance aside, avoiding Haden. "Because it was nothing. A drunken mistake."

"Well, it's not nothing since you're having a baby together!" He slams his fist against the countertop. Ouch! It looks painful, but nothing in Marcus' expression, aside from pure hatred, makes me think he feels a single thing.

Looking much like death himself, the Jerk is dressed in all black. If one didn't know his life was turned upside down less than twenty-four hours ago, you would think he's attending a funeral. Maybe it is a funeral, a farewell to his carefree life of no responsibilities and only having to worry about himself.

Finally, he steps in. "Back off, Marcus. This is hard on all of us."

Marcus jumps to his feet and stumbles to where Haden is standing. Head on, Marcus sways the bottle, taking another swig and throwing it into the sink behind him. The sound of the glass smashing startles me, and I know shit is about to get real.

With shaky hands, Marcus latches onto Haden's shirt and presses against him.

"You fucking knew she was with me. You fucking knew I loved her!" He almost spits into Haden's face.

Being somewhat sober gives Haden the advantage, and he pushes Marcus off, watching him fall backward. I reach out to help him up, and with a shrill, he laughs as he wraps his arms around me.

"Get rid of it. You can have another baby with me. We're in love. We can get married if you want. Just get rid of it," he demands in a calm yet dominant tone.

Shocked at the harshness of his words, I set the record straight once and for all. "I'm seventeen weeks along. If I wanted that, no one would make that decision for me," I angrily yell at him, annoyed at his lack of morals and willingness to voice them. "I don't expect you to understand, but it's happening, whether you like it or not."

"Of course, I don't fucking like it! I love you, and this is how you repay me?"

Did he really say those words? This is getting worse by the minute. Marcus has no clue what love is. Love to him is mind-blowing orgasms at night followed by a morning blowjob. I don't know how else to spell it out for him without being the wicked witch and breaking his heart.

"Put yourself in my shoes for a second. I'm raising this baby alone. I'm terrified. I didn't purposely do this to hurt you."

Marcus turns to face Haden with an arctic glare. "You're not even helping her?"

"Back the fuck off. Let me deal with this shit," Haden warns him.

I sit in silence, listening to the argument unfold before me. Like a strong force gravitating me toward my stomach, I rest my palms on top of the baby. Suddenly, the protector instinct kicks in, and I can no longer sit here and listen to what is being said about this tiny human growing inside me.

"Now the baby is 'shit'?" As I raise my voice above the incessant noise, they both stop and turn to face me. I grab my purse and hop off the stool. I think about saying a few final words, but instead, I leave their apartment and the mess behind me.

Turning the corner amongst the other pedestrians, my phone vibrates, and I contemplate reading the text. Whoever it is can wait. Finding myself a small café a few blocks down the street, I order myself a tea and *the* most expensive chocolate cake that ever existed. It is a slice of heaven and exactly what I need at a moment when alcohol isn't an option.

I try calling Vicky, but all the calls lead to voicemail, so then I call Gemma. We have a long chat about everything, and by the end, she reminds me again that she will always be there to help the baby and me, even suggesting I move to California.

After ending the call, I sit for a long time thinking about my options. In five months, I will have a baby to raise.

Maybe moving to California isn't such a bad idea. I need help despite having too much pride to ask for it, and I have to consider what future I want for my baby. Even though I love the city, it may not be the best place to settle down. A child needs a home, not a shoebox apartment, which is all I can afford at this moment.

In the midst of this train of thought, there is Jason to consider. It seems like common courtesy to tell him I am pregnant, but every time I attempt to type a message or even make that call, my body starts to dry heave. One goddamn problem at a time, and he is perhaps the least of my worries.

Back at home, I avoid reading that text and dive into some housework. Cranking up the music as loud as my neighbors will tolerate, I grab a bucket and some gloves to do some major scrubbing on my bathroom tiles. When I can practically see my reflection, I decide to take a long shower and climb into bed with a good book. I keep reading the same line over and over again, and I know that I have to read that text because it's eating away at me.

Haden: *I didn't mean it. This is a lot.*

The asshole wasn't saying anything that I didn't already know. Caught up in the heat of the moment, I am able to understand how overwhelming this is for him. The difference is that I have no choice but to accept my actions. This baby is growing inside of me, and every minute that ticks by, I am reminded of that.

～

Haden didn't show up at work for two weeks. When I asked Mr. Sadler of his whereabouts, he simply informed me Haden has taken some personal time off. I didn't question further, and our resident National Inquirer, Clive, told me he was in Maui at some surfing gig and scouting wedding locations with Eloise.

Seriously, what a fucking dick.

Marcus didn't call me except for last Friday night when he was obviously drunk and asked if he could come over, so I could give him a blowjob. It was laughable, and a polite 'no' was all I could manage. He then proceeded to rant on and tell me that I'm a no-good bitch, and he could get better head elsewhere. That was my cue to disconnect the call, but not before he threw the apologies in and professed his love for me, again.

Talk about being a hormonal mess, and I mean Marcus, not me.

Project *Fallen Baby* is in my hands, so I spent time tying up all the loose ends. The author would be attending our yearly publisher's event on Friday night. It will be a great chance for her to meet fellow authors and for us to let our hair down at a fully paid catered event. Too bad I couldn't drink, though Clive will no doubt drink enough for the entire office.

My biggest dilemma is finding a dress to wear to the party since my belly now pops out, and my current wardrobe is no longer an option. Vicky offers to go shopping with me, but her voluptuous figure fits perfectly into every dress she tries on. I, on the other hand, give up shopping in the 'normal' women's stores and hit up the maternity shop. I expected ugly frocks, so I am quite surprised when the shop assistant shows me some fabulous evening wear.

It doesn't stop me from feeling sorry for myself, though.

"You're silly. You haven't put on a pound apart from this little stomach forming," Vicky tries to reassure me, rubbing my belly while cooing at the baby.

"I feel like a beached whale."

"You feel like a beached whale now? Wait until the end."

"Thanks. So much to look forward to," I answer back sarcastically.

"It's all part of the experience, Pres," she reminds me.

As the shop assistant bags the items, I lean into Vicky, whispering, "My breasts are huge, and my nipples... I can't even begin to tell you what's happening with them."

Vicky raises her eyebrows, and the nipple-talk is put on hold until we leave the store.

Having found a black cocktail dress in a stretchy fabric, I am all set and ready to go. Most of the office will attend, and Vicky is certain on there being some eligible bachelors she can get her hands on.

The event is being held at a rooftop bar consisting of a small and intimate crowd. The view is sensational, the bright lights and city skyline surrounding us. Clive is terrified of heights. Standing beside me with a fierce grip on my arm, his face pales from the sheer terror of being thirty stories high.

"I'm scared I'll shit my pants, Pres."

"You won't shit your pants, and you know why? Because they cost you a whole paycheck, and what would Gianni Versace say if he knew you shit in his ridiculously expensive pants?"

"Okay, you have a point. At least if there was some good eye candy here, then I could distract myself." Clive shrivels his face in discontent as a not-so-attractive waiter walks by carrying some shrimp.

"I need to go talk to Mr. Sadler," I tell him. "Look, here comes Vicky. If there's anyone who has found the hot guys, it'll be her."

"Okay, so here's the lowdown. A bunch of guys near the bar who belong to that party over there are single. The guy with the black slicked-back hair is gay," Vicky informs us.

"Vicky, your gaydar has been off so many times," Clive complains.

"Well, this time I straight-up asked him if he wanted to come home with me. He said he likes playing with snakes, not beavers and pussies."

I snort out my club soda, laughing at Vicky. Clive disappears into thin air, then reappears at the bar trying to make conversation with the animal lover.

"Is that true?" I ask, still unable to contain my laughter.

"Of course not! As if I'd ask him to come home with me. You know my rule... minimum two drinks first, then always at his place."

"Oh, that's right, your rules," I mock.

"Maybe if you stuck to your seven-week rule, you wouldn't be in this predicament," she points out in jest.

I poke my tongue out at her, juvenile but called for. Leaving her to complete her man mission, I wander around until I find Mr. Sadler standing near the small stage.

"You look beautiful, Presley. And I guess congratulations are in order. When are you due?" Mr. Sadler smiles, asking in a fatherly and concerned way.

During the week, news broke about the pregnancy. It was the biggest scandal to rock the office. With Vicky busy on an assignment, Clive was my informer. Dee wasn't talking to me, backstabbing and calling me every name she could think of. Trina had joined forces with her, calling me a traitor and a homewrecker. Not sure how, since they weren't a couple, but that's her warped imagination for you.

"Five months. I'm sorry I didn't get a chance to tell you myself. It's been... overwhelming, and I was waiting for the right time," I admit.

"Understandable, my dear. If you need anything, my wife and I are only a phone call away," he pats my arms, reassuring me.

Something about the way he looks at me mirrors the look my dad gives me. You know when your dad has that my-baby-girl-is-all-grown-up speech followed by a heartfelt smile and glassy eyes? It was a nice gesture. He is—and has always been—a great boss to everyone in the office, always attentive and making sure his employees are happy. I had met Mrs. Sadler at the event last year and could tell she was of a similar nature.

I give him my thanks and kindly excuse myself to mingle with the authors and other guests. The night itself is a success, and just when I think about pulling out the I'm-pregnant-and-need-to-call-it- an-early-night card, Haden is standing at the doorway dressed in a fitted navy suit and looking exceptionally handsome. His hair is brushed toward the side, and his tan looks fresh from the Hawaiian sun. And those glasses, what the hell is it about those damn reading glasses?

I have to pull up my jaw from the floor, ignoring the throb between my legs because he is completely off-limits. I blamed the pregnancy hormones, again, especially after Vicky called me out for thinking the pretzel guy on the corner of Fifth looked sexy in his stained shirt.

Haden is pulled to a group and shakes hands with each person while scanning the room. When his eyes find me, something changes. His face softens yet stills, staring at me deeply as if he is lost in a trance. I beg my eyes to turn away, but the way he is looking at me—something in the way his eyes pierce through me—sends the butterflies into overdrive, much to my discontent. My butterflies can't fly for him. They need to be saved for the one I will spend the rest of my life with, not the ass standing at the opposite side of the room with a rocking tan from his pre-honeymoon in Maui with the evil witch.

Whoa, calm down already!

He appears to be excusing himself, and moments later, he is walking toward me. Something in his stride exudes way too much confidence. God, he does have a good stride, though.

"Can we go somewhere quiet to talk?"

I nod, and he leads the way to a secluded part of the terrace. There are a few scattered tables and chairs unattended, so I take a seat and wait for him to begin the conversation. He doesn't say anything, and I'm expecting the worst. Just don't cry.

"I'm sorry for the way I reacted. This was a shock," he says in a cemented tone, not sounding like an apology whatsoever.

I remain tightlipped, waiting for the whole I'm-not-ready-to-be-a-dad speech.

"I took some time off to consider this, and I just don't know how this is going to work," he concedes.

"You think *you* were in shock. I almost had a coronary," I confess. "It's probably best we come up with a plan and expectations. That way neither of us is disappointed. So, let me set the record straight to avoid any confusion. I'm not looking for a husband, boyfriend, whatever. I'm not here to tie you down."

He appears taken aback by my forwardness and

perhaps slightly offended by my quick stance on not getting romantically involved. *He is engaged—what the hell did he expect to happen?*

"I'm getting married. Eloise... she knows..." he trails off, staring into the night's dark sky.

"And she still wants to get married?" I ask, annoyed at myself that a hint of jealousy accompanied my question.

"Yes, she wants to be involved."

"But... but how can I allow someone else to be involved in my child's life? I don't know her," I tell him, trying to calm myself down. I hadn't even thought about that being a possibility, and now the reality of it frightens me to the core.

"You don't know me either," he reminds me.

"No, I don't, but you're the father."

"And that's another thing..." he hesitates, avoiding further eye contact until he has no choice but to look me straight in the eyes. "I'd like to have a paternity test done."

Deeply staring at me, his facial expressions remain stagnant as he waits for me to rationally respond to his request. *Fat fucking chance.* He outright called me a whore, again. The anger is bubbling at the surface, and I am gripping my clutch so tightly under the table, I expect the contents to explode. Emotions are difficult to disguise at the best of times, and this moment is far from the best of times.

I stand up, and with shaky hands, give him the reality check he needs. "You know what, Haden? I don't get you. One minute I think you're not such a bad guy and may actually have a heart beating somewhere, then the next, you act like the biggest asshole to walk this earth."

My pride, dignity, and lack of self-control are the reasons I have to walk away.

"I'm leaving. You can have your test. In fact, I'll be

booking it as soon as possible, so maybe then you'll get it through your thick skull that you *are* the father."

Saying goodbye to everyone is difficult in the state of anger I'm in, but I manage to plaster on a fake smile, doing my rounds until I can go home and officially climb into a dark hole.

This isn't going to work.

This complete stranger walks into my life, and every time we are in the same air space, it ends disastrously.

I blame him—immature and stubborn like the rest of that generation.

Jason, on the other hand, he was mature, polite, respectful. That means crap right now because it isn't his sperm doing laps in my uterus.

A quick taxi ride home, I strip and get into bed. I don't attempt reading, hoping the exhaustion will knock me out. Staring at the dark ceiling, my mind is playing tricks on me, and when the light of my phone brightens the room, I welcome the distraction.

Haden: *I don't know what I'm thinking when I'm around you. Seeing your stomach tonight was a reality check. I don't know how to be a dad.*

I quickly type the first thing that comes to mind with no filter from this hormonal pregnant woman.

Me: *I'll book the appointment first thing next week. You'll get your answers. Then I'm off to visit my family for a few days. You don't have to see me which is probably for the best.*

. . .

Just when I place the phone down on my nightstand, there is a knock on my door. Late-night knocks aren't exactly safe unless, of course, Vicky's been out on the town. So, armed with my frying pan and baseball bat for safe measures, I walk toward the door and stare through the peephole.

It's him.

I unlock the deadbolt and pull off the chain to open the door. He is leaning against the door frame with no jacket and his hair a wild mess. I can't detect any alcohol on his breath, and his eyes appear crystal clear behind his frames.

"You don't need to do the test. I shouldn't have asked for it."

"Too late. You did, and well, maybe it's for the best." I cross my arms, noticing his stare fixated on my tank top that is semi see-through. He's a guy, they are like magnets to breasts, and my breasts could qualify to be their own planets right now.

Don't read anything more into this.

Quick to bring his tortured gaze back up to my face, he carries on. "I want to come with you to visit your family."

Shocked by the change of subject, I stare back at him oddly. "Why would you want to do that? They know the whole story."

"Because they need to meet me. I'm going to be around their grandchild every day. Surely, that counts for something."

Did he just tell me he's going to be around the baby every day? This is getting more complicated by the minute. I am confused, to say the least, plus it's after midnight and well past my bedtime. No good can come from this conversation.

"I really don't think—"

"I'm going. Either you tell them I'll be there, or I will," he threatens, eyeing me dubiously.

"Are you threatening me?" I raise my voice.

"Honestly, Malone, why do you have to be so fucking stubborn all the time?"

I call defeat. "Fine. Your funeral. My dad once shot a deer on top of the mountain range from our front porch. Just saying."

He appears amused, the corners of his lips curving upward. To disguise his moment of weakness, he moves his hand toward his stubble and rubs his chin gently.

"I have a black belt in martial arts. Plus, I can wrestle a boar in the wild. But's that a story for another time."

I let out a small laugh. Maybe this won't be so bad, and just maybe there is a side to him that I haven't seen yet.

But that's the thing about maybes. They leave you with a ray of hope when chances are you're bound to get hurt one way or another.

TWELVE

The plan to visit my parents came to a screeching halt when Jason called to inform me that the apartment has sold. It happened late Sunday, and I missed his call while taking the longest nap that ever existed. Fatigue is a bitch. My new routine gym effort was proving difficult as was my ability to curb my coffee cravings. Tea is coffee's bitch.

Yes, I am *that* tired.

I contemplate calling him back, but I'm weak and extremely aroused. The stupid what-to-expect-when-you're-expecting books were spot on. My hormones have turned into a sorority of college boys all trying to get me to succumb to a wild orgy. I knew if I talked to Jason, I would invite him over one last time and take him on the kitchen bench, armed with a tub of maple syrup.

Cravings are also a bitch.

But texting can only get you so far, so I swallow my pride, hormones, and all the other crap and call him.

"Long time no speak," he greets warmly.

My body involuntarily sinks into my bed at the sound of

his voice. I miss him, I miss his voice. I can almost smell him over the phone.

"So, it's sold? I'll sure miss this place."

"The buyers are a young couple. Nice enough. Anyway, they want to move in next month."

Add more stress to my growing ball of stress twine. "That's quick. I'm half packed. I guess it shouldn't be a problem," I respond calmly.

There is an awkward silence, and I hear a shuffle over the phone. "So how have you been?"

"Good," I reply. "And you?"

"Yeah, good. I'm seeing someone," he admits quietly.

"I figured. You're something special, and it was only a matter of time." I smile into the receiver.

He laughs, and it's familiar and comforting. "And you?"

I had thought about telling him about the baby but decided against it. It doesn't matter anyway. He has moved on. Sooner or later, he will find out, but for now, I'm downright exhausted and can't find the energy to have that long-winded conversation which will probably end up with me in tears.

"No, still single. Just working and stuff."

We talk for another hour about work, family, and life. It's like visiting an old friend, and during the conversation, it becomes even clearer to me we made the right decision. He hasn't changed one bit, but that's Jason. Happy to live in the same bubble, just screwing someone else instead of me.

In my mad rush to find somewhere to live, Vicky comes to my rescue. She has a friend living not too far away who has a room available. Her name is Kate, and she's renting the apartment from a friend. I call her first thing on Monday and have a long chat about the room and apartment. She's super nice, and even with her British accent, I sometimes have no clue what she's saying.

We agree to meet at her apartment later in the afternoon so she can show me around.

"So that's the kitchen, and just over on the right will be your room."

Kate opens the door to a sunlit room with a view of a small park. It's furnished with a double bed and dark wooden dresser that match the floors. There's a walk-in closet that's the perfect size to fit all my clothes, not that I have many now since I morphed into a hippopotamus.

"It's gorgeous. But I wouldn't be here for long, Kate. With the baby and all, I'll need to find my own place."

"That's totally fine. The room's always been vacant. The only time it gets used is when my friends from L.A. fly over, but even then, the lot of them prefer to stay at the Waldorf, so they can have a gander at the cute bellhops."

I wasn't quite sure what gander means, but I laughed anyway because the bellhops are indeed cute.

We sit in the kitchen and talk for a bit, getting to know each other. Kate is from Manchester and moved here permanently a few years back. She is head of a division in her company and is completely career-obsessed, which she blames for her lack of relationships.

"So, no boyfriend?" I grin, taking a sip of my tea.

"Uh... I wouldn't call it that. It's complicated."

"It could be worse... look at me."

Kate states she's dying to know my story, and given that we're roommates now, I tell her the truth. All of it, holding nothing back.

"Wow! All my friends are married with kids or getting married, except for Vicky. Vicky is a hoot. Did she tell you about our weekend in Atlantic City?"

"That was you?" I laugh.

I remember the story vividly. Vicky and a friend had met these guys at the craps table, and they weren't shy about letting them know they wanted to spoil them for the whole weekend. They were taken to the fanciest restaurants and showered with lavish gifts. Then when it came time for the intimate dinner in the hotel room, Vicky and Kate both did a runner and checked into another hotel. They even bought wigs in case they ran into them.

When they got to the airport, the men happened to be there and were super pissed. The only thing that saved Vicky and Kate was that the airport security detained the men because of the large amount of cash they were carrying. The girls got on their flight, lucky to get away from them.

"That was me, all right. It was totally hilarious. No partying for you, though. So, if you don't mind me asking, where's baby daddy now?"

"Around, somewhere. As I said, we don't really communicate well."

"So, is he still getting married? What kinda bird would wanna get hitched after hearing that news?"

"The kinda bird who must really love him, I guess."

Kate pulls the keys out of her purse and removes a spare from the key ring. "Here you go. Feel free to move your stuff in whenever. I'll be working late most nights this week because my boss is in town. Maybe you can join us for dinner one night?"

"Sure." I smile back in return.

With that problem sorted, I focus on packing up my apartment and tying up some loose ends at work before I leave to visit my folks. Haden booked a flight the day after mine and will be staying only for the weekend. He tried to book a motel, but my mother insisted he could sleep in the guestroom. He thought it was very nice of her, but deep down, I knew it was her way of watching him and asking a thousand questions. She reminds me every day that he's the father, and this is who my child will look up to.

Great, my child will wrestle boars.

The day before I'm scheduled to leave, I am met by an unusual surprise. As I'm just about to grab a quick lunch, I look up and see Eloise standing at my cubicle. Wearing a pale pink knitted top and a gray pencil skirt, she stands proudly in her high patent pumps. Her long blonde hair is parted to one side, and even I have to admit, she is drop-dead gorgeous.

"Hi, Presley. I don't mean to intrude. I was hoping you were free for lunch?"

Keeping my expression fixed, I smile forcefully and nod my head in agreeance. I wondered if this had been Haden's idea—get the mother of his child and future wife to bond in order to make his role in all of this easier. I would give her an hour, at most. Then find some pregnant excuse to leave.

We head to some 'healthy living' restaurant not too far from the office. Salads aren't really on my agenda, considering all I can think about is a big fat juicy hamburger and a bowl of syrup on the side. Nevertheless, I order a warm chicken salad. Eloise orders a soup that looks like mushed lawn.

"Haden told me everything," she opens up. "It was quite a shock, and definitely took me some time to take it all in."

I remain quiet, not sure where she's going with this.

"I love Haden. Meeting him was like fate, you know? Everything was just perfect, and he's just so... I don't know, it's hard to explain."

Maybe she can't explain it, but it is written all over her face—that constant glow of happiness, the eyes dancing in delight, the smile that cannot be erased. She's in love, and here I sit without a man in my life and the very real possibility I will never find love because I'll be a single mother.

"We want to help you, both Haden and me. I know he has difficulty showing it, but he's a kind person, Presley. You just have to be patient with him," she says softly.

"Eloise, despite what happened, I don't know him aside from my dealings with him in our office. You have to understand that I need to be able to trust both of you with my child."

"But it's Haden's child, too," she reminds me.

"Yes," I admit. "But I'm carrying this baby. I'm the primary parent."

"So that's another thing. We'd like to talk about putting together a schedule. You know, what days and weekends we can have the baby."

My warm chicken salad might as well have been a bowl of jagged-edged rocks. Swallowing a mouthful, the sharp edges painfully slide down along with my overwhelming desire to tell them to fuck off. The baby is still inside me, and we're planning out schedules?

She reminds me of myself, and maybe if she weren't his fiancée, I would think this is a good idea, especially since I plan everything out and even mentioned this to him. But I'm a hormonal monster. This baby is mine, and there is no chance in hell they will steal this baby away from me.

"While your suggestions are appreciated, I'd like to discuss all this with Haden," I say in my polite yet gritty voice.

"I'm sorry." She places her hand on mine, making me feel very uncomfortable. "This weekend will be great for both of you. Give you time to talk about plans and schedules."

"You won't be joining us?" I ask, pretending to play dumb.

"No, I have a dress fitting, plus my bachelorette night." She smiles playfully.

The looming wedding is a dark gray cloud hovering over me. None of it made sense, but it's also none of my business. Haden obviously had his reasons for proposing marriage and nothing should stop him marrying someone he loves. But despite my ignorance of his upcoming nuptials, I'd be a fool to think it didn't affect me. I found myself caring one minute, then not caring the next.

"Oh, I didn't realize you were getting married so soon."

"Still six months away, but my schedule is so busy, and my best friend is getting married in two months, so it's the only free weekend I have."

I look at my watch, praying the time is up, and thank my lucky stars it is.

"Listen, I have to head back to work. It was really nice chatting with you, Eloise."

She places her hand on mine again, and this time I wait with patience. "No, thank you, Presley. Haden told me how nice you were and that we'd get along."

"I highly doubt that." I chuckle while shaking my head. "He doesn't think very highly of me."

"That's where you're wrong." She pulls back almost immediately, her perfectly-shaped brows furrowing in concern. "When we met in London, he never stopped talking about you. Sure, it was work-related, but it was your name that I heard and with admiration."

"Honestly, Eloise, you must be mistaken. Maybe he was

talking about Dee. Haden and I don't see eye to eye on a lot of things."

"I know what I heard. Frankly, I thought you guys had dated by the way he spoke about you. I was even jealous for a while." With a disturbingly fake laugh, she continues, "Anyway, timing was perfect for us. He met me, and look, we're getting married."

Is this true? Shell-shocked by her comment, I pass it off as nothing, but my brain is going into overdrive.

"Anyway, thanks for lunch, Eloise."

Back in the office, I stare at my screen in a daze. So much of what she told me doesn't add up. Obviously, she knows Haden better than I do. Actually, I don't know him at all, yet the conversation on the way he talked about me fills me with a desire to find out more.

So what if he said nice things? It doesn't mean anything.

Remember, he said I meant nothing to him.

Those were his exact words to Marcus.

"Hey." Haden is leaning against my partition, and the smell of his aftershave hits me. God, he smells so good. And why is that deep burgundy shirt accentuating his perfectly-toned forearms.

"Oh, hey."

"Sorry I didn't warn you about lunch. It was kind of sprung on me after many arguments."

"No, it's okay. I'm sorry if it caused arguments."

"So, you're leaving tomorrow?" He swiftly changes the subject.

"Yeah, an early morning flight. So, I'll pick you up Saturday morning from the airport?"

He appears calm, but again that stare leaves me breathless. I need to remember he is nothing but the sperm donor in this equation. These stupid thoughts and feelings, they need to be buried along with my libido.

"I've hired a car. I'll just meet you at your parents' in the morning," he responds quietly. "I've got a meeting all afternoon, so I'll see you then?"

"Right."

He begins to walk away, and I let out the huge breath I'd been holding until he turns around, forcing me to suck it back in.

"And, Presley..." Our eyes meet, and something catches me off guard, a force or pull making my stomach flutter or perhaps that was the baby. Whatever it is, I need to ignore it, or I'll be in trouble. It's a slippery slope once this shit starts.

With a deep penetrating stare, his eyes narrow and his lips twitch nervously. "Have a safe flight."

THIRTEEN

The second my feet land on my parents' front porch, it's a bittersweet moment. Having grown up in this house as a child, I am now standing here as a grown woman with child. Yeah, let's blame the hormones again, but it is definitely worth a good cry.

I have nothing but sweet memories of this house. The pale-yellow paint and white shutters have remained the same throughout the years. The garden is covered in roses and carnations, my mom's favorite, of course. The rockers are sitting on the porch, the same ones that belonged to my gramps and grammy. Carved in some fancy wood, they've been passed down through the generations. The warm air touches my skin, and just when I'm about to shed some more tears, my dad comes out carrying what looks like roadkill.

"Here's my little poodle!"

I cringe at the nickname, stepping forward and walking into his arms. His overbearing hug and scent of wooden musk engulf me, and I burst into tears, once again.

"I missed you, Dad," I babble like a baby through my tears.

"Aww, you got those damn hormones your mother did," he says, kissing the top of my head.

He lets go and takes a good look at me. I'm wearing a pair of cotton shorts and a shirt that has 'Turkey Baking' written on it. My belly is popping out. In fact, over the past week, it's grown tremendously and can no longer be concealed no matter what I wear.

"You're looking beautiful, poodle. You got that glow to you."

"Step away, George, and let me see my daughter."

My mom is standing behind him. Much to my surprise, she is wearing a fluorescent pink yoga outfit. She hasn't changed much since I saw her last with her bangs still cut like she's rocking an '80s video clip, and it wouldn't hurt her to wear a bra once in a while. Nevertheless on numerous occasions, I've been told we looked like sisters. Apparently, she has a youthful glow, or perhaps I look like an old soul. Let's stick to the youthful glow story to boost my ego.

"Come here, give me a hug." She smiles.

I step forward and embrace her. Leaning my head on her shoulder, I'm happy to admit that it's good to come home. What I need is some quality time with my family. That, and to get ridiculously spoiled.

"George, take her bags up to her room. Honey, you have to eat something. It's not about you anymore. I know you city girls are into all these fad diets, but if you don't eat and gain nutrients, the baby could be born with God knows what."

"Mom, I've been eating. And would it kill you to wear a bra?"

"I read an article about how bras can increase your risk of breast cancer. Your dad seems to enjoy it."

I wince at the mental image, shaking my head with disgust. "Oh my God! You didn't just say that."

As I walk through the house, I see that nothing has changed apart from a ridiculous-looking exercise thinga-majig in the living room. Hanging on the walls are several photographs of Gemma and me throughout our childhood. I take a moment to stand in the hallway and look at the pictures, so much fun and laughter hanging on this one wall. I rest my hands on my stomach and hope that one day my child will get to experience everything I did. That will most likely require me finding a husband and having more children. *Do not have this conversation with yourself now, you sadistic fool.*

There is a picture of Jason and me sitting in a small frame amongst the others. I remember the day clearly—it was the first summer I brought him here to meet my family. We're sitting in a boat, him behind me with his arms wrapped around my waist. Laughing out loud, I recall just afterward when we both fell into the lake accidentally. It's a great memory, and so as not to get too caught up in nostalgia, I go in search of my mom.

I settle into the kitchen as my mom prepares lunch for us. As we all sit to enjoy the meal, my mom takes this oppor-tunity to lecture me on everything I should have done, should be doing, and basically how I should raise this kid until he or she is in college. Only my mom could have an entire conversation with herself while I devour the home-made pie in front of me. My dad polishes off three beers as she rambles on. By the end, we both stare at her until she realizes she's been talking to herself.

"Honestly, the two of you are like peas in a pod. Can't

get anyone to listen in this household," she rattles off, moving toward the sink as she starts to wash up.

My dad shrugs his shoulders and heads out the back door with his fishing hat on.

Even at the sink, my mom continues to talk a mile a minute. I take my phone out of my pocket looking for some social media relief when I see a text on the front screen.

Haden: *Hope you got there safe. I've got my black belt packed.*

With Mom still going on about breastfeeding versus bottle feeding, I scramble to send him a text before she realizes I'm not paying attention.

Me: *Pack a new set of ears. My mom has not stopped talking since I got here. Apparently, I should be looking at colleges now because there's a waiting list.*

The exhaustion from traveling finally catches up with me, so I excuse myself to take a short nap. I wake up in a blind panic and disorientated realizing I have slept through to the morning. My mom didn't even have the heart to wake me. The time on my phone says eight, and another text is sitting on my homescreen.

Haden: *We, Presley. We should be looking. We're both parents to this baby.*

. . .

Huh? There is no time to think about his text as I race out of bed and into the shower. Within minutes, I've hopped out and dressed in a simple white dress that sits a lot shorter than normal. With my wedges on and my hair tied into a bun to avoid the sweltering heat, I make my way downstairs. The aroma of pancakes lingers in the air, which can only mean one thing—maple syrup. I'm eating for two, and boy does my mother stack them on the plate.

As predicted, my mom eyes my dress. "That dress is a bit short, don't you think?"

Rolling my eyes at her, the stupid side of me mentions that I haven't really purchased any maternity wear apart from that black dress. With a light bulb going off in her head, she rushes to the bottom of the stairs.

"I've got a box of stuff in the attic. George," she yells to my dad.

Why, oh why, did I say that? I just know she'll pull out some muumuu with a horrific pattern from the '80s.

"I'll be back in a jiffy." She darts out of the room, leaving me alone with my almost finished stack of pancakes.

Knowing Haden will be here soon, I use the moment to relax and read the local paper. Nothing much has changed, a few new marriages and births, but as usual, the town carries on without much excitement. There is a whole page about a carnival coming in for the night. Sounds like fun if you're ten.

My mom is talking to herself again, carrying some boxes down the stairs. The sound of an engine pulls up at the house, and I look at my mom to see her reaction. She has her stern parental face on, and Dad is walking down the stairs with his rifle in hand. All right, he doesn't, and that's a bit overboard, but I do know he has a pocketknife ready.

I wipe my mouth with the napkin and make my way to the porch. There is the sound of the trunk shutting closed and behind it, Haden appears. That stupid flutter, the one that gets all my panties in a twist, makes another appearance. With every fiber of my being, I'm trying to ignore how gorgeous he looks in his natural-colored denim shorts, light gray tee, and a pair of Chucks—my damn weakness. Jason hated them. He called them skater shoes and also wore Jesus sandals.

For someone who just traveled on a plane, he looks refreshed, his hair perfectly styled to the side, and a freshly shaven face. With a warm smile, he greets me, fully aware that my parents are standing right behind me.

"Mr. and Mrs. Malone, it's a pleasure to meet you." He reaches out his hand, but my mom embraces him instead. *What the hell?* What happened to this lecture on how utterly disappointed she was that such a young man would be irresponsible enough to have sex with an older woman, and if his parents didn't teach him to have any morals, then maybe she should?

What a load of bullshit from the woman smiling and acting all friendly with him.

My dad, on the other hand... well, his face says it all.

"So, you're the one who knocked up my poodle?"

Haden pulls away from my mom and looks at me confused. "Um, I like women, sir. I'm not into bestiality."

"He means me," I complain. "Dad has called me poodle since forever. You know, 'cause of my curly hair."

"Oh... right, I get it. I guess I'm the one who knocked up your poodle then," he says, amused.

"So, what are you going to do about it?"

"George, please. Let the boy at least place his bags down before you get all wound up." My mom ushers him into the house, asking him how his trip went and if he wants a drink.

My dad, on the other hand, pulls me aside. "Jesus, poodle, is he still in college?"

"Dad!" I groan. "He's twenty-six."

"Back in my day, you didn't marry women older than you."

"Oh my God." I stop him, raising my palm to his face. "Who the hell is talking about marriage here?"

"I just assumed because the two of you are single—"

"He's not single. Have you not listened to Mom at all?"

"I try not to. It's what happens when you've been married for forty years. You tend to zone out. Your mother could talk a glass eye to sleep," he says, scratching his belly.

I ignore his ramblings and move on inside to join them in the kitchen. Mom has stacked a plate of pancakes in front of Haden. Looking quite pleased with his hefty appetite, she pours him some coffee, and I nearly grab the cup from him.

God, I miss it so much.

"Your sister will be arriving this afternoon with her friend, Melissa," Mom tells us.

"My sister is a lesbian," I mention casually to Haden.

"Presley Victoria Malone!" Mom scolds.

"Well, it's the truth, Deidre," Dad says with a mouthful of toast. "God gives ya what He gives ya. Gemma is a good girl."

"So, you're saying I'm not?"

"Poodle, truth be it... this baby wasn't exactly planned. Besides, what happened with you two? Because Reverend Keith could sure have a word with the both of you."

I groan at the mention of Reverend Keith. If my parents' grand plan is to try to marry me off to the Jerk, it's time to set the record straight. Unlike my usual opinionated self, I struggle to get a single word out and look at Haden for answers. His eyes lift while grabbing a napkin to wipe his mouth. My gaze wanders down to his full lips, glazed in maple syrup. Gliding his tongue along his lips, his eyes continue to watch me with a quizzical stare.

Oh my God, Presley, look away. I shake my head to pull myself out of this pornographic maple syrup fantasy and focus on the question. We hadn't really come up with a story, so I guess there's no better way than stating the obvious, and Haden takes charge by leading the explanation.

"Presley and I have been friends for a while, but, of course, she was engaged. I'd always had a thing for her but respected her relationship. When she broke it off, I wanted to take things further."

With a steady gaze, I look at him thinking what a lie he's spun. Apparently, I hadn't been privy to his talents yet.

"Presley has told us you're engaged to someone else?" Mom interrogates.

"Yes, I am."

This is probably the moment I need to throw him a life-jacket. But this is fun, so I sit back and watch the show unfold. Let's see what other *lie* he can come up with.

"Well, I'm sorry if I'm out of place but marrying another woman when expecting a child is somewhat confusing?" Mom continues to pry.

Haden takes a long sip of his coffee and places the cup on the knitted coaster. "I can understand why you think that. Eloise came into my life before I knew about the baby."

He shuffles awkwardly, so I throw him that much-needed lifejacket.

"Look, Mom and Dad, Haden and I had our fun and well... this is what happened. If you don't mind, I'd like to give him a tour of the house, then maybe show him around town."

I don't wait for their response and motion for him to follow me. As soon as he catches on, we make our way upstairs, and I show him to the guest room.

"I'm apologizing in advance for the plaid. Mom is a little, um..."

He laughs. "She's a mom. She'd get along great with my mom. It was the plaid generation."

I let out a similar laugh. "And my sister, Gemma... sorry about blurting that out."

"It's okay. You don't need to apologize for everything."

I lean against the wall as he sorts out his bags. "This is weird."

"Sure is. Look, it's only a weekend... *poodle.*" He bursts out laughing again, then walks over to where I'm standing, allowing me to swat him across the arm.

"And ignore my dad. Laugh all you want, but if you saw me in bed, I represent a poodle vacationing in the tropics quite accurately."

He stops laughing, and his expression looks pained.

"I guess I'm going to be seeing a lot of you. After all, you're carrying *my* baby."

My eyes move to the hideous plaid duvet. "The paternity test is booked for next Thursday."

He doesn't say a word, completely ignoring what I just said. "So, show me your room."

"You want to see my room?"

"Yeah, I want to see who Presley Malone really is."

I'm not sure exactly what he means, but I walk down the hall and open the door to my room. I moved out of here when I left for college, which feels like a lifetime ago. My parents really haven't change it. It still has the single bed positioned in the middle of the room with a bookshelf above it. Sitting on the shelf are my favorite books, all-time classics that I read throughout my teens. And yes, somewhere buried in the row of books is my collection of *The Babysitter's Club*. I walk toward the shelf and pull out the one book that was my bible as a teen.

"Have you ever read this?" I hand him the book.

"*Forever* by Judy Blume," he says. "Can't say I have."

I take a seat by the bay window, and he follows me.

"I'd curl up in this exact spot and read it over and over again. I was so curious and wondered if I'd feel the same about a boy one day. You know, in love and wanting to have sex with him."

He looks at me oddly, lips pressed together in a slight grimace, and doesn't say anything.

"Too girly of a conversation for you?" I tease.

"Not at all," he quips, lowering his gaze. "It's part of teen sexuality. That curiosity. And so, then you obviously took the plunge one day?"

"I was seventeen, and it was at some party. Nothing more to tell other than it was over in a minute, and the guy moved away. His dad was in the military. And you?"

"And me, what?" He stares at me, confused.

"How old were you when you lost your virginity?"

"I don't know... like twenty," he mumbles.

"Twenty!" I raise my voice despite his embarrassed look. "I'm sorry. Twenty? Really? Isn't that kinda old for your generation?"

"I wasn't into girls at school. I had other things to worry about."

"Like what?"

He quickly stands up and stretches his arms. "So, what do you want to do now?"

Once again, I'm taken aback by the swift change in subjects. Something I said, or the topic at hand, appears to be deeper than I thought. Not wanting to cause another argument, I let it go for now.

"How about a walk around town, then maybe lunch by the lake?" I offer.

"Sure, lead the way."

My parents live in a small town east of Virginia. It was the same place I grew up in, and much like me, they don't like change. Over the years, people have moved on, and the generations that followed occupy most of the town now. It is small, friendly, and mostly trouble-free.

Gemma was the first to fly the coop by skipping college altogether and heading out to California. From there, she enrolled in a few classes and met Melissa. My parents knew I didn't like change, but college was a huge deal, and I knew if I wanted to pursue a career in publishing, I needed to head to the city.

"See that school across the street? That's where I went." I show him. "And that church, it was built by my great, great grandfather. I always dreamed of getting married there," I say loudly, forgetting that he's standing right beside me.

"Is that where you and what's his face were getting married?" he asks with a bitter tone, while continuing to stare at the church.

"Jason, and no. Jason wanted to get married at his priest's church out in Jersey."

Since he has decided to bring up weddings, I can't think of a better time to ask.

"And you? Eloise says you'll be getting married soon."

"Did she?" He appears agitated. "I don't know. I don't get involved."

"But it's your wedding," I state, slightly confused.

"I'm just not interested in the finer details," he tells me, hesitating a little.

"I know how you feel. I was excited about Jason proposing, but when it came time to planning, I lost interest. I guess that's how I knew something wasn't right. I always thought it would be the most exciting time in my life."

He exhales, rolling his eyes like an immature brat. "That's a stupid woman thing. Men don't care. Plan all you want as long we're told when and where to turn up, that's all that matters. Oh, and the bachelor party."

"Ugh, that's such a guy thing. I don't understand why you need to see strippers as a send-off into marriage. It's not like you can do anything with the strippers. You've pretty much been tied down since the moment you asked someone on that first date," I argue.

"You're delusional. Do you know how many of my friends had sex with a stripper the night before their wedding?"

"Are... are you serious? First of all, I thought you weren't even allowed to touch a stripper. Second, what's the point of getting married, then? Just stay single and play the field."

He stops mid-step, running his hands through his hair then turns to face me. "Some people don't have a choice, Presley."

I look at him and laugh. "Everyone has a choice, Haden. It's called decision-making. It's part of being a grown-up."

Walking toward the park bench, we take a seat in front of the church.

"And now what? You're going to have a baby. What about finding yourself someone?" he asks uncomfortably.

I hate this question because even when I ask myself the same thing, it always ends badly.

Cats. Cats... everywhere.

"I have no clue. I know why it's good to be married while you're pregnant," I say without even thinking.

He turns to me, resting his arm along the top of the bench. "Why?"

"Why? We're both adults. It's not hard to figure out why. Pregnancy hands you a bag of hormones, and somehow, you're expected to carry on and pretend it does not affect you whatsoever. Plus, everything is aching, swollen, and I swear, I'm this close to getting a membership at the sketchy massage joint downtown."

Haden shakes his head while grinning. "You have no problem being honest, do you?"

"We crossed the secrets bridge when you took your pants off."

"I think you took my pants off." He smirks.

"What?" My cheeks are flushed, but it's also hot out and below. "We were both drunk, but I swear it was all you."

"I wasn't drunk."

I look at him. "Yes, you were."

"I rode my bike. I never ride my bike if I've been drinking."

I let out a panicked laugh. "I saw you drinking."

"That was root beer."

"I don't get it, then. You weren't drunk, but you..."

The penny drops, and I stare into his eyes to read the truth behind his admission. He wasn't drinking. Therefore, he knew full well what he was doing. Unlike myself, I kind of just went with the flow, and let my body succumb to the moment. Does this mean he wanted it to happen? Did he plan for this to happen? Was what he said in my parents' kitchen true?

"Presley..."

"Haden, what the hell does this mean?"

In a quick change of emotions, his momentary sympathetic expression changes as he sucks his cheeks in with a wide-eyed look. "I wasn't drunk, but I was angry with you. That was it."

"If you're angry with someone, you throw a martini in their face or throw shade on social media. You don't fuck them in the alley!" I turn to face away from him. Just when I thought there was more to this, he reminds me why I am a hormonal mess. The tears are building, and I watch the people strolling past as a distraction.

He places his hand on my shoulder as a kind gesture, but I shake it off, not wanting him to touch me. And so, we sit in silence for a very long time while I try to calm myself down. A good hour later, my stomach rumbles, and all I can think about is food.

"It's done, okay?" I mumble, hoping to redeem myself. "How about we grab some lunch and head to the lake? My treat."

Haden smiles cautiously, then stands to take his ringing phone out of his pocket. Excusing himself, he walks toward the tree, and the moment he answers the call, his face lights up. He then speaks, saying something about the wedding and honeymoon, but shortly after, his smile fades, and an argument erupts.

"I told you I don't want to go there. Why won't you fucking listen to me?"

He is talking loudly enough for me to hear the conversation, but I pretend to be engrossed in the kids running near the church entrance, ignoring the pang inside my chest.

"Eloise, I don't give a shit what you want. You said this wedding was going to be small and uncomplicated, not the splashy affair you're turning it into."

He is kicking the tree with the toe of his shoe and utters more words. "I need to go, okay?" His face softens again, and a small smile escapes him. "Yeah, me, too."

I remember the '*me, too*' at the end of the conversation. It's the reply to '*I love you*.'

It's like a stab into my fantasy bubble.

A reality check.

No matter what he does or says, he's marrying *her*.

And I'm just the woman carrying his baby.

FOURTEEN

Awkward lunch partners. Someone should create a reality show based on that.

After returning from his phone call, something between us changes. Haden seems less friendly and almost annoyed that he was forced to have lunch with me. That, in turn, puts me in a foul mood. We still have another day left in each other's company, so I take the mature approach. Or so I thought.

"Okay, I'll bite. Why are you acting like a jerk?"

Chewing his mouthful of bread at a slow and annoying pace, he eventually swallows to answer my question. "Nothing's wrong," he mumbles, taking another bite to avoid talking.

"God, you're such a woman. Whenever someone says 'nothing's wrong,' there's always something wrong," I complain.

"Geez, you nag like the rest of them."

"Did you say that I nag like the rest of them? You know what?" Whether it is the stifling heat or the anger consuming me, my body temperature rises, and suddenly I feel woozy. "I'm jumping into the lake."

His knee-jerk reaction is laughable. I've jumped into this lake a million times, and today is no exception. Taking my wedges off, I carry them and place them on a rock. It would have been a good idea to wear my swimmers, but this heat is overbearing, and my dress will dry within minutes.

"There could be anything in that lake," he warns me.

"Can't be as bad as what's beside me," I mutter under my breath.

My feet move toward the shoreline, and instantly, cool water graces my skin as I breathe a sigh of relief. Moving further in, my muscles relax as I sink my entire body. A couple of kids are playing in the water not too far away, and on this hot summer day, I can't think of a better way to pass the time.

Haden is standing on the sandbank, watching me in amusement.

"What?" I yell out. "Worried you'll get that pretty hairstyle of yours wet?"

Didn't Vicky say he's into extreme sports? Not that lake swimming is an extreme sport, but reality is that anything could be lurking in this water.

He takes off his shoes and places them beside mine. Next, he pulls his shirt off, revealing his perfect—and I mean perfect—set of abs. *Shit, maybe this wasn't such a good idea.* Wearing only his shorts, he takes his glasses off and hides them in his shoes. Moving toward the edge of the rock, he dives in, causing a huge splash before he resurfaces right beside me.

"FYI, I'm not afraid to get my hair wet," he says, out of breath and way too close to me.

"Could have fooled me. Thought you were an adrenaline junkie... or what was it your Facebook page said?"

"You've stalked me?" He grins, swimming around me like a hunter circling its prey.

"Uh... no, not *me*. Vicky did. She's the social media addict."

"You stalked me," he gloats.

"I didn't stalk you. But I have no idea who you are. So yes, Vicky stalked you, and I may have listened, but I want to point out that I resisted." I'm folding my arms like a petulant child as he continues to grin like he is winning this battle.

Well, two can play at this game.

"Two Yorkshire Terriers... really?" I tease.

"Harry Potter... really, Malone?"

"Wait." I grin unwillingly. "You've stalked me?"

"I had no idea who *you* are." His smile remains fixed. "Let's see, aside from Harry Potter, you're into swimming, extreme cleaning, and what's the other thing..." He continues, "Oh, that's right, you're obsessed with cats."

"No, no," I correct him. "I'm not into cats. I just have a lot of crazy cat-lady friends. Personally, becoming a crazy cat lady is *my* worst fear."

He laughs with ease. "You're too beautiful to be a crazy cat lady."

I respond quickly to avoid my embarassment, "Didn't you watch that episode of *The Simpsons* where they show how Crazy Cat Lady became just that? She was beautiful, graduated with a doctorate and law degree, and then became so burned out she began drinking. She got one cat... then another... and so on."

His expression remains fixed as he watches me in a curious yet heartwarming way.

"Why are you looking at me that way?"

"You're cute when you're quoting *The Simpsons.*"

"Um... thank you? So anyway, anyone can become a crazy cat lady."

Continuing to swim circles around me, he appears to be unable to wipe the smirk off his face. I'm not quite sure what's so funny, but the looming gray clouds followed by thunder in the distance divert my attention.

"Time to get out," I suggest, eyeing the clouds again. "Plus, I'm hungry."

"You just ate," he points out, swimming beside me to the rock.

I walk out slowly and squeeze my dress to wring out the excess water. It's an excuse to ignore his wet body right beside me. Bending down to grab his shoes, the muscles of his back tense, causing me to lick my lips unknowingly. With quick reflexes, he catches me looking and gives me a wink. Okay, what a cocky thing to do. I let out a huff, then tell him to hurry his ass up.

We head back home to find that Gemma and Melissa have arrived early. Seeing both of them makes me super excited. It's been a while, and I've missed their fun-loving ways so much.

Gemma is also known as the Chameleon in our family. The last time I saw her, she had black hair with streaks of blue. Today she's rocking a new, shorter style dyed gray. People often say she looks like Dad, which isn't such a bad thing unless she had inherited his beer gut. Thank God, she hasn't.

"Lil' sis!" She rushes up to me and squeezes me tightly. I forgot to mention that she's only five feet tall, making her the shortest in our family. I hold onto her until she pulls away and rubs my belly until it bugs me, forcing me to swat her hands away.

"I can't believe I'm going to be an auntie!" She hands me a green gift bag, and I stare back at her, confused. "For the baby, silly."

Finally catching on, I place my hand in the bag and pull out a white onesie. It's tiny, and I mean one-of-my-boobs-could-barely-fit-in-there kind of tiny.

I hold the onesie up and read out the print. "My aunt is hotter than your aunt."

Everyone around me breaks into laughter, and even though it's lame, I laugh along with them.

Melissa pushes Gemma aside and reaches out her arms. I happily embrace her, and she gently whispers in my ear, "He's cute, Pres... *real cute.*"

No shit. That is half my problem. If he were drop-dead ugly, I wouldn't be in this mess to begin with.

The obligatory introductions begin, and already Gemma has found something in common with the Jerk—they both love horror flicks—something I despise. We move into the living room, and Gemma pops in a DVD since my parents were behind in technology. It's something about a lunatic murdering people in some rural town. It's gory, unpleasant, and by the time the second person is killed within ten minutes of the movie starting, I jump ship and escape to the kitchen where my sanity and will to live remain intact.

"Since you're in here, how about you peel those potatoes for me?"

Mom hands me the bag of potatoes as I happily chat away about work, life in the city, and Vicky.

"That girl sounds like a bad influence," Mom scowls.

"Honestly, Mom, I'm not ten. If anything, maybe I'm the bad influence. Uh, hello!" I point to my belly.

Mom simply shakes her head, then entertains me with the latest family gossip. Before I know it, the food is ready, and I am famished just smelling the enticing aromas.

An array of food is spread out on the dinner table. My mom, a.k.a. Martha Stewart, has gone all out, even using her fancy silverware. Everyone else enters the room, talking animatedly about the movie. I take a seat beside my dad, and Haden follows by sitting on my other side. We say grace, then dig in, all the while talking about random topics including Gemma and Melissa's house in L.A.

"I love L.A. There's a nice buzz to it. Plus, I love surfing," Haden says.

"You'll love our new place," Melissa adds. "We're a block from the beach, and there's plenty of cafes and shops along the boardwalk. Maybe Presley can bring you along next time?"

"I'd love that." He grins, shoving a piece of chicken into his mouth while he watches me.

What the hell just happened? Now he's taking vacations with me.

When did it cross over from enemy to friend?

Note to self—do not rely on your family to hate him because clearly, he has them under some magic spell.

"So, Haden, tell us about your family?" My mom moves to the subject that I so desperately want to ask about but have never found the courage to do so. He places his fork down and appears to change his demeanor. His smile whittles to nothing but a bleak stare. The light in his eyes almost darkens.

"My family lives in New Jersey. Mom works at the local

library in her spare time, and my twin sisters, Lucy and Lennie, are in college."

"You have twin sisters?" I blurt out, almost spitting out my peas.

"Yes. Annoying twin sisters, but yes."

"Oh my God, Pres, you could be carrying twins," Gemma cries out loud.

I shut her down immediately. "No, there's definitely only one baby inside."

I take my phone out of my pocket and produce the picture I had taken of the ultrasound. I point out the baby as my phone is passed around the table until it lands into Haden's palms.

Quietly, he stares at the photograph, and I realize only then that he hasn't seen the picture of the baby yet. That's partly my fault. For a man who yo-yos from giving a shit to not giving a shit, I figured he didn't care about stuff like ultrasounds.

I watch his facial expression, the look of curiosity as his eyes narrow in on the baby, and the way his lips purse contently. He turns to face me and, embarrassed, I try to look away, but he has caught me staring.

"Do you know what the sex is?" he asks, just short of a whisper.

"Uh... no. I could have found out, but the baby decided to do this somersault thing and covered its bits. I'd say it's either a boy or girl," I state, trying to lighten the conversation and ending with a short chuckle.

"Our friends, Ella and Jess, were told they were having a girl and bought everything pink. Turned out to be a boy," Gemma tells us. "Let's just say that kid may give Elton John a run for his money, what with all the pretty colors and sparkly fabrics."

"Happened to your Aunt Kathy, too," Mom adds.

"It doesn't matter what sex the baby is," I mumble as the conversation continues around me.

"Of course not. As long as the baby is healthy, that's all that matters." Mom smiles.

I hate to admit it, and I feel like the worst person in the world, but it kind of does matter. I'm terrified of having a girl because I am one, and I know how high-maintenance they can be. My dad once told me that having two girls was a sure-fire way of dying from an early stroke. It was around the time we were both in high school and felt the need to disregard our curfew multiple times.

On top of that, I had joined part of an online group made up of single mothers. A lot of them talked about how raising a girl in their teens is difficult and how boys tend to protect their mothers. Now, I don't know if that's all bull-shit, but one mother posted about her fourteen-year-old daughter running off with her twenty-five-year-old boyfriend one night. I decided then and there that if the universe cared for me at all, just the slightest bit, I would have a happy little boy.

With dinner almost over, the conversation moves to sports, and I leave the table to clear the dishes. At the sink, my mom stands alongside me and places her arm around my shoulders.

"One step at a time, Presley. You have your whole family here to support you," she reminds me. "And by the look of it, you've got Haden's support, too."

"I don't even know him, Mom."

"Then, get to know him, Presley. He's going to be in your life whether you like it or not."

"How is that even going to work, Mom?" I whisper beside her. "He's getting married. Does the baby stay at his place on weekends? What about when they have their own kids?"

"Honey, you'll work it out. You always do. You're my little planner," she reassures me. "And besides, have you thought about moving back home so Dad and I can help you?"

I try not to laugh. Living with my parents again would only highlight how pathetic my life has become. I am used to being a strong, independent woman, even in my relationship with Jason. I don't need a man. Hand me a toolbox, and I'm Miss Fix-It. Turn the television to ESPN, and I'll talk stats with the best of them. No, I don't need a man, except for sex. Greedy Kitty down below needs more than a flick of the bean.

"The offer is there, Presley. Pride aside, consider what's best for your child."

I place my hands in the water and think about what Mom had just said as I listen to the conversation at the table about baseball. When Dad starts to talk about the Yankees, and Haden expresses his love for the team, there's a shift in my Dad's voice, and soon he's calling him 'son' and inviting him out to the range tomorrow.

They both ramble on, the conversation turning to extreme fishing. Haden whips out his phone and loads a video from YouTube. *Really? Extreme fishing.*

With the final plate put away, my mom calls it a night with my dad at her tail. Haden follows me to the living room to join everyone else. Much to my disapproval, Gemma decides to put on a Stephen King movie, and the only seat available is on the two-seater sofa beside Haden. I take a seat beside him and brace myself for the worst.

Honestly, I could kill Gemma and Haden right now with the nightmares that will plague me because of this damn clown. I swear I am so close to shitting in my pants. The moment the face pops up from the drain, I jump in fear, and at the same time, that familiar flutter pokes my belly, and I'm almost one hundred percent certain the baby just moved.

"I think the baby just kicked."

Gemma pauses the movie, rushing to my belly and placing her hands across it. Melissa is also waiting and places her hands near Gemma's. I feel like a science project with all hands on me but Haden's. He looks uncertain and waits for me to allow him to place his hands on there too. I tell him it's okay, and I guide his hand to the part where I felt the last flutter. Of course, nothing happens, and everyone grows bored, including me, so the movie is turned back on. With the lights turned off and the volume cranked up so loud, my body tenses in anticipation. Then again... that little prod.

I don't waste the moment, so I inch closer to Haden. Grabbing his hand, I place it on top of my stomach, and within seconds, the baby kicks again.

I hear him gasp, followed by a heartwarming on-top-of-the-world type of smile. With his hand still on my stomach, we watch the rest of the movie until the credits start to roll. When the lights are turned back on, he removes his hand, and I feel an instant loss.

Don't get attached, Presley.

We all call it a night, especially because Haden is waking up early the next day to go out with Dad.

In my room, dressed in my tank and boxers, I toss and turn, unable to sleep with the face of that fucking clown taunting me. Stupid Gemma. Even as a child, she would do this to me, and the worst part was, she never got scared.

I try to busy myself with my phone, reading some articles on post-partum routines and retweeting some interesting facts, until I look at the clock and see that it's past midnight. Everything in my room is freaking me out, from the shadow of my curtains to the swaying tree outside. I need to pee but dare not get up for the bathroom. When I am sure my bladder is on the verge of exploding, I run to use it but refuse to look inside the drain, paranoid about a certain clown murdering me.

I am no closer to falling asleep, so I decide to do the unthinkable and send him a text.

Me: *Are you awake? FuckingPennywise*

That little bubble appears on my screen.

Haden: *Yes.*

I jump out of bed and, without thinking, walk down the hall and tap on his door. He says to come in, and when I enter the room, I'm surprised to see him shirtless and reading a book. I'm not surprised it's a Stephen King novel.

Don't look at his abs, even though they deserve to be looked at.

"I can't sleep."

"I figured since you were on Twitter for the last hour."

"You follow me?"

He nods and pats the bed beside him. I move closer to the edge of the bed, trying to create some much-needed distance between us.

"I hate that movie. Who writes a book about clowns killing children?"

"A very talented author." He chuckles.

"Our kid is never watching that movie," I tell him.

He keeps still, and I turn to look at him, wondering why he remains silent. Okay, avoid the fucking six-pack because you know it's only the hormones. If I wasn't pregnant, I wouldn't look at him this way.

"Is the baby moving now?" he asks.

"Uh, no... why?"

"You're squirming."

"Oh... just uncomfortable." *Great lie.*

His eyebrows raise in concern. "What's wrong?"

"My back is stiff from the extra weight." *Fantastic lie!*

"Here," he says, then shuffles behind me.

I feel his hands press against my upper back rubbing the spot that needs the most attention. I let out an involuntary moan and regret it almost immediately. The warmth of his breath is only inches from my ear, and I feel the goose-bumps settle across my skin.

"Are you cold?"

"No." I almost choke.

Allowing my body to relax, I close my eyes and enjoy his gentle caress until the baby moves again. Quickly, I grab his hand and move it toward the spot where the baby kicked. He moves in closer behind me until his chest is pressed up against my back. The echoes of our heavy breathing are the only sounds heard, and his soft breaths are inching along my skin, taunting me, teasing me until I am feeling things I know I shouldn't.

Barely above a whisper and under his touch, I warn him that we shouldn't be doing this.

"We're not doing anything," he murmurs back.

"Are you sure about that?"

I know I'm not sure about anything, except for how right he feels at this very moment. How right he *always* feels when he touches me. How my body does this thing I cannot explain. It is almost like it's possessed with feelings and desire for a man who's unattainable, a man I loathe because he is a downright jerk.

"All I'm doing is letting the baby know who I am."

With my eyes closed, I respond quietly, "The baby knows. I wonder why it moves every time I'm near you?"

His hands move around my stomach, tracing my skin like a fragile piece of broken glass until he has his arm around my torso, pulling me in closer to him. I close my eyes again, and this time I swear it's his lips against the base of my neck brushing along, warm, teasing me with a slight flick of the tongue. Maybe I'm just imagining things. I open my eyes the second his phone vibrates on the bed. The cool air grazes my skin instantly, and I know he has pulled away.

"Hey, baby," he answers.

Baby? He has the nerve to call her baby while he is licking my skin?

The room suddenly feels warm as my skin begins to crawl. I shuffle away until I am off the bed and standing near the door. He doesn't look my way, and instead, stares amused at the floor. There is a loud noise coming off the phone speaker, and his laughter, along with his complete disregard for what just happened between us, angers and forces me to take whatever dignity I have left and exit the room.

Instead of heading back to my room, I open the door to Gemma and Melissa's room, climbing into bed beside them. Gemma wraps her arm around me and mumbles, half asleep, "You're falling in love with him, Pres."

She has no idea what she's talking about. Pfft, *love*. Haden isn't capable of loving anyone but himself. Though Gemma said *I* was falling in love with him, there is zero truth to that. I know what love is. After all, I had it with Jason, and this in no way can be compared to my relationship with him.

Love is feeling secure, knowing you can count on that person no matter what. There is comfort, happiness, and a feeling of being content.

Haden's expressed none of that, and what do I expect, anyway? A twenty-six-year-old jerk who loves himself is going to be my kid's dad.

But not the man I am spending the rest of my life with.

There is a huge difference.

Or maybe, there's absolutely no difference at all.

FIFTEEN

D ad and Haden left early to go hunting, leaving us girls for the day. Mom thought it would be 'swell' to take us shopping.

Jumping from store to store, the three of them "ooh" and "aah" over anything baby related, while I sit in the corner of the store allowing my tired feet to rest. Shopping and pregnancy do not mix. I am ready to say yes to everything they shove at my face just so we can get out of here.

"So, Pres, have you made a list of all the things you need?" Gemma asks, holding up two sailor outfits.

I cringe at the outfits. "No."

"Stop the press! You're so anal with your lists and need to be organized," Melissa points out, this time holding up two lamb onesies which, I have to admit, are adorable.

"Just busy and stuff."

"Presley Malone. Since when are you ever this blasé?" Mom takes the sailor outfit from Gemma and places it in her basket.

Great. My kid is going to look like one of the Village People.

"Mom, I'm busy with work. I don't have time to plan these things. I'm sure there's some website that, with a click of a button, will deliver everything to my door."

The three of them stare at me, wide-eyed in shock.

"What have you done with the real Presley?" Gemma inquires, raising her eyebrows at me curiously while holding up a cowboy outfit, frills and all. I shake my head in disapproval.

"Why are you all making a big deal out of this?" I answer defensively.

"Because you're having a baby. It's the biggest deal there could ever be," Mom intervenes.

Now they're ganging up on me. I can't please anyone, and right now that diner across the road with the awesome banana fudge sundae is the only thing I can think about.

"Are we done? I'm hungry."

The three of them nod and pay for the items before we head out of the store. They don't raise the subject again, and they don't realize that I'm completely terrified. Every day I'm experiencing something new, whether it's exciting or unpleasant, and even though I'm surrounded by family, I feel so alone—even more so after the Jerk's willingness to abandon the intimate moment between us, proving again he's unreliable.

The banana fudge sundae is a temporary cure before we head back home to pack.

When Dad and Haden pull up in the old pickup truck, I greet them outside, instantly hit by a godawful stench.

"What the hell is that?" I scowl.

"Don't look in the back, poodle."

Too late. I do and run straight for the bathroom to empty the contents of my stomach. There is a gentle tap on the door, followed by an, "Are you okay... *poodle?*"

"Go away!" I yell, head in the basin, saying goodbye to that banana fudge sundae.

I don't realize the door has opened, but there is a gentle creaking sound as the door is shut. My stomach is still weak, and the Jerk grabs all my hair and holds it back with his hand. Whether it's because of the roadkill smell or his caring gesture, I hurl one last time into the toilet.

Flushing it, I sit back on my knees, facing away from him.

"Do you need me to get you anything?"

I shake my head as he continues to hold onto my hair.

"I think I puked in my hair," I almost cry.

He leans in, and he is smelling my hair. "It still smells like coconut."

"Coconut? Oh, that's my shampoo to stop me from looking like Diana Ross."

This is awkward. Do I tell him to let go of my hair? Then I remember last night and how he so easily just ignored what happened between us. I shuffle my head to the side and loosen my hair from the grip of his hand. "I'm going to take a shower."

I stand, avoiding eye contact, then walk out of the bathroom and head upstairs to escape him.

After spending a good hour thoroughly rinsing my hair, I head back downstairs but halt just before the bottom step where Haden is standing, staring at the pictures on the wall.

"There's a picture here of you and him," he tells me, staring at the wall disconcertedly.

"Yes. He was my fiancé, and my parents considered him family."

"Do they still see him, talk to him?"

"I don't know. I haven't asked them. If they do, it wouldn't bother me. Jason is great, and it's not fair for anyone to have to cut ties just because we aren't romantically involved."

His eyes are boring into the picture. Unsure of why it's bothering him so much, I move my gaze to the picture itself to see if I'm missing something. It's still the same picture I saw yesterday, nothing out of the ordinary.

"Is there a problem? You look annoyed."

Abruptly, he turns to face me. "How would you like it if you went to my parents' house and saw a picture of me and my ex on the wall?"

"I wouldn't care because it's your ex. And since we aren't together, I really wouldn't give a goddamn shit. That would be more appropriate wording for it. Besides, you're with Eloise now. If I did care for you, which I don't in the slightest bit, you being with her would be like adding salt to a wound," I rant.

He exhales with a slight snicker. "Well, I'm glad you cleared up the confusion."

Haden walks away from the conversation, and I see him disappear down the hall. How am I going to survive being on the same flight as him? Thank God, we didn't book seats next to each other because I can't handle any more of his childish outbursts.

We have an early meal before it's time to pack and head out. With my suitcase ready to go, Mom knocks on the door before entering.

"Hey, Mom, what's up?"

She comes in carrying a small bag. "Here, honey. I want you to have this."

Inside, I pull out a small yellow blanket. It's soft and covered in colorful stripes on one side. I press it against my cheek, and a very familiar emotion overwhelms me. It smells a little like mothballs, but judging by the age of the blanket, it's probably been sitting in some trunk in the attic.

"This was your blankie," she tells me. "You carried this around with you everywhere you went until you were five."

"Thanks, Mom." I almost tear up. "What else is in the bag?"

"Oh! Here you go. I kept it all these years."

She pulls out this yellow bottle-looking thing with a suction cup attached. For some unknown reason, I place the suction cup on my cheek until Mom informs me of its use. "That's my breast pump."

I throw it back at her. "Eww, Mom! I can't use your breast pump!"

"Why not? It's still in perfect condition." She places it against her breast, mimicking the sucking motion.

"You know what, Mom? I'll start a list right now. And a new breast pump can go at the top."

"Have it your way. I just don't know why you would waste money when this is in perfectly good working order."

I don't say another thing. Instead, I wrap my arms around her and hug her tight. I don't want to let go, frightened that the next time I see her, I'll be in the hospital bed pushing out a watermelon from my lemon-size vagina.

"I know you're scared, honey. I'll be right by your side the whole time."

Letting out small sobs, I nod my head, trying to translate my fears into words. "Just promise you'll be there, Mom. I don't want to be alone."

"I promise. You won't be alone."

We let go of each other, and even my mom's eyes have gone glassy. She carries my suitcase downstairs where everyone else has already congregated on the porch.

Gemma and Melissa hug me, and I'm sandwiched between them as they are promising to visit. They are quick to push me aside to fuss over their new favorite person. They exchange something with Haden—phone numbers, I suppose.

Dad loads the car, then moves toward me to give me one of his big bear hugs. "Take care of yourself, poodle. We'll see you when we get back from Fiji."

"Oh, that's right. Your second honeymoon." I cringe.

"I've got a new bikini. I forgot to show you," Mom says excitedly.

"It's quite a piece of string. I'm going to have to shoo those Fijian men away," Dad jokes.

Gemma and I both groan at the same time before I walk toward the car and give my final wave goodbye.

"What do you mean the flight's canceled?"

The crack of the thunder startles both of us as we stand at the crowded check-in desk. The attendant gives us a dumb look. Haden is angry and slamming his fists on the counter to no avail. The line behind us is out the door, and it appears everyone is as frustrated as we are.

Annoyed, I lean against the counter with my back to the attendant as she punches stuff into her computer.

"You okay?" Haden calms down enough to ask the question.

"Yeah, just tired."

Apparently, due to this wretched storm, all flights are canceled. Haden is still mouthing off, and I turn around and push him out of the way since he is getting nowhere with this.

"What are you going to do to compensate us? Accommodations for starters?" I take charge.

She clicks away on her computer and makes a few phone calls. A minute later, we are booked at the hotel by the airport. According to her, it's the last room available. Now it's my turn to panic.

"What do you mean, only one room?" I raise my voice.

"Well, I assumed you were a cou—"

I interrupt her. "Never assume! It makes an ass—"

Haden places his hand on my shoulder. "Okay, calm down," he says coolly. "No big deal, you take the bed, and I'll take the chair."

"You can't sleep in a chair, Haden."

"We shouldn't be in the same bed..."

She is staring wide-eyed at us, watching our conversation unfold. Unable to control my anger once again, I unleash my frustrations on her. "See, that's why you don't assume."

I grab the tickets she issues us for the next flight and walk away without thanking her.

Geez, Presley, calm down the hormones. A growl escapes me, and I think it's my anger, but it turns out to be my stomach. This day—or should I say weekend—has gone from terrible to disastrous.

"Let's get you something to eat," Haden suggests, taking both our bags and walking toward the exit.

We head outside the airport and straight to the hotel across the road. It is no five-star, but it's acceptable for a night's rest.

"You want to go to the restaurant?" he asks.

"Room service. We've got vouchers." I smile in delight.

As soon as we settle in, I'm on the phone with the restaurant, ordering everything on the menu. And I mean everything. Haden announces that he's going to change in the bathroom. Moments later, he emerges with his PJ bottoms on and no top.

"Do you always parade around shirtless?" I pry, trying to come off annoyed rather than interested.

"Does it bother you?"

"No... yes... it must be your generation," I say, mostly to myself.

"I'm sure you oldies do it. Try it some time? Why not now?" he drags with an inviting smirk.

I exhale loudly to cover my embarrassment.

Haden one.

Presley *zero*.

I grab my clothes and head to the shower. The steaming hot water is exactly what I need, and as my body relaxes, my skin begins to prune. Getting changed into my tank and boxers, I cringe at having to wear a bra to bed. It's extremely uncomfortable with the size of these bazookas, but what choice do I have? The tank I'm wearing is light pink, and my nipples have darkened from the pregnancy, not to mention their size. I could have given the Amazonian ladies on *National Geographic* a run for their money.

Exiting the room, I see that Haden has taken the lids off the plates, and my stomach rumbles embarrassingly. The plates surround the bed, and I jump on it, immediately devouring everything in sight. On my last bite, I let out a sigh.

"Jesus, I thought you were kidding when you said you could eat all that." He finishes taking his last bite.

"Baby needed it," I tell him.

"The buffalo wings as well?"

"Yes."

"And the cheesy fries?"

"Yes," I repeat.

"The pizza with extra toppings and salad on the side?"

"Yes, and yes." I smile, satisfied.

"The chocolate mud cake?"

"No, that was for me."

He shakes his head in disbelief, curling his lips as he laughs. "Well, you still look beautiful. Eloise would never eat anything like that. She's into this stupid diet where everything has to be green. Even the wedding menu is all green."

I stop laughing and stare at the television uncomfortably. Firstly, who invented green diets? What a waste of perfectly good and delicious colorful food. Secondly, that's twice he has mentioned my looks. At what point do I classify that as infatuation instead of just admiration? Both times he's done it, I have frozen up with no following comment to offer. After last night's misadventures, I am extremely cautious about being in the same room as him. It would be silly of me to take these passing comments to heart.

"Look, don't take this the wrong way, but you can sleep on the bed, too. Just no scary movies?"

He smiles. "Deal."

We still argue over each movie before finally settling on *Father of the Bride*. Haden appears bored by my choice but continues to watch with a chuckle every now and then at Steve Martin's ridiculous antics.

"Marcus loves this movie," I blurt out, regretting it immediately.

In the dark room, his body stiffens beside me. His stare is fixated on the screen.

"Do you still talk to him?" he asks in a slightly aggravated tone.

"Um... not really, apart from a text here and there."

"So, you do talk to him?"

Confused by his question, I simply agree. "If you consider that talking, then yes. Why?"

Crossing his arms to cover his bare chest, he continues to watch the television, refusing to make eye contact with me. "I just don't see why you still talk to him. You told him it's over."

"Because we're friends. It wasn't just about sex."

The tension in the room thickens, and I have no idea why this is still an issue. It's almost like he's jealous, but that notion is ridiculous because again, we're not together.

With an undermining stare, his eyes bore into me, followed by a deep growl. "So, you weren't just fucking him?"

"Do you have a problem? Because the last time I checked, you were engaged. My sex life is of no concern to you, especially what's in the past."

"He's my cousin!" he raises his voice, startling me.

"How does that matter? You and I weren't dating. Geez, Haden, it was one night—"

He interrupts me, dead cold. "That you regret."

"I did regret it, but—"

"But what?" he demands.

"Will you let me finish?" I exhale. "But now I have this baby growing inside me. I can't regret something that feels so right. This is my life now."

"Our life," he corrects me.

I don't understand him, and I have no idea what triggers his erratic behavior. This is getting more complicated by the minute. Now, we are sitting here side by side with a whole night ahead of us. I'm pretty sure one of us won't come out of this alive.

We continue to watch the rest of the movie in silence. Toward the end, I twist my back against the headboard of the bed, scratching the itch that my bra strap is giving me. For starters, it's two sizes too small, and my breasts grew to double their size overnight. Trying to remain inconspicuous, I move in subtle yet slow twists.

Haden turns his head to watch me, his eyes peering like a curious meerkat. I still my body movements, not wanting to draw further attention. Stupid big nipples.

"Why do you look like you've got a spider down your back?" he questions with dark amusement.

"It's my bra," I tell him, fed up with the persistent itch. "It's uncomfortable, and the stupid strap is driving me insane."

"Then, take it off."

"Honestly, you got a screw loose. That's so awkward, and no, I won't do that."

"Just do it. I won't look, okay? Besides, there's going to be more uncomfortable moments than that when the baby comes barreling out of your vagina."

"You're *not* going to be in the room."

"Why not?" he argues back. "I'm the father. I have that right."

I laugh at his comment. "You don't have the right to look at my vagina. If you have to be in there, then you're standing in the corner."

"But don't I have to hold your hand and shit?"

"Maybe you need to watch *Father of the Bride II*."

The credits roll on, the illumination from the television screen providing the only light in the room. All of a sudden, some foreign film comes on with nudity. Breasts, to be exact. It is laughable and extremely tacky. Oh, and downright awkward. There is bush... plenty of bush.

"This is so lame. People don't screw like that," I say to myself.

"I'm sure people do."

"Yeah, smartass, name one."

He hesitates for a brief moment. "Me."

Silence.

The movie is showing a couple having sex against the wall in the shower. The man has lifted the woman, and with her legs wrapped around his waist, he continues to drill into her while she lets out the fakest moans.

I can't take my eyes off the bush. You could run a brush through it and style it with cornrows, it's *that* long.

"What's wrong? You don't believe me?" he continues, not letting go of this awkward subject.

"Oh no, I do," I mutter. "It's just the type of conversation you don't have with a pregnant woman without a partner. You know, it's just not advisable."

"Oh, right, the hormones." He grimaces hopelessly. "Is it that bad?"

He's asking the question that should remain unanswered because the more I think about it, the more I work myself up.

"Yeah, pretty bad. Bad enough I'd probably do you again." I swat him with a pillow, teasing him in a friendly and relaxed way.

He doesn't respond immediately, and when I glance at him, he is removing his glasses and placing them on the nightstand. He's roughly running his hands through his hair, and I feel the sheets move until the heat attacks my skin, and his body is in line with mine.

My heart is beating a million times a minute, and my vocal cords appear to be out of order as I beg him silently to back off, knowing full well I am the weak one.

"Presley?" he murmurs gently into my ear.

With his body close, the words cannot be communicated, so I turn my head until our eyes are locked onto each other.

"Then do it," he whispers, against my lips.

Three little words and my world comes undone.

SIXTEEN

Did he just say he wanted to have sex with me? Baby brain, a miscommunication, or maybe I'm reading this all wrong?

His lips are feverishly locked onto mine, our tongues twisting in a manic frenzy. The suction is strong. I attempt to pull away to maintain my morals, yet his grip around my shoulders pushes me further into the mattress, unable to break free.

I reach for a quick breath and try to stop him.

"Haden, we can't... you have—"

His lips find their way back onto mine, and without answering me, he continues to passionately tease my mouth with his. I beg myself to stop, but every flick, every swirl of his perfectly soft tongue is signaling every inch of my body to react with desire.

The ache below is taunting me, but I need to be the strong one here, the mature person who can push him away because I have self-control. His strong weight against my body overpowers any self-control I have though, and my feeble attempts to wriggle away from him appear fruitless.

"No one will know," he whispers against my lips, offering me a bite of the poisonous apple he is holding. It is red, delicious, and with just one bite, I know I cannot stop.

"We'll know."

The cool air graces my mouth, and he has pulled away, yet still lingers only inches from my face. Staring deeply into my eyes, his pupils dilate, and I see the fire burning deep within, the passion and desperation reflecting back at me. With his glasses removed, his bare face draws me in, and this intimate moment between us allows me to study his face in a way I have previously only dreamed about. Running my fingertips along the contour of his cheekbones, I teasingly drag my finger against his bottom lip. I adore his lips.

"Presley," he commands my name, owning it as if I belong to him, but then he bites the corner of his lip and softens his gaze. "I want to do this for you."

Wait, he wants to do it for me?

Rational Presley would punch the Jerk in the face for such a comment!

How dare he turn this around on me, like *he* is doing *me* a favor. My body automatically tenses, and my fists curl. That beautiful face of his is about to see stars.

I place my hands against his chest to open the distance between us.

"I just think that—"

Frustratingly, he interrupts me once again. "Don't think, Presley."

He's resting his palm against my cheek, and I lean into it, uncertain how my emotions have so quickly shifted. I've longed for the comfort and touch of the man who was inside me. His blood is running through the veins of our unborn child. This intimate moment between us, this simple touch, is the validation I need to allow my body to completely give into him—once again.

The tip of his tongue runs across my bottom lip until it sneaks into my mouth and slowly gains momentum. Soft, sensual swirls heighten the throbs persisting in all the spots that haven't been touched for a long time. I can't control the way my body is responding to him, and being pregnant is surprisingly driving my hormones to a level of pure insanity from how much I want him inside me right now.

He knows what he does to me.

I know he knows.

But do I do the same for him?

Moving his palm to the base of my neck, I gasp into his mouth at the sheer intimacy of his touch. His mouth lingers around my chin, moving slightly to his left until he is positioned at the base of my earlobe. The anticipation, his words, they will no doubt destroy me and take me to a place of pure ecstasy that I have never experienced in all my years.

"I want to take this slow. Make every fantasy I've had of you come alive."

My breath hitches, and my body presses against his. His hardness against my thigh is driving me crazy. The fantasy of his cock, *pierced* and sitting in my mouth, is becoming a reality, and my patience wears thin. My hands move on their own accord, running through his soft hair and scratching down his back, causing him to arch and flex his muscles into my hands. Burying his weak moans into my shoulder, his teeth grip onto my skin with a gentle bite, and his hands lose all sense of control as they travel into the gap of my tank, exposing my breasts.

Even in the dark, his eyes glow fiercely, and the ravaging noises escaping his throat drown with the frantic kisses placed all over my very full breasts. My nipples are hard, and every flick of his tongue drives me to moan louder into his hair as I try to control the way my body is reacting.

"Let yourself go, Presley. Let me have all of you."

He continues to fondle my breasts, taking turns, not wanting to unfairly leave any part of me unattended. I allow my body to relax, enjoying the attention and new sensations. I shift to the side, and my sudden movement throws him off. Without a word, he searches my face for an explanation.

"The baby... I don't want to squash the baby."

Truth be told, I'm terrified of it happening.

Haden appears amused yet continues his mission of having all of me. His hands slowly wander down my torso, caressing the bump in my stomach.

"So beautiful," he murmurs. "And mine."

Trailing kisses down my body, he stops at the top of my boxers and waits, leaving me to do the unthinkable—beg him to go down.

With a playful grin, he tells me, "You don't play fair, Malone."

"Who said anything about playing fair?" I smirk, gently tugging his hair.

"I don't want to hurt you."

Simple words that stop me in my tracks. *Is he talking about the baby or my feelings?* I thought we covered hurting the baby already. Emotionally, I am resilient, or at least that's the lie Kitty feeds me. This is a pity fuck, a spur-of-the moment-need-to-release-the-tension fuck. We aren't going to get married and live happily ever after. Physically, I want him to give it all to me.

"You won't," I almost beg of him.

Momentarily, his hands slide past the edge of my shorts

and into my panties. The low grumbling sound he makes, followed by a deep moan, push him further against my clit until his fingers find their way inside.

I gasp at the pure pleasure of the deep thrusts, moving my body in a slow rhythmic motion, bucking my hips against his hand.

"Hot fucking damn, Malone, you're completely soaked," he tells me, thrusting a third finger deep within.

I'm going to explode. I'm just one finger away from gushing all over his hands. In an attempt to control my breathing, I relax my body and enjoy how good it feels until he warns me that he's about to enter me.

"I need to be inside you now," he demands, and with a swift and steady drop of his shorts, he commands me to sit on top of him. "I want to see all of you, riding me, hard, till you can't take it any longer and explode all over my cock."

I'm quick to jump on top of him as he holds his cock with that shining silver barbell, teasing me before gently sliding it inside me. The fullness of him completes the emptiness that I felt earlier. He moves slowly, gaining momentum as I arch my back, gripping his thighs for support.

His hands trace the base of my neck and follow down my chest and between my full breasts, stopping just shy of my nipples. The anticipation becomes frustrating, so I take control, resting my palm on his and dragging it on top of my nipples.

He moans in delight. "You feel just as I've always imagined you... tight, wet... your body craves me to fuck you."

My head won't even nod, so possessed by the strong build-up of pressure forming below that I cannot string together my thoughts or words.

He stops, and instantly my eyes flick open, staring

widely at him, wanting to know why. This better not be his signature calling card—abandoning women on the brink of an orgasm.

"Tell me you want me," he demands quietly, running his hands along my thigh. His beautiful eyes stare back at me oddly, and I can only imagine he is riddled with guilt.

I lift his hand and kiss his fingertips. "I want you."

"Tell me it's only me that you want to fuck this beautiful pussy of yours."

"It's only you."

My uneven breaths echo throughout the quiet room, and I move against him, only for him to stop me once again.

"Tell me," he whispers. "Tell me it's only me that will ever be inside you from this moment on."

My eyes connect with his, attempting to understand what he's just demanded of me.

He wants me for the rest of his life. Or am I signing a contract to dance with the devil in the pale moonlight?

His eyes show no mercy, fixated on my lips and waiting impatiently for my answer.

This is a heavy question from someone buried inside me, and from someone who's engaged. Everything we are doing is completely and morally wrong. We are hurting others. We are the driving force in this sick and twisted game, leaving the pawns to hurt and suffer from our indiscretion.

But I don't care.

I want him.

All of him.

And right now, in this deep and intimate moment, I want only him for the rest of my life.

"It's only you... you will be the only one ever to be inside me and make me feel this way from this moment on."

Promises are just promises made to be broken if they are built on lies.

Not wasting any time, he pushes me back as the tip of his pierced cock rubs against my wall. He pulls me forward again, this time fast and steady. I ride him, and just when I know my body is ready to explode, I warn him in a high-pitched breath, "Haden, I'm going to..." Releasing my inhibitions, I scream as the orgasm spreads throughout my whole body, causing me to see only stars in the dark room.

He follows, picking up the pace, holding a deep breath until he releases and cries out, "Fuck!"

Slowing down the pace until I'm at a standstill, my tired body falls onto his, careful of my protruding stomach.

In silence, with him still inside me, we lay together, my head lying against his chest. His heart is beating loud, and I wonder if it beats for me. Maybe only me?

"Presley," he murmurs, running his hands through my hair.

"Mmm..."

"Presley..."

~

I open my eyes, and Haden is sitting on the chair beside the table, dressed in his jeans and a tee. The sunlight is filtering through the sheer white curtains and into the room. I squint my eyes and then open them abruptly.

"We need to leave in an hour, and I've already ordered your breakfast." He moves his attention to his phone, typing without looking at me.

It was just a dream.

Shit! What the hell did my imagination go and do? It made me think Haden would give me the best sex of my life, and worst of all, that he wanted only me, and I was in love with him.

In my awkward and compromising position, I roll toward the other side of the bed which is closer to the bathroom door. I quickly get out and lock the door behind me. Staring in the mirror while I allow the water to run, my body appears flushed, my hair is a tangled wild mess, and my lips look swollen and plump. I have no choice but to take a cold shower to wash off the intense desire I have for him.

It all felt so real.

The way he touched me.

The words he spoke.

I exit the bathroom, dressed and with my hair pulled back into a ponytail. Food sits on the table, and if it weren't for the baby, I would be out of this room so fast, hungry or not. I eat my toast in silence and follow by polishing off some juice.

"You ready to go?" he asks, a little too politely for my liking.

I simply nod, unable to make conversation.

"Are you okay? You were having a restless sleep."

I grab my purse and pull my suitcase along. "Just a nightmare."

"Me, too. Must be the heat in the room."

"Maybe. Thank God it wasn't real."

It's the last thing I mumble before we exit the room and head back to reality.

SEVENTEEN

I was quiet the entire flight home, trying my damnedest to ignore a dream that felt entirely real. Luckily, we weren't sitting together. The overweight man next to me and his body odor were more pleasing than the Jerk himself.

At the airport, it was an obligatory goodbye before we parted our ways.

I made it my priority upon our return to attend to the paternity test. It was the only communication we've had, and even then, it was short and to the point. Soon, he would have the answer he so desperately craves, and maybe luck would be on both our sides, and the baby's Jason's.

Yes, I am that screwed up that I prayed for the easier way out of this whole mess.

Days passed without us talking at work or even via text, and after a week, I let it all go. Whatever bond, friendship, or connection we had over that weekend has now passed. It's strictly business, and even then, he won't make eye contact with me. I am not sure what I did wrong. After all, he was the one who invaded my dreams and gave me the best sex of my life.

Distracting myself came easy when I focused my energy on moving into Kate's. Boxes were all packed and ready to go, neatly organized into categories, color-coded, and alphabetically in order. I placed the remaining boxes into storage along with some furniture until I can figure out my next move. The apartments are overpriced in the city, and while we got top dollar for ours, I have a child to think about—a whole new life I need to think about for at least eighteen years.

It begged the question of whether or not I will settle down in the city. I do have a job to think about but am certain I can pick one up on the West Coast. I also took the liberty of researching my rights as the primary parent and whether or not I can make a decision like that.

Still in my second trimester, what I thought would be a walk in the park is turning out to be more like a trip down Agony Lane. My ankles, or should I say 'cankles,' have disappeared along with my waistline. The only thing that keeps me sane is Kate. She's a hell of a lot of fun, tells ridiculous stories about herself and her wild friends, plus she is a great listener.

"So, did the Jerk speak to you today?" she asks, biting into a stick of celery.

"Yes, but it was only to ask me where we kept the scissors in the stationary room. Trust me, it was as formal as any stationary room exchange could be."

"Then you didn't tell him about the scan next week? Presley, I can come if you need me," she offers.

I have learned a very important thing about Kate—she is a great friend. Not only does she listen to me complain about the Jerk for countless hours, she is willing to rearrange her schedule to attend my appointment with me. In all fairness, I spent countless hours listening to the drama unfold with her secret lover. The thing I didn't get about the whole situation is, why Kate allows this pathetic excuse of a man to manipulate her. She is gorgeous and tall with an athletic build. Her shimmering blonde hair is cut just below her chin, perfectly straightened like she just stepped out of a salon. She has these cute freckles that spread across her cheeks and nose, covering her pale British skin. Plus, she has this cheeky smile with a dimple on the left side of her face.

Yet something about this man, the power he holds, or the fact he's some secret underground boss, has drawn her in to the point she's under his bewitching spell and can't break free.

"I promise I'll tell him, and thanks for the offer."

"We have sucky love lives," she complains, sinking into the couch with the remote.

"Yep, we sure do. What's the latest on your secret mystery man?"

She lets out a huge sigh. "Nothing. I texted him and asked if he wanted to have dinner tonight, and he never responded."

"So then, why didn't you call him?"

"Because he made it clear that he doesn't date. He doesn't do relationships. I was just hoping he might change for me."

"Are you sure he isn't gay, Kate?"

"Maybe. Who knows? He only wants to screw me from behind. What the hell does that mean? He's gay, or he doesn't like my face."

I give her a sympathetic smile. "Why are you still hung up on him? You can have any guy, Kate. He sounds so—"

"Disinterested?"

I simply nod.

"Because, Presley, the way he makes me feel. Even

though he acts that way, when we're alone, I feel so empowered. He teaches my body to do things I've never experienced, and sexually, he takes me to a level that's beyond words."

I can sense it in her voice. It's not love as such but an uncanny connection to someone who's unattainable.

The next day at work, I decide I need to ask Haden about the ultrasound. Somehow, I chicken out again. So, I text him from my desk to his and throw in the invitation to a last-minute farewell lunch for Clive. Because that's mature.

Me: *I have an ultrasound on Monday at 9am. You're welcome to come.*

Me: *Oh, and there is a farewell lunch for Clive today at the diner round the corner. You're welcome to come to that too if you wanna bang.*

He is chatting away to another colleague, and I don't expect it when my phone beeps instantly.

Haden: *Sure why not. And about the bang part... gladly, if you're offering.*

Huh? I scroll back up to my text.

Oh, fucking hell!

Stupid fat pregnancy fingers. Great, now his idiotic man brain is probably playing porn music in the background already.

Me: *Hang! I meant hang!! #duck*

Me: *I mean #FUCK*

The bubble appears, and I throw my head down in shame. Serves me right.

Haden: *Wait, are you still offering?*

I respond at a very slow pace, checking all my words before I hit send.

Me: *Round two. I'm not offering. HANG out with us if you want.*

I hit send and jump when I see him standing beside me with a grin on his bearded face. I hadn't paid close enough attention to see that he had grown it out until now.

"What's with the beehive, Jerk?"

He rubs his beard making a scratching sound. "Just something new I'm trying out."

"If it makes you feel better, you look like Bigfoot." I turn back around abruptly.

"Actually, that does make me feel better."

He continues to linger, making me feel very uncomfortable.

"So, are you over your little drama now?" he chastises.

"What drama?"

"The drama that made you ignore me from the moment you woke up at the hotel."

What excuse can I come up with that was plausible?

"I don't know what you're talking about. You must be talking about yourself," I say in a clear and nonchalant tone.

He lets out a loose chuckle, scratching his scruff again. "Women."

It's the last thing he says before walking back to his desk.

Clive's last-minute lunch got canceled, and thankfully, it gave me an excuse to avoid Haden until Monday.

Friday has officially become my favorite day for two reasons.

One, I can wear my unattractive muumuu at night and stay indoors.

Two, I don't have to see Haden, which means I can stop thinking about how that beard would feel brushing against my thighs.

As soon as I walk through the door on Friday night, I'm surprised to see Kate already home. She tells me to get dressed quickly because we are going out to dinner with her boss. I only agree because she said the restaurant makes the best enchiladas in the city, so we head off.

"Lex," Kate yells amid the small crowd sitting in the restaurant.

Her boss, Lex, is no doubt one of *the* most gorgeous men I have ever seen. Dressed in a crisp navy suit and a white linen shirt, he stands up and opens his arms to hug Kate. His eyes are like emeralds. And wow, he is all types of beautiful.

"Lex, this is my roommate, Presley Malone," Kate introduces, taking a seat at the small, round table.

He reaches out his hand and shakes mine, and when I pull back, I notice the white gold band on his wedding finger. I remember now how Kate told me he was married with kids. Go figure. The good ones are always taken.

"Nice to meet you, Presley. Kate's told me a lot about you." He pulls out the chair beside him, and I take a seat, giving him a nod in thanks.

"And vice versa. So, Kate has raved on about these enchiladas, and I'd like to point out that I am eating for two, so no judgment from either of you."

Lex laughs as he scours the menu. "My wife used to always say that. It's how she justified ordering the whole menu."

"Oh, that's right, Kate mentioned you had two daughters." I smile.

Kate's face lights up immediately. "Yes, two of the most beautiful girls ever to exist."

He is quick to scowl but follows it with a warm smile. "That's what she says, but Kate hasn't experienced Ava during her teething stage."

"Don't scare her, Lex," Kate scolds.

"No, scare me. I'm too naïve, and I want to expect the worse. That way I'm not in for too much of a shock."

It's nice to finally chat with another parent because no

matter how many textbooks I read, experience can only be told from those who are wise because they've gone through it.

Lex enjoys talking about his family, and I enjoy hearing his stories.

"My oldest daughter, Amelia, is the tomboy. She's always getting into mischief. Almost broken limbs, jumping off things." He raises a Corona to his lips and takes a long drink before continuing, "Ava is my quiet princess. She's happy just to sit quietly and observe others. Never causes trouble. Sometimes she'll just sit in a room, and you'll have no idea she's there."

"I need a baby like that." I sigh.

Kate finishes his sentence. "Lex and Charlie's surprise baby."

"Technically, they were both surprise babies," he adds.

"I've said it once, but I'll say it again... it's because you don't keep your hands off your missus. And the two of you combined are like some baby-making factory." Kate laughs.

Lex doesn't appear offended and instead laughs along with Kate as if it's a longstanding joke between the two of them. They appear to be relaxed in each other's company. Kate told me about how things used to be different. That Lex was one of those horrible bosses up until he ran into the love of his life. It's such a romantic story—they were high school-college sweethearts who broke up years ago, then fate stepped in when they coincidentally ran into each other at a restaurant one day. She told me how everything about him changed the moment his love walked backed into his life, but not without drama, of course. Kate now considers them family, and I can see just by sitting here how true that is.

"Two kids feel like a lot. How did your wife cope with being pregnant twice? It's hard enough this once."

"She enjoys it, but toward the end, she's a bit of a hormonal demon," he adds.

With a mouthful of food, Kate is quick to admonish him. "How dare you say that about my best friend."

"You were the one who called her that," Lex points out.

"Oh, right. Yes, I did."

Hearing these stories brings to the surface my unresolved feelings about my situation. I force myself to be strong, independent, and rely on no one but myself. I am going to be a single mom, whether I like it or not. I will have to raise this child for the rest of my life and make decisions that will either be wrong or right. Haden will eventually start his own family with Eloise, and this child will become less important to him. I will be both the mom and dad when that time comes. I'll be doing it all alone.

Lost in these thoughts, I blurt out, "I don't know how I'm going to be a single mom."

With a sympathetic smile, Kate moves her hand and places it on top of mine.

Lex puts his fork down and clears his throat. "If I'm getting too personal, tell me to back off. The father's not around?"

"He's around. It's just... this was a one-night stand with a work colleague. He's now engaged. It's just not your normal relationship," I admit wholeheartedly.

"I see. Enough said."

"So anyway, I was telling Lex you work at Lantern Publishing. His brother-in-law..." Lex's eyes turn to Kate with an evil stare, "... published his manuscripts with the Californian branch."

"What's his name?" I ask curiously.

"Julian Baker," Kate replies.

"What? Are you kidding me? I love his work, not to mention he's... oh wait, pregnant hormonal lady on the loose. He is gorgeous." I fan myself with a napkin, a wide smile on my face.

Lex's eyes narrow, and Kate is quick to jump in. "Sorry, Pres, he's now married to Lex's sister."

I laugh loosely. "I'm always missing the boat. So yes, he has done a great deal for Lantern Publishing and has opened up avenues for other authors. He's never visited our New York office, but hopefully, he will one day."

"So, correct me if I'm wrong, Mr. Sadler owns and operates this branch?" Lex questions in a more business-like manner, quick to get off the topic of Julian Baker.

"Yes, I've been working for him for about ten years now," I tell him.

"I met him last year at a conference. Kate and I discussed branching out into publishing. With business thriving in our production company, we're looking to expand once again. He's quite knowledgeable as is his son."

"Son? Mr. Sadler doesn't have a son," I answer, puzzled.

Lex furrows his brows. "He introduced him to us. What was his name again, Kate?"

"Had... oh my God, Presley! Why didn't I put two and two together?" she almost yells.

I am confused by Kate's outburst. "What are you talking about?"

She drops her cutlery immediately, leaning back into her chair and folding her arms with a surprised look on her face. "Haden, he's Mr. Sadler's son... your baby daddy."

This time Lex looks confused. "Wait, the father is Haden Cooper?"

I quickly shoot the ridiculous notion down. "You guys are mistaken. Haden isn't his son."

"Stepson," Lex corrects me. "He married Haden's mom when Haden was young. That's what he told me."

Now it's my turn to sit here in disbelief. I'm staring blankly at my plate, trying to piece the puzzle together. I didn't understand why Mr. Sadler never said anything, even after he congratulated me at the party. Surely, he would have known from all the office gossip that Haden knocked me up. It explains why he got away with murder, but what doesn't make sense is why he would hide this from me. It's not a big deal.

"Presley, you look pale. Are you okay? Do you want me to take you home?" Kate's worried face pulls me out of my confused daze.

I smile at them and lie easily. "I'm fine."

The conversation carries on, and I immerse myself in business talk distracting me for a while. Lex Edwards is a very powerful and smart man. I have never met someone so driven, yet so family-oriented at the same time. I understand why Kate speaks so highly of him, and together they are such a dynamic duo with the ideas they are bouncing off each other during dinner.

As the night winds down, Lex says his goodbyes before an early flight back home. Prior to him leaving, he offers his support should I ever need it.

"This is my wife's number and email. If ever you want to ask questions or have a chat, please feel free to contact her. She comes to the city often, and I'm sure Kate will take you girls out." He hands me a business card. "Now, here is my contact information if ever you need anything or if the two of them get up to no good."

I laugh. "Thank you, Lex, for being so kind. It was really nice to meet you."

On our way home that night, I can tell Kate knows something isn't right.

"You had no idea his stepfather was your boss, did you?"

"None whatsoever," I answer bluntly. "Why would he keep this from me?"

"I have no clue. Is it a big deal, though?"

"It just doesn't make sense. Listen, I'm going to his place. I need answers."

She nods. "Want me to come with?"

"No." I smile at her. "You've got your secret date tonight."

She returns the smile. "I'm just a phone call away, okay?"

I hop into a taxi and give the driver the address. Ten minutes later, I am standing outside Haden's door hoping Marcus isn't home, or worse, Eloise isn't there. Music is playing in the background, a gangsta rap of some sort.

I knock on the door and wait.

Nothing.

I bang harder, and some guy I don't recognize opens the door.

"Hey, Mama, who you here for?" He smirks, laughing oddly at the question.

Mama? Jesus, there's a first time for everything.

I try to look past his shoulders, but he is quite tall.

"Who does she belong to?" he yells back into the room.

He moves his body, and I can see directly into the dim room. Marcus is lying on the sofa with some random chick straddling him. As I scan the room for Haden, a godawful stench invades my lungs, causing me to cough and heave.

It's like a trip down memory lane, or should I say college lane more like it.

It smells like weed.

This can't be good for the baby, so to make this quick, I search again and find Haden sitting against the wall. He spots me, and with a crooked smile, he raises his head to greet me.

"Can I please speak to you out here in the hall?"

I walk out of the apartment but not before Marcus jumps up and pushes the girl off him. "Presley, baby, I still love you." His pathetic attempt at speaking to me deserves no response.

Haden stumbles out of the room, and I realize this isn't the best time, but stupid me asks anyway.

"Why didn't you tell me Mr. Sadler's your stepdad?" Annoyed and keeping my distance, I stand against the wall.

"You know what?" He points his index finger at me. "You're beautiful."

It's followed by a delirious laugh, and I throw my hands up in the air, frustrated that I am wasting my time. I turn away and walk toward the stairwell, and just when I think I've escaped, he grips my shoulder and swiftly turns me around.

His eyes are wild, seriously dark, and the laughter he showcased only moments ago has disappeared. My eyes are drawn to his stained shirt and ripped jeans. It's very unlike him to be so unkempt, especially with a rugged beard and scruffy hair.

"Why don't you answer me when I tell you, you're beautiful?" he grits, pinning me closer to the wall.

"Because you're a jerk who's clearly stoned right now."

"It's not an answer," he raises his voice.

Startled, but refusing to show it, I bite back, "Fine. Thank you. Now let me go."

His hands trail across my collarbone and directly down my chest, and I don't stop him, only because I'm gearing up to kick him in the nuts if my Kitty can stop drooling long enough.

"Why do you make life so hard for me? What is it about you, Malone?" He refuses to look me in the eye, talking to himself rather than to me. "If only I hadn't gone to London..."

"Haden, I need to go. This is pointless."

"Where are you going? Let me come with you," he pleads.

Underneath his strong and arrogant persona lies desperation and turmoil. I can't tell whether he has a hidden agenda or just needs a friend right now. Then I remember that men don't like to talk, so I'm guessing the hidden agenda may be sex for all the wrong reasons.

I stand tall and lean forward to kiss him on the cheek, a gesture of goodwill before walking away, but he swiftly locks his lips onto mine.

He forces his tongue into my mouth, but the intensity and longing are torn away as my protective instinct for the baby fogs any passion toward him.

Pushing him back, I catch some air before telling him no. "We can't do that, and you've been smoking. That can't be good for my baby."

He smashes his fist against the wall, screaming in agony, "*Our!* Why won't you fucking get it through your head that it's *our* baby?"

"Because you haven't stepped up and proven to me you're responsible. If you can turn up on Monday morning without being stoned or acting like a jerk, maybe then I can take you seriously."

I push him out of the way and walk down the stairs, praying he won't follow.

He doesn't.

And first thing on Monday morning, I get the call we've been waiting for.

The paternity results are finally in.

EIGHTEEN

I slam the envelope down on his desk, trying to draw a reaction from him. Nothing but a sideways glance, then he refocuses on his computer screen. I'm irritated by his stubbornness and disregard for a clean and sanitary working environment—it drives me fucking nuts. Papers are stacked in no specific order, and pens are missing their lids, not to mention chewed at their ends. An empty coffee mug sits beside his desk phone, growing some green species inside it, unwashed and smeared with lipstick. Gross, it's not even his.

"We need to talk," I grit, barely able to contain my anger.

"I'm busy."

"You're drinking a can of Coke and playing solitaire."

"Exactly. I'm in the middle of something."

"Fine, I'll do it here," I bellow, crossing my arms in frustration. "Thanks for not showing up at the ultrasound. I had to fucking reschedule. Would it have hurt you to pick up the phone? Or even send a text? Since clearly, you have no balls whatsoever."

The king lines up to his final card, and the screen shows his victory win. He shuts the page down, then turns to face me. He looks ghastly with deep, dark circles shadowing his dull eyes, not to mention his beard that has truly taken on a life of its own. He was obviously stoned and drunk all weekend.

Looking uninterested, he takes a drink, then throws the can into the trash. "Are you done now?"

I exhale at his insensitivity. "No, I'm not done. This is exactly why I don't want you in *my* child's life. Once again, you've proven you have no desire to be a father, and I'm really sorry that your name sits inside that envelope."

His face falls, and he quickly opens it to read the answer he is undoubtedly hoping isn't true. His expression turns to pity, fear, and most noticeably, regret. The quick stabbing pains in my heart make me wish he had reacted differently, that may be in some universe filled with rainbows and unicorns, he would have jumped for joy.

But he didn't.

And sometimes, one look can say a thousand words.

What did I seriously expect? He is twenty-six. He rides a motorcycle and gets stoned on the weekends. I couldn't have picked a less desirable sperm donor if I had plucked one from a hat.

Whatever part of me still clings to some sort of pathetic miracle should have read all the signs by now. I only rile myself up the more I dwell on it.

Where did smart, level-headed Presley run off to? Well, it is time for her to come back. Guns blazing.

"So, you have your proof now, but it doesn't matter," I tell him, trying to remain strong. "On top of all this, I don't know why you hid the fact that Mr. Sadler is your stepfather. And, you know what?" My heated words and my irritable behavior should forewarn him of the storm that's about to hit. "I don't know you at all, Haden. Your mood swings are worse than a fifteen-year-old girl's. I know you're hiding something, but who knows what? And I have no clue why you're getting married to someone you barely know. I'm really over all your immature games. I've got a child to raise, and frankly, I don't care whether you're a part of it or not."

I storm off not waiting for an answer. This day's just gone from bad to complete and utter hell. To add to it, I am pissed at myself for even mentioning the marriage thing. Yeah, in hindsight, what does it matter? What he does with his life is his business. Why do I want some an answer or insight into why he is marrying a woman he has known for such a short time?

Back at my desk, I struggle to get any tasks done. Everything in my life feels like a giant mess. When these moods appear, there is only one solution—clean. I grab some disinfectant and wipe my entire desk down including my keyboard, removing the keys one by one, wiping, replacing. I file away the two papers sitting on my desk and sharpen all my pencils to the same height. Then I reorganize my filing cabinet and archive some old paperwork.

That was too easy.

So, I sneak into the main kitchen and start cleaning out the fridge. I was wrong about the Jerk's cup and the new species growing inside it because there is something ten times worse in this fridge. Someone has left a moldy apple, a rotten banana, and some cheese in a plastic container. It's now green, furry, and I swear on my unborn child's life, I see movement in the box. I shiver and pinch the sides of the container, throwing it in the trash.

Breathing a sigh of relief when I can practically see my

reflection in the countertops, I head back to my desk, much calmer now. Sitting in my chair with a fresh cup of tea, I take in the peace and quiet for just a moment. It is short-lived as my phone starts to dance across my desk. I recognize the number and pick it up. The receptionist at the ultrasound place had a last-minute cancellation this afternoon, and I'm quick to accept her timeslot. This morning was bad enough, showing up and waiting like an idiot. I've learned my lesson and have no desire to tell him about this second appointment.

"Guess what?" Vicky is sitting on my freshly-disinfected desk with her God-knows-where-it's- been ass.

Frowning, I eventually indulge her. "Let me guess, the Jerk came and saw you and is trying to worm his way back as Mr. Nice Guy?"

She stops mid-smile and grimaces. "Are you in love with him?"

"Wh... why would you say that?" I stutter, wanting to slap myself in the face for making her think I am. Because I'm not.

"Just asking... so, anyway, Patrick called me," she says excitedly.

Welcoming the switch of topic and avoiding the awkward conversation about love, I am shocked and surprised to learn the weasel is contacting Vicky again. Here's the thing about Patrick—he's the ultimate jerk. The amount of pain and humiliation he's caused Vicky is downright inexcusable. There is no logical reason for him to call Vicky apart from wanting to screw her one more time, then send her off on a shame parade down the highway to hell.

"Patrick? Your ex? The man who was married with kids and fucked you till all hell broke loose? That Patrick?"

She grins, and automatically I worry she will if she

hasn't already jumped on the boat to Brokenheartsville. Again.

"Vicky, don't go there again. You were a mess last time," I gently warn her.

"But this time I'm over him. I'm just curious to find out what he wants." She tries to reassure me.

This isn't good. I have half a mind to call him up and tell him to fuck off, or I'll chop his balls up and feed it to the snappy dog that lives next door. But, of course, I try to be the mature and ever-so-caring friend. I was there through it all, from the snotty sobs to plotting the ultimate revenge. What I didn't expect was to be back here two years later and for Vicky to so eagerly jump back in.

"What else would he want but to get you into bed?"

"Closure," she replies.

"Guys don't want closure. They just go find some new jackrabbit to fuck... or something along those lines," I mumble.

"What?"

"Never mind."

Vicky continues to justify her reasons for responding to him, and I continue to play the friend who tries to stop her from making another wrong decision. But it's her decision to make, and no amount of persuasion from me will change her mind.

Mental note—stock up on ice cream because it's all downhill from here.

"I'm guessing we'll continue this conversation tonight. Listen, I love you, but if he hurts you in the slightest way, I'll go all psycho on his ass."

"I know you got my back," she simpers, leaning in to kiss my forehead as reassurance. "Are you going somewhere now?"

"The Jerk stood me up this morning, so I missed my appointment. The ultrasound place has another opening this afternoon, so once I finish this report I'm working on, I'm heading out."

"Uh-oh... I need the whole story." She glances at her watch. "But I've got a meeting I need to get to. I'll call you tonight, okay?" She raises her eyes, then quickly says goodbye and disappears.

I make it to the appointment with only a minute to spare. The sonographer, Sandra, invites me into the room, and just as I'm about to close the door behind me, there is chaos in the waiting room.

"Am I late?"

Panting and out of breath, the Jerk bends, resting his body against the door and trying to redeem himself. His hair is a wild mess, and sweat is visibly dripping down his forehead.

"Why are you here? I didn't tell you..."

Damn Vicky! That conniving little witch!

"I'm here, okay? Quit giving me grief."

Secretly, I am glad he is here. Whatever the reason he felt the need to see *our* baby, I don't care. It's the first moment throughout the pregnancy where I feel normal, and when I say normal, I mean with a partner right beside me. Sure, it's all fantasy, but just for this short time, I can pretend it's real.

But, of course, I wouldn't think of telling him that, and instead, I poke fun at him.

"Geez, Jerk, wouldn't hurt you to hit the gym once in a while."

"I ran ten blocks," he responds, exasperated. "In an Armani suit."

I roll my eyes at his melodrama and walk into the room. My cheeks start to flush as I think of having to change into the gown. Thankfully, Sandra senses my embarrassment and leads me to the bathroom inside the room where I quickly change into my gown. Walking back into the area, my bare body lays beneath the thin material and feels extremely exposed.

I cross to the other side of the bed as Sandra assists me with getting comfortable. The sheets are placed strategically over my private parts, and Haden takes a seat beside me as the warm gel is spread all over my belly.

"That's a lot of lube," he snickers under his breath.

"So mature, Jerk."

The volume is turned up on the machine, and Sandra moves around my uterus until the baby's heartbeat echoes throughout the room. It's like music to my ears, and my eyes move toward the screen as I watch the images of what looks like a happy little baby cooped up inside.

"So, the baby is measuring correctly," she tells us, typing in the measurements as she speaks.

Haden is staring at the screen, fixated on the baby. "Can you tell us what the sex is?"

"I sure can." She smiles.

"Don't tell him. I don't want to know." I shake my head.

"You can't decide that for me."

"Seriously, what the hell is your problem? You think I'm hormonal, what about you? You're such an ass."

Sandra pauses and looks at both of us. "So yes... no?"

"No," I say at the same time he says, "Yes."

I speak up again. "Absolutely not. If you want to know, then I'll leave the room."

"Not yet, Miss Malone. I just wanted to talk about the position. The baby is breech. However, there's still time to turn."

In a blind panic, I ask, "Is there anything I can do to help the baby turn?"

"Your obstetrician may be able to assist, but the best thing you can do is relax and enjoy the rest of the pregnancy."

Any previous concerns about the sex of the baby don't seem to be an issue anymore. She spends longer checking the baby and its progress, and I forget Haden is even in the room. I only remember he is here when he clears his throat. Something about the way he is amorously staring at the screen consumes me. He's lost in a moment where his soul becomes an open book, and I see a man who is capable of loving this unborn child more than himself. It moves me, yet I break away from these thoughts. This line of thinking is dangerous because deep inside, my walls are breaking down, and he is the giant wrecking ball ready to do enormous damage.

It takes every part of me to turn away from this beautiful sight and move off the bed.

Haden reaches out his hand to help me, but stubborn old me refuses to touch him, and I almost fall off the bed.

"Jesus, can you seriously stop being so stubborn and allow me to help you?"

I hold onto my stomach as a small cramp hits.

"I told you. I don't want anything from you. My goddamn mailman is more reliable than you," I snap, unsure of where it's coming from after such a special moment.

In his typical signature move, he runs his hands through his hair, disheartened. I am tired of arguing with him, and something tells me this is only the beginning.

The two of us just can't get along, it's that plain and simple.

"I didn't tell you that David, or as you call him, Mr. Sadler, is my stepdad because I don't like anyone knowing."

Thrown off by the change of subject, I attempt to listen rather than open my big fat mouth for once. Sandra gives us some time alone to gather our things and leaves the room to attend to another appointment.

"Today is the anniversary of my dad's death." He falls into a digestive silence, eyes staring at the screen where the picture of the baby remains frozen.

I'm never sure what to say in these circumstances, never having experienced the death of anyone close to me besides my grandparents. This is why Hallmark runs a successful business—they sell a card for every occasion when you have nothing appropriate to say.

I need a Hallmark quote right now.

"I'm sorry, Haden," I apologize quietly.

His eyes focus on my stomach, then move toward my face. He's like a little lost boy, the vulnerability and sadness weighing heavily in that one glance. I want to reach out to him, but I know it's inappropriate. Instead, I keep my distance and try to offer some support by listening.

"He died when I was fifteen. A car accident," he tells me in a low voice. "Presley, I run away from this because I'm scared I'll never be the dad he was to me."

I have no choice but to be nice now because I'm not a cold-hearted bitch. I hate the way my feelings toward him shift. I knew there was a reason why he acted like a jerk all the time. I just never expected it to be this.

"Do you want to go somewhere and talk?" I offer.

"I have to attend this dinner with Eloise."

I don't say anything, and he quickly adds, "But I can cancel. Can we go back to your place?"

"Sure."

～

Eloise doesn't take the cancellation well. The argument in the taxi ride home echoes through the speaker.

Some mouth she has on her.

His patience is wearing thin, and the grinding from his teeth is audible, not to mention his repetitive tapping of the door handle, which is driving me insane. When he directs the driver to stop at the corner pizza place, I welcome the interruption.

When we walk through the door of the apartment, the exhaustion of the day hits me like a ton of bricks, and I fall onto the sofa effortlessly.

The one thing I love about Kate's apartment is how cozy and warm it feels. There is something about this place that makes you feel like you are home. It could be the one-of-a-kind vintage pieces or the comfortable natural-colored sofa that practically begs your body to sink into it. Either way, I'm happy to be here.

"Nice place. Who did you say owns it?" He takes a slice of pizza, practically inhaling it in one bite.

"My roommate, Kate, but actually her best friend, Charlie Edwards, owns the place."

"Name sounds familiar," he casually responds.

"Maybe you know her husband, Lex Edwards? He was the one who told me about Mr. Sadler being your stepdad."

Haden lets out a long whistle. "I remember her. How could I forget?" He chuckles at what appears to be his own private joke. "She was at this event, some business thing. I believe I tried to, um... anyway, Lex was quick to set me straight."

I have to laugh at this. I can only imagine how possessive Lex could be. He and his wife are stunning—at least from Kate's photographs they are. From what Kate told me, no one, and I mean no one, gets near Lex's wife.

"Always the player, aren't you?" I tease, grabbing another slice of pepperoni pizza that I am certain is calling my name.

"Was," he corrects me. "What am I now? I don't even know who I am."

Taking slow bites, I drink some soda and wipe my mouth with a napkin. "You're the same person to me. A big fat jerk. Well, not the fat part because actually, you're quite muscular and lean, but you ..." I trail off as he stares at me in bewilderment.

"What? Sauce on my face?" I ask, paranoid.

"No... it's nothing."

I let it go for now, finishing off the last bite and holding in the burp that wants to escape.

"It's nice to just pig out on pizza," he says out of the blue.

"It's one of life's greatest pleasures. You don't pig out on pizza? I thought guys were all about pizza."

"I used to be. Eloise doesn't like it."

I laugh on cue. "If I were with someone who didn't like pizza, there would be no future for us."

"Yes, well, that's the difference between you and her," he boldly states.

"I'm sorry, Haden. Please just once and for all tell me... why are you marrying her?"

He shuffles uncomfortably. "I told you. I love her. It's all about timing, right?"

"I know you said that," I hate to admit. "But you just met her. How does a guy who's used to jumping into random panties suddenly tie himself down?"

I watch him wringing the napkin between his hands. Staring at the floor, he lets out a long breath, then opens his mouth to speak. "She happened to be there at a time when I needed someone. I can't forget that. Despite what you might think, she's a really good person."

I quickly defend his allegation against me. "I never said she wasn't. I simply don't understand why you're rushing into marriage."

"Well, I just told you. She's great. My mom loves her, and so it makes sense."

I don't pry further because, truth be told, he sounds completely unsure of himself. So, after that revelation, we continue to sit in silence.

"Why did you stop talking to me that morning you woke up?" he questions, this time holding my gaze.

It's the second time he's asked me that, and this time I call defeat. Honesty is something I base all of my relationships on whether they be partners or friends.

"The truth? And don't get a big head. And when I say head, I mean down below because, no chance, buddy." Looking puzzled, he waits for my explanation. "I had a dream about you. About us."

With a smug look, he pries further. "What was I doing in the dream?"

"Stop playing dumb. I don't need to spell it out for you. It's awkward, and I really don't want to discuss it further."

With a wide cocky grin, he licks his lips before asking, "Was I at least good?"

Still in his suit with his shirt partially unbuttoned and

flashing me his tanned skin, I realize my strong will can only be pushed so far.

"Have some faith in yourself, Jerk. Yes, you were. Totally sweeping this convo under the rug now," I mumble.

With a sly smile, he leans in a little further. "I had a similar dream that night."

I almost spit out my drink and choke on the liquid stuck in my throat. I cough involuntarily until Haden realizes I need assistance and pats me on the back repeatedly. "You okay?"

I nod, embarrassed he thinks I am this affected by his admission.

"I don't know what to say. This is really awkward."

"What else is there to say besides the fact we're clearly attracted to each other?"

I have no idea how to respond to this, mindful my cheeks are flushed and despite my eyes falling towards the floor, he can see there may be some truth to his admission. Panicking, I try to come up with something witty to say but *nada*.

"Haden, I don't think—"

"Let me finish. It was bound to happen, and I blame curiosity," he claims. "We both know it can't happen."

My heart slightly sinks as he says the words which add salt to an exposed wound. Of course, it can't happen—my emotions are running wild as usual. Tired of feeling like this, I lift my gaze as our eyes meet, his lingering stare causing my breath to hitch.

"It can't happen because you're getting married." There, I said it again. "Haden, we've got to stop playing these games."

He seems to acknowledge the truth, and although it hurts more than I thought it would, it has to come out. We have to focus on raising this baby. That will forever be our top priority.

"I'll stop playing these games on one condition."

"What's that?"

His eyes are practically dancing, and I subconsciously look around the room wondering why he is watching me this way. Under his stare, my cheeks flush, and my body temperature rises.

"I want to kiss you. Just one kiss. Nothing more."

I laugh, thinking it's a joke until his expression tells me to shut the fuck up because he is dead serious.

"But you're—"

He doesn't allow me to finish, moving his body close to mine and cupping my chin in his masculine hands. My uneven breaths are terrified and anticipating his next move. He runs his nose along my chin and moves his face slightly upward until his lips press gently onto mine.

One kiss.

That's all.

Just one little peck won't hurt, right?

I part my lips until our tongues meet midway and intertwine. With a slow and tantalizing pace, our lips move in sync, and the taste of him melts away at my body, reacting instantly.

My hands mimic his and find their way to his chiseled cheekbones. We continue to kiss like this for what feels like forever, and much like high school, my jaw starts to get sore. With a final moan, we both slow the pace and pull away simultaneously.

I look directly at his pants, a bad move since he's obviously hard.

We catch our breath, and suddenly, feeling shy, I struggle to look into his eyes, avoiding them until it's impossible. Everything I see there is filled with forbidden feelings —lust, sex, desire, and maybe traces of something deeper. The silence deepens, and neither of us say a word for what feels like minutes.

"See, it was just a kiss," he insists, adjusting his pants.

"Yep, just a kiss. A kiss that will never happen again."

"Never ever happen again. And that was the point I was trying to prove."

I turn to face him, and with curiosity, I ask, "You had a point to prove?"

"Yes," he quietly chokes. "The awkward part is over. No more curiosity. So, now we can be normal... be friends."

What planet is he on? Not the same horny planet I'm on, that's for sure.

"Okay, so we can be friends," I say, unsure.

"Great." He claps his hands, surprising me. "So, what are you up to this weekend?"

Really? We both just had the most intense kiss ever, and now this is what we are discussing? It's such a bizarre reaction.

"Just shopping for last-minute stuff for the baby, and that's about it. You?"

"Before I forget, my mom wants to meet you. Well, she's been begging to meet you since I told her, but I think now's the time."

"Okay..."

"David wants me in L.A. next month for three weeks to manage the office while the senior editor is having an operation."

"David? Oh! Mr. Sadler, right?"

"Then, I'll be spending a week in Vegas for my bachelor party," he adds.

Whoa, rewind. Again, he gives me the most intense kiss

only to tell me he's going to party all week and probably get laid by a stripper.

My blood rises, and that unusual bout of jealousy is consuming me. I stare at my feet, trying to control these fucked-up feelings. Don't say anything, just keep it to yourself.

"Strippers? Weren't you the one who told me about fucking them or something?"

He smiles softly and raises his hand to stroke my cheek. "I'd never do that to you."

My eyes dart to his, and he is seemingly unaware of the words he's just spoken.

"Don't you mean Eloise?"

His grin disappears, and suddenly he looks agitated. "Yes, I meant Eloise."

Silence falls between us, and when no more words are left to be said, I realize my feelings need a massive reality check.

A fucking astronomical reality check.

"So, I better be going. I'll see you tomorrow at work."

Standing, he heads toward the door, and I follow. He turns to look at me one more time, but this time his eyes are heavily fixated on my lips. With my chest pounding hard, I pray my face isn't flushed, showing how aroused I am and how much I want him to stay.

"So, I guess it's goodbye..." He speaks barely above a breath, unable to pull his focus away from my lips.

Biting the corner of my mouth, I struggle to keep my hands by my side, itching to reach out and caress his face one more time. Finally, I return his smile, and just like that, he turns away and walks to the elevator. Urgently, I call the name my heart can no longer hold in.

"Haden?"

He turns back around, standing still in his perfect pose as my body aches for his beauty. His posture stands tall, showing off his masculine presence. His eyes are bewitching, and behind his frames, his beautiful, light brown eyes are capturing me, not wanting me to let go. But I have to because he doesn't belong to me.

"You're going to make a great dad."

His beautiful face beams instantly. "Thank you. It's exactly what I needed to hear."

Walking away, I shut the door and run for my room. Lying on my bed, I raise my fingertips and run them along my sensitive lips as I close my eyes. Every sensation, every feeling of what happened only minutes ago, is ingrained in my memory. It's all too much, and my heart can't take it, terrified of the one thing I promised myself I would never do.

I am falling in love with the Jerk.

NINETEEN

The night Haden left my apartment, things changed in my head. I couldn't get over the kiss we shared, and while his intention was to get it over and done with and eliminate that awkward tension between us, it had the exact opposite effect on me.

I can't stop thinking about him.

I can't stop thinking about that *kiss.*

As much as I try to talk myself into thinking it is the pregnancy, deep down, it's gnawing at me. You know, that moment when you look at someone in a different light, and all of a sudden you think to yourself, Holy shit, but that person's been in front of me all along. It reminds me of my teenage years watching *Dawson's Creek.* Nobody had a crush on Pacey, then all of a sudden Dawson became an afterthought, and Pacey was *the* guy everyone crushed on.

Geez, you know you have loose marbles in your head when you're comparing your adult life to *Dawson's Creek.*

As the weeks go on, we seem to get along better, never mentioning what happened between us. He is busy wrapping up parts of *Fallen Baby* before heading to L.A., and I am busy trying to get as much done as I possibly can and hand over any ongoing projects to Dee.

I must admit, we get along much better since she started dating this sugar daddy. Not to mention, she is covered in bling.

True to form, I made a list of all the things I need for the baby. After researching baby sites and emailing Lex's wife, Charlie, back and forth, I have a pretty good idea of everything I need. She was extremely helpful, nice, and went out of her way to send me some stuff she hadn't used—extra bits and pieces still new in their packaging. We talk long and hard about the need to attend Lamaze classes. Given that I am trying to limit my contact outside of work with Haden, I settled for a small intimate class for mothers without partners. It is refreshing to be surrounded by women in the same situation, even though the majority of them chose to be inseminated by an anonymous sperm donor.

The day Haden is scheduled to fly out to L.A., I have officially hit thirty-one weeks. Now I am really a beached whale, uncomfortable everywhere, and the worst part is, I still have nine weeks to go.

"Don't go having that baby while I'm gone." He chuckles.

"I'll stay away from the spicy food," I joke.

"And sex," he adds with sarcasm.

"Ha, ha... fat chance of that happening," I mock. "So, Gemma tells me you guys are going to some surfing gig on the weekend?"

"Yes. I can't wait. The best in the world will be there."

"Well, give them a hug for me."

"The surfers?" he teases.

I punch his arm, enjoying the relaxed conversation between us.

"No! Gemma and Melissa."

He continues to smile, shutting down his computer and packing his things. He will be gone for four weeks, and I hate to admit that I'll miss him.

Yes, we get along much better.

Yes, I try very hard to curb any feelings I have toward him.

I am certain that once the baby comes, I will feel differently about him. I am certain everything that is consuming me now is because of the hormones. Take hormones out of the equation, and all he will be in my eyes is my child's father.

"Have a safe trip," I say with a genuine smile.

"I'll text you once I'm there. Just take care of my baby, okay?"

"Our baby," I correct him.

His face breaks out into a wide smile before he walks to the elevator and disappears.

"Surprise!"

I walk into the apartment, and there are balloons everywhere. Standing around are Kate, Vicky, Gemma, Melissa, Charlie, a couple of girls from the office, and my mom.

Aside from the mint-green balloons floating in the room, there is a long table covered in finger food, and a giant stork sits in the middle of the room. Toward the left wall, another makeshift table stands with a ton of presents.

"Happy baby shower," Vicky and Kate sing in unison.

I smile, still in shock, and walk around the room greeting everyone. It's the first time I'm meeting Charlie in person, and just like in her photographs, she is beautiful.

With long, wavy brown hair just above her waist, her toned physique blows me away, especially considering she's had two kids.

"It's so nice to finally meet you." She smiles, leaning in to hug me.

"And you. Where are the girls?"

"Lex took them to the zoo today. I've already gotten a dozen texts and calls." She pulls out her phone and proudly shows me a picture of the two girls sitting in front of the bird enclosure. "Anyway," she continues, "we're here to celebrate you."

Having been dragged to a number of these events in the past, I'm surprised it turns out to be a fun couple of hours, playing games, eating delicious food and, of course, opening presents.

Mom, as promised, got me a new breast pump, and pretty much the rest of the baby store back home. Among the other gifts are clothes, toys, and other much-needed items.

Hidden behind the last bag I open is a flat present wrapped in brown paper. I take it off the table and search for a card, which is on the opposite side. I open the envelope, take out the small card, and slowly read the inscription.

My dad would read this to me every night.
Now it's my turn to read it to our child.

With everyone in the room focused on me, I unwrap the present carefully. It's a storybook with a picture of two bears on the front. The title reads, *Why I Love My Dad So Much*. As I open the first page to have a glimpse, there, in a child's writing, are the words, *This book belongs to Haden Cooper*.

I know everyone is watching me, and I'm barely able to choke back the tears. I think I mumble something like 'thank you all for coming,' and fortunately, Gemma distracts everyone with party favors.

When the last guest leaves, I head to my room, utterly exhausted. Vicky and Kate are happy to clean up, and Gemma, Melissa, and Mom head back to their hotel for some sleep before an early morning flight home.

Flopping onto the bed with Haden's book in hand, I grab my phone and try to call him. It goes to voicemail after a few rings, and with heavy eyes, I send a follow-up text.

Me: *Your gift was beautiful. Thank you for giving this to our child.*

It's the following morning when I read his reply.

Haden: *Sorry I missed your call. I didn't hear my phone at dinner. My dad read that to me every night till I was ten years old. I'm hoping I'll be able to do the same.*

It wasn't until a week later that I went back and absorbed his words. My heart sank for him, that he won't be able to read to our child every night because we aren't together. He will live with his wife, Eloise, and I will live somewhere else. There is no point dwelling on that fact, and so I choose to move on. Well, at least I *try* to move on.

He may have been in Vegas, but it feels like a million miles away, and my memory forgets what he looks like, having not seen him in almost a month. So, becoming a crazed, obsessed stalker seems only natural. I hit up social media, searching every photograph he is in and the general comments he posts. Just like Vicky said, he's an extreme sports junkie with countless pictures of him jumping out of planes and off cliffs. He doesn't post many status updates, but it's the link to a video that he posted only hours ago which catches my attention.

I press play, and it's him playing a guitar and singing. In what looks like a hotel room balcony with the night's sky above him, the guitar is positioned on his lap as he sits on the floor against the railing. Wearing a ratty Rolling Stones tank, gray sweats, and an army-green beanie, his arms are flexed and fuck, does he look gobsmackingly beautiful.

He plays the chords and hums along to a familiar beat. I wrack my brain trying to figure out the song, and by the time he reaches the chorus, I recognize it. It's an Eagles' song, 'I Can't Tell You Why,' and I remember it from my childhood when Dad would play the album on repeat.

Haden's voice is soft and sexy, perfectly in tune with the song. It's over so quickly that I press play again, but this time I close my eyes. The lyrics are sinking deep within me —every word, every emotion, fueling this burning fire I am trying so hard to contain. What is it about him that does these things to my body and soul?

I let out a breath to stop my heart from racing, and I click on the comments below. Several friends have commented, shared, and liked his post. In fact, there are over a hundred comments. By the end of the night, I feel like a complete loser for reading more into it. He probably sings it about Eloise, and that thought makes me head straight to the tub of ice cream I had reserved for Vicky.

Kate and Vicky notice a change in my mood, and they are quick to figure it out.

"You porked him, didn't you?" Kate sighs, using her over-the-top British slang.

"For the millionth time, *no!*"

"Something happened," Vicky coerces, watching me intently. "You're acting odd. You're in love with him... aren't you?"

Frustrated, I pull myself up from the couch with the assistance of Kate. Being heavily pregnant at just under thirty-five weeks is taking its toll on my body.

"We kissed... okay? That's it," I barely admit. "And I'm not in love with him. Just feel guilty because we shouldn't have. It's not fair to Eloise."

The damage is done, and the worst part is that it damaged me. I have enough on my plate without throwing a pile of guilt on there. I should have known this would happen. I'm not as strong as I thought I am. Love has this stupid way of creeping under your skin when you least expect it.

Shit, I did not just use the word *love.*

"Sweetie," Vicky says soothingly, rubbing the base of my back like the good friend she is. I welcome the massage, especially because of the extra weight I'm carrying. "Why don't you just admit there's something there between you?"

I want to ugly cry, and I'm not an overly emotional person. I didn't even cry when watching *Steel Magnolias* or even *Beaches*, and everyone cries watching those movies.

"I really want to drop this subject."

Thankfully, they drop the subject at that, but not

without offering to hang out with me for the night. I reassure them I'm okay because I have to be, and I carry on, asking them about their plans for the evening.

Vicky is meeting up with Patrick, which no doubt will result in her coming back here two hours later in tears. Kate has a rendezvous planned with mystery man. She's dressed in a short, fitted leather dress and really high leather pumps, and I'm dying to ask if it's at some underground bondage club. I also wonder if the mystery package that arrived earlier in the week from a place called *Betty's Sweet Things* has something to do with tonight.

Alone and on the couch with a bowl of popcorn, I'm entertained by Reese Witherspoon in *Sweet Home Alabama*. As one of my favorite movies, it is normally a great distraction, but tonight, I can't stop thinking about what Haden is up to. No doubt, men surrounded by feral kitties and cheap booze won't end well. Argh. I shove a handful of popcorn in my mouth, ignoring the images that taunt me. Vegas is a sleaze hole.

Moments later, my phone beeps, and Vicky's name pops up.

Vicky: *Oh my god Pres! Quick bathroom break, Patrick just told me he is leaving his wife and gave me a key to his new apartment!*

I cringe and let out an annoyed sigh. Here we go again. No matter what I say, Vicky is going to ignore my advice anyway. To avoid the confrontation, I put my phone aside until I have some sort of response that will satisfy both of us.

When it beeps a minute later, I know she won't give up, so I pick it up and see that it's not from her.

Haden: *Just checking in to make sure you haven't given birth and ran away to some enchanted forest to raise my kid.*

I laugh out loud to myself, sinking further into the sofa with a deep smile on my face. As I type a response, nerves suddenly appear, and my usual witty comebacks aren't occurring to me like they usually do. He's miles away, yet I feel like he's right beside me.

Me: *Still THE giant elephant in the room. Surprised you found time out of your busy stripper schedule to say hello.*

I sit and wait for him to respond, but nothing. An hour later, I've deemed myself pathetic and make my way to bed, cursing the living daylights out of him.

Why did he have to text me, only to leave me hanging like this. It's my own fault, I shouldn't get so giddy at a simple text.

I try to fall asleep, but my restless legs and weak bladder call for a sleepless night, so I get to reading. Somewhere in my pregnancy book, I fall asleep only to be woken shortly after from another text.

Haden: *Can I call you?*

. . .

These four simple words make my heart race so fast that I'm unable to respond immediately. The second I do, my phone rings.

"Hey, giant elephant in the room," he whispers.

"Thanks. You sure know how to make a woman feel better."

He lets out a raspy laugh. "I think I left my charm along with my wallet in some stripper's panties."

"Sounds like you're behaving yourself. What time is it there?"

"Beer o'clock," he responds humorously. "The sun will greet me soon."

"I can't sleep either but for very different reasons."

His heavy breathing comes through the phone, and for a brief moment, I think he is asleep.

"Soon, the baby will be here, and you can sleep better."

"Ha," I exclaim. "News flash, babies wake up all through the night. I wonder if Kate would like to do the a.m. shift."

With a slight hesitation, he responds sincerely, "You don't have to do that. Maybe some nights I can stay over... like on the couch or something?"

It's my turn to hesitate. It was inevitable that this would come up. We still haven't agreed as to how things will work once the baby is here. I'm still staying at Kate's because I can't decide whether to stay in the city or not. Kate reassures me that having a baby around will not cramp her style. She has even offered to help out whenever she can, especially at night since she's a night owl.

I don't cope well with no sleep. In fact, I'm the grumpiest person ever if I don't get eight straight hours of sleep. Haden can't sleep on the couch forever, but it's not like I'm ready to have the baby sleep at his place, either. I feel a migraine coming on.

"I guess we could do that..."

"You sound unsure."

"I just haven't thought about it much. I've been preoccupied with this birthing plan I'm supposed to come up with."

It seems like the most awkward conversation ever, and it goes on for ages. He then proceeds to tell me stories about the past few nights, many of which leave me in stitches. Although he doesn't talk much about Marcus, he eludes to the fact that Marcus is somewhat not over me.

"You need to ignore his texts and calls," he warns me.

Coincidentally, it's then that a beep comes through the line. I quickly pull my phone away from my ear and open the text.

It's from Marcus and holy shit! It's a picture of his cock. Nothing good ever comes from being drunk and your ex's number still stored in your contacts.

"He just texted me. Do you have ESP or something?"

There is a low growl over the speaker. "What did he say?"

I laugh because it is funny when you think about it. "It's not what he *said* but more what he *showed.*"

"Are you fucking kidding me?" Haden snaps.

"Don't worry, I can handle him. I'm not looking to start things up with Marcus again if that's what you're worried about."

More silence.

"I'm not worried. Marcus is relentless when he wants something he can't have. He shouldn't send shit like that to you."

"Sounds like someone else I know," I blurt out without thinking.

He laughs on cue. "You mean me? I'm not like that."

"Yeah, and I'm not going to turn into a crazy cat lady."

"I won't let you get a cat. So there, you can't become a crazy cat lady."

I shake my head and realize he can't see me. "It only takes one visit to the shelter and *bam*, you're coming home with a kitty and a bag of litter."

"What if I told you I'm allergic to kitties?"

I almost choke into the phone as I fall into a fit of laughter. "Um... I don't think you're allergic to kitties because if you were, you might as well call me Immaculate Mary."

Even through the phone, I know he is smiling. "Mind in the gutter, Malone. I think you're long overdue to get some."

God, is that the truth. *Don't you dare mention that you want some from him.*

"That would involve dating," I state in a serious tone.

His breathing becomes heavy and thick. "You're thinking about dating already?"

"No. But maybe one day. I can't stay a nun forever, although I'm not sure how desirable I'll be. Single mom, and the guy would have to deal with you?" I joke lightly. "Talk about excess baggage."

"Why would you need to date? Is it just about sex?" he barks.

Taken aback by his change of tone, I go into defense mode. "Are we really having this conversation?"

"Yes. I want to know why."

"Then, yes," I almost yell. "This is the longest time I have ever gone without sex. I'm so fucking horny, it's depressing, and I miss the smell and touch of a man beside me in bed every night. Being single sucks big time."

"I have to go," he quickly tells me.

Great, another awkward ending between the Jerk and Presley. It's a broken record, so overplayed.

Before I can say goodbye, he hangs up on me.

What the hell was that?

Lying flat on my bed, I let out a loud growl and shake my body in frustration. The nerve of him to put me on the spot and then back out mid-conversation. When my phone beeps a minute later, I am wondering what pathetic excuse he'll use this time.

Haden: *I'm sorry I had to do that. There's something about you... I don't know what it is. I just don't want you seeing anyone else. Yes I know I'm selfish but it's the truth and I'm sick of hiding it.*

I read the text over and over to make sure I get the words right. What exactly is that supposed to mean? He's confusing me. Throw Eloise into the mix, and I really have no idea what's going on.

Me: *You're going to have your own life soon with Eloise. I don't think you'll be bothered with what I'm doing or who I'm seeing.*

I haven't even hit send yet when his next text comes through.

. . .

Haden: *This is complicated. You're my kid's mom. You'll be in my life forever. Every man that touches you will have some bearing on our kid. I don't want anyone else being my kid's dad or stepdad. Only me.*

His words anger me. How hypocritical of him! Does he honestly expect that I will never have a boyfriend again or get married? But it's okay for him? I am typing so fast with zero self-control as the words pour out onto the screen.

Me: *I'm not turning into a nun Haden so you can feel good about yourself. I have needs too. Just like you do. You need to get over it because your stupid demands mean nothing to me. I will do whatever the hell I want.*

I wait for his reply for what feels like forever. I expect a long-winded message, but instead, it's only a few words.

Haden: *Then why won't you let me help you?*

What the hell is he talking about? He wants to help me find someone to date or marry? This is ridiculous, and I am growing bored with his antics.

Me: *Help me do what?*

. . .

I wait impatiently for his response.

Haden: *Let me take care of your needs. Nobody has to know. It can remain our secret. Maybe you need to just release and you'll feel different about the whole situation.*

Now I am completely lost, so I dial his number, and he picks up immediately.

"I don't understand."

"You're smart. What part of having a mind-blowing orgasm don't you understand?"

Did he just say mind-blowing orgasm?

"Are you talking about phone sex? I don't think that's a good idea. Besides, you're in Vegas... and did I mention already that it's probably not a good idea?"

"It doesn't matter where I am. I'm right here talking to just you, Presley. Get comfortable."

I laugh nervously. "How? I'm pregnant."

"Sorry, I mean naked."

Shit. It just got real. And why am I peeling off my clothes at his command? Maybe he is right, this could be our little secret. It's only phone sex, no physical touching involved.

"If I have to get comfortable, then so must you."

"I already am... naked, that is."

My palms start to sweat, and I focus on his uneven breaths as I close my eyes and listen intently. My body is betraying me, reacting with pleasure even in my uncomfortable state.

Phone sex is something I've never dabbled in. When Jason went off on trips, the only sexual interactions between us were quick I'm-horny-so-I'll-jerk-off-when-we-hang-up-and-catch-you-later types of calls.

This is unfamiliar, nerve-wracking yet incredibly hot.

"Relax," he whispers calmly. "It's just you and me. But I'm warning you, I don't play fair, and this will be over really quick."

"I don't play fair, either, Haden. I'm assuming your cock is out and hard as a rock. I'm also guessing that this is driving you insane, and as we've been speaking, you've been stroking it gently, trying to control the mind-blowing orgasm you're about to have."

His silence only confirms what I've just said.

"So, what if I were to tell you that I've been lying here, pussy soaked and throbbing, thinking about how your hand moves slowly from your shaft up to the tip of your cock as your back arches and your eyes close feverishly with pleasure? Tell me, what would you do next?"

A low grumble escapes his throat. "I'd tell you that all I can think about is how fucking wet your pussy is and how I never got to taste it. How my tongue wants to slide all over your clit and suck it till you beg me to fuck you."

Dammit! He got me.

I squeeze my legs to contain the persistent throb to no avail. My arms weaken, and the tingling sensation spreading throughout my body intensifies. Shit, this is torture. My hands don't reach that area comfortably, and when they do, I am mortified at the amount of bush forming and blush in embarrassment. Talk about a distraction. Thank God he can't see it.

Shit, where was I?

"I wouldn't beg you to fuck me. I can see how desperate you are. It's all you've been thinking about."

His moan deepens. "Tell me now how fucking wet you are again."

"Soaking wet..." I moan, rubbing my fingers across my swollen clit. I gasp unwillingly at the heightened arousal. "You've got me so wet I can't stop thinking about how perfect your cock would feel inside me right now." My eyes are closed, and I allow those words to escape without thinking.

"Tell me how you taste," he begs me.

I raise my fingers to my lips and gently lick the tips. "I taste... sweet."

The echo shifts and there is a moan followed by a growl. Without a doubt, he is just about there. I speed up the motion and know that I have about five seconds before I am seeing stars.

"I want you to come, Haden. Come all over that beautiful, pierced cock of yours. Imagine my mouth is there waiting to take you all in."

Three, two, one, and I'm fucking done.

I moan loudly as my body jerks back. I forget he's on the phone, and as my eyes flick open, reality hits, and I think about what the hell I've just done.

As the communication between us goes stagnant, I have no choice but to speak first. "Well, that was..."

"Hot?" he teases.

"Hot... interesting... different."

"Needed."

I sigh. "Yes, fine. Very needed."

"You hate admitting that, don't you?"

"That I'm horny? Sure. Doesn't everyone?"

"No. I'll admit it," he tells me.

"First of all, you're a guy who's seen strippers nonstop for three days. Second, you're in a relationship. You can pretty much get laid anytime. I'm only human, I have needs, too, and I seriously didn't think this single-mom stuff through. I'll never get laid again," I ramble.

"Are you done?"

"What? Yes," I concede.

"Yes, I have seen strippers nonstop for three days, but my dick was as soft as a marshmallow. Yes, I'm in a relationship, but it's just..." he trails off. "I don't want to go into that part. Third, you're fucking beautiful, and you don't see it. Every guy in our office was waiting for you to break it off with James—"

"Jason," I correct him.

"Whatever," he grumbles. "Because they wanted to fuck the living daylights out of you."

I laugh, thinking it's a joke. "C'mon, Haden. Joke's over. No one in the office shows interest in me. I wish."

"You don't realize what you do to men. You're like this untouchable goddess walking around with a fucking wand that makes everyone's dick hard."

"Jesus, Haden, I'm pregnant. What planet are you on?"

"And thank God you are because now they've backed off."

"What did you just say?" I ask, nervously.

"I'm saying that this is a good thing."

"I didn't know this is a let's-lay-all-the-cards-out-on-the-table type of conversation, but then again, you just made me come over the phone, so no more hiding stuff anymore."

"My cards are out if yours are."

"They're out," I breathe into the phone, tired and exhausted.

"Why are you worried about getting laid once the baby is born?"

"I'm not worried about getting laid straight away. I'm

saying that one day I'm going to crave the touch of a man, and it's going to be difficult since I have a child to think about. It's not just about me anymore."

"But I told you I don't want anyone touching you."

"And I told you that's too bad because you're getting married and getting laid every night, so stop being a jerk."

"I don't want anyone touching you."

"Why are we even arguing about this? Let's deal with it when the time comes."

"I want to deal with it now. I don't want anyone touching you."

"Yeah, well, I don't want anyone touching you, but life is unfair," I shoot back.

"Then no one will," he states confidently.

"Empty promises, Haden. You're a guy, and I respect that your cock needs to get laid."

"By you," he confirms.

Whoa. This conversation is taking a turn, a major turn, to God knows where. The whole dynamic of our conversation has changed, and I'm rendered speechless. He has no idea the enormity of his words, and being the rational one, I feel I have no choice but to bring him back down to reality.

"Haden," I whisper. "We need to talk about this when you're back. Right now, I'm tired, and I have to get up for work in a couple of hours."

"I'll be back on Sunday. I want to see you then."

"Okay."

I hang up the phone, bewildered. Not even a minute later, I receive a text.

Haden: *I meant what I said.*

. . .

I know he means it. I'm just not ready to deal with it.

Vicky and Kate come home not even ten minutes later. Vicky has decided to sleep over, and the second I see her walk through the door, I run to her with a razor in my hands.

She yawns. "Pres, it's three in the morning, and you want me to shave your kitty?"

"This is an emergency situation! You don't understand."

"I understand that it's three in the morning, and there's a possibility I may give you a mullet."

I drag her to the bathroom and close the door behind us. Kate is already in her room, drunk on her bed.

"This really can't wait till tomorrow?"

"No, I can't sleep knowing I've let it turn into the Amazon Rainforest."

"I must really love you to do this..." she mumbles to herself, armed with a razor, soap, and water.

Ten minutes later, she's done.

"You wanna see? Geez, I think the razor went dull."

I laugh. "No, I'm fine. Thank you."

"Honestly, the things I do for you."

I wake up the next day, incredibly happy despite the lack of sleep. With a shaved kitty and a refreshing cup of tea, life has become a bed of sweet roses. Not to mention, I get another text from Haden which makes me smile.

Haden: *I still mean what I said.*

I don't respond just yet, and when I receive a bouquet of flowers ten minutes later, my day gets even better. It's a bunch of rainbow-colored roses with a card attached that says, "From your Jerk."

I can't help but smile until I notice Eloise walking toward my cubicle. Perfectly dressed in a pristine white, turtleneck dress, she appears somewhat cheerful as she greets me hello and bends down to kiss me like we're the best of friends.

My conscience is on the run like a fugitive, leaving me to deal with that godawful emotion called guilt.

"Hi, Presley, are you free for lunch?"

"Uh... I'm kinda busy," I lie.

"It's really important. Hey, nice roses."

She leans in to sniff them, and I thank God the card is still in my hands.

Reluctantly, I join her for lunch at another one of her green diet-friendly restaurants. She sits across from me sipping her lawn in a glass, flashing her bright white teeth.

"So, first, I know we haven't had a chance to catch up, but I heard everything went well with your trip to visit your parents."

"Yes, it did, thank you."

"I've been so preoccupied with the wedding, so I haven't been able to give you this." She slides an envelope in front of me, and I see the fancy cursive writing on the front. Opening it slowly, I see that it's their wedding invitation.

"The date on there is next week," I say, trying to control my nervous stutter.

"Yes, we decided to move it closer. It's only very close family and friends at my parents' house, so changing the date wasn't really an issue."

"I'm not sure what to say. I feel like it would be uncomfortable for me to be there."

"But you're family. We'd really love to have you there." She smiles.

My mind is reeling. Did he know this information last night? Surely, he had to. Then why did he go on and on about it just being us. Or is my brain reading way too much into this?

"How're things going with the pregnancy?"

"Fine. Five weeks to go," I respond with my best poker face.

"I'm kind of excited to say this, but since we're like family, and I feel like I can really open up to you... Haden and I are trying to have a family."

"You're trying for a family?" I stare at her in disbelief.

"Yes. We spoke about it briefly, but I thought, why not go off the pill now? Anyway, before he left for L.A., we had quite a night." She leans in. "We did it three times that night. I really think we made a baby."

The sound of my heart shattering into a million pieces echoes throughout the room, or at least that's how it feels. I feel a stabbing pain, its persistent jabs creating deep, unfounded wounds. I'm infuriated with him, with her, at myself for believing that this fucked-up story would become a fairy tale.

"It will be perfect. Our babies can grow up together. I told Haden this morning that I had a gut feeling about it."

"What did he say?" I can barely speak.

"He seemed pretty tired, but he said that if I'm pregnant, then we probably should get a bigger place for both of the babies."

"Both babies?" This time I don't hold back my animosity.

"He didn't tell you?" Her face falls. "I was really hoping

he did. He wants to file for joint custody. A week on, a week off type of arrangement."

Under the table, my hands sweat profusely as my blood begins to boil. "When did he tell you this?"

"We've been speaking about it for a while, but late last night we talked about it again. He's got the papers drawn up." She pulls an envelope out of her bag.

I can barely see. I'm fueled by anger, and every shade of red is blinding me. My stomach is twisted into heavy knots, and I feel like I'm going to be sick. "I need to go."

Dizzy, I stand and leave her behind as she calls after me.

Somehow, I make my way back to work, confused and utterly disappointed. At my desk, I throw the flowers into the trash and grab my scissors, angrily cutting every stem to pieces. I take a picture of it and send it to him.

Me: *YOU JERK*

My hands are shaking, and I see Vicky standing over me, mouthing something. I try to hear her, but the warm gush of liquid running down my legs confuses me.

"Holy fuck, Pres! Your water just broke," Vicky screams.

I look down and then back up at her in a blind panic, only to hear her yell to the office, "It's showtime, baby."

TWENTY

I'*m staring at this face.*
   It's soft and wrinkly and everything is so small.
Ten tiny fingers, ten tiny toes.
It's my baby.

My life does a complete one-eighty in just twenty-four short hours.

It all happens so fast from the moment my water breaks.

In a state of denial, I want to go home, but Vicky shoves me into a taxi with her, and we head straight to the hospital. I am not experiencing any pain physically, but emotionally I am angry, hurt, and humiliated by what the Jerk did. The delusional fog I am in, which I blame on the hormones, has come to a screeching halt, and there is no time to even think about that as I lay in the hospital bed, tied up to several of drips and monitors.

"I've tried to call Haden," Vicky tells me.

"Why would you do that?"

"Because you're having this baby, and he needs to be

here." She shakes her head at my question, gently patting my forehead with a cold washcloth.

"I'm not having this baby. I'm only thirty-five weeks along. It's not going anywhere."

Denial only gets you so far. No matter how much I try to talk myself out of it, the contractions are a motherfucking giant slap of reality. The pain ricochets across my back, then moves toward the front. Gritting my teeth in this unbearable state, I'm given a jug of ice cubes to suck on for the next lot of contractions. I want to throw the jug at the nurse, but physical abuse won't help me, and I shouldn't be mean to the person who has the drugs.

"It keeps going to voicemail," Vicky says in a worried tone.

"Well, fucking good! He doesn't deserve to be here, anyway," I yell mid-contraction.

The second the contraction winds down, I start to cry, and I mean ugly-sob cry. Even with Vicky by my side, I feel so alone and terrified. She holds onto me for what feels like forever until I manage to calm myself down.

Mom and Dad are honeymooning in Fiji—they only just arrived there yesterday. Gemma and Melissa are staying at some B&B, and their phones have no coverage. To add to everything else, the crib hasn't arrived yet, and I haven't washed all the clothes like you're supposed to, plus my hospital bag is sitting beside my bed at home.

This was not my plan.

This is so unplanned it makes me want to cry even more.

"Shhh." Vicky strokes my hair at the same time Kate rushes into the room with Lex right behind her.

"Oh my God, what the hell happened? Lex and I were in a taxi when I got your text. I had the taxi driver rush us right over here." Panicked and out of breath, she is by my side, riddled with worry.

Still in an emotional state and unable to communicate effectively, I let Vicky do all the talking. She starts with my lunch with Eloise, how the Jerk screwed me over, and the taxi ride over here. Both of them offer their opinions on Eloise, but I immediately tune out, not wanting to deal with that.

"Did the Jerk really knock Eloise up, too?" Kate whispers to Vicky.

Vicky nods and proceeds to tell her the rest of the story. Lex walks over to the end of the bed and lifts the chart off the railing to read it.

Curious, I continue to watch him. "Can you read charts?"

"He used to be a doctor," Kate adds.

"Intern," he corrects her.

"What does it say? Is something wrong with my baby?"

He continues to read, then puts it down. "Well, your water broke, but you knew that. The baby's heart rate is high, and it appears to be distressed. Basically, if it continues, they will need to do a C-section."

"But... but I can't be cut open." I panic. Not once have I thought this was a possibility. "I don't handle blood very well or knives and scalpels. And what about if they can't close me up? What happens if my organs fail?"

Lex moves over to Kate's side, and with a calm demeanor, tries to ease my worries. "You'll have well-trained surgeons taking care of you. Women bounce back without too much trouble. Aside from no driving for a while, you'll just need to take it slow. No heavy lifting or strenuous exercise. But let's see what your doctor says first.

In the meantime, is there anything I can get you from the nurses' station?"

I shake my head and thank him.

"I'll be right outside if you want me, just need to make a few work calls."

He goes off into the hallway, and I rest my head back and close my eyes. The second he is out of sight Vicky is quick to comment. "Shit, Kate, why didn't you tell me he was gorgeous?"

"Because he's married and totally off the market."

"Does he have any brothers? Or even cousins? Hell, what about his dad? I'm quite open." Vicky winks.

Even in my despair, I laugh out loud at her comment. "You're very open."

"Like a twenty-four-hour convenience store," Kate roars.

"Hey!" Vicky hollers. "That's not nice... but *so* true."

Kate grabs the chair behind her and pulls it in, still holding onto my hand. "I hope you don't mind that Lex is here. It was hard enough getting a taxi at this hour without having to drop him off first, plus he was worried about you. He called Charlie straight away, and she sends her best wishes and a message for you... ask for the drugs."

I manage to laugh out loud again, not plagued with another contraction yet. They appear to be inconsistent, which is probably a good thing. The doctor still hasn't turned up, but according to the last nurse who came in, he will be here shortly. It's a waiting game, and uncertainty is something that makes me extremely anxious. I haven't even taken the time to research Caesareans, believing I would have a normal vaginal birth. My body temperature begins to rise again, so I shove some ice cubes in my mouth, biting hard to stop panic-ridden Presley from blacking out.

Vicky checks her phone again before placing it back in her purse, turning her attention back to me. "I get why you're pissed off at him after what Eloise told you. But what did he say or do the night before for you to get so worked up, Pres?"

"Nothing," I mumble. "It's not even worth talking about. Just distract me. Tell me what happened with Patrick."

Once Vicky gets started on Patrick, it's like listening to a soap opera. Apparently, he separated from his wife because she busted him cheating with some secretary at his firm. Although they aren't divorced yet, he's eager to move on with his single life, and Vicky's name is at the top of his list.

"You'll be proud of me... I didn't touch him whatsoever."

"Good, because I'd hate for you to be here one day, pushing out a baby that belongs to a jerk!" I scream suddenly, riding out another contraction that catches me by surprise.

I squeeze both Kate's and Vicky's hands, and I only let go when the pain subsides. They let go as soon as I relax again and shake their hands to stop the numbing. I hadn't realized how tight I was squeezing until I saw their pale white hands.

Exhausted from the tides of pain, I manage to close my eyes for what feels like only a brief moment. Time is lost on me, and when Lex walks back into the room with the doctor, I pray for pain relievers and a positive solution.

"Miss Malone, you've gone into early labor, and the baby is distressed. We need to operate shortly," the doctor informs me.

"Wait, operate? You can't cut me open! That's why I have a vagina," I yell, out of breath as I choke, panicking.

The midwife strolls in and takes Vicky's spot, patting my forehead with a cloth. She talks to me, but all I hear is blah, blah, blah. I'm certain I'm going to pass out from the sheer terror. I begin to cry, wanting my mom or sister, someone familiar to comfort me and not this stranger. With Vicky and Kate sent to the waiting area, the pain mixed with my desperate pleas drown out an army of nurses who come into the room and unlock the wheels to my bed.

"We're going to wheel you to the operating room now."

The doors open, and my girls are at my side with Lex behind them. The sobbing starts again, and I desperately hold onto their arms, not wanting to let go.

"It's gonna be okay, Pres," Vicky whispers. "The Jerk hasn't picked up his phone, but I'll keep trying."

"I'm scared," I cry through small, strained sobs.

"I know, sweetie, but I promise you'll be okay."

"How do you know?"

"Because you're my best friend, and you have to be." She kisses my forehead with tears falling down her cheeks. Kate looks equally distraught but is attempting to smile, reassuring me everything's going to be okay. Lex stands beside Kate and offers his kind words.

"It'll be over before you know it, and you'll be holding that beautiful baby of yours in your arms." He smiles, looking somewhat nostalgic.

"Great, someone just got baby fever again," Kate says as she rolls her eyes at him.

I manage to smile through my tears before their faces disappear down the hall.

There's something to be said for being a patient in an operating room. It's the most surreal out-of-body experience there is. The sterile walls and bright lights somehow create a calm before the storm. I've zoned out, only barely hearing the distant voices. Things are thrown over me and poke and prod me. When a contraction rocks me to the core, they warn me they are giving me an epidural, and the pain is suddenly washed away.

I want to smile.

I want to laugh and run through the fields, dancing and carefree.

What a fucking relief.

In a sea of calm, I stare into the light, blissfully dazed until the doors burst open, and the Jerk rushes in. The guards behind the surgeons are trying to catch him, and when the nurse figures out who he is, they give him a gown and mask and make him sanitize his hands. He is by my side so fast with bloodshot eyes surrounded by a thick black bruise. He looks a complete wreck.

The stale stench of alcohol lingers on his breath as he sits closer to me. *Jesus, he is drunk.*

"Really? This is how you welcome our child into the world? Drunk and covered in dried blood?" I whisper.

"It's a long story."

"We've got time. In case you haven't noticed, I ain't going anywhere anytime soon."

"I don't want to get into it now."

"Why? Because Eloise is pregnant, too?" I spit back, accusing him in front of the entire medical team.

The anesthesiologist tries not to smile, but it's obvious behind her mask. It doesn't stop me from asking the questions the Jerk doesn't want to answer.

"She's not pregnant, okay? I don't know why she told you all that," he answers, sounding short-tempered. "We have a baby to bring into this world, so enough questions, Malone."

"Well, you're still a jerk, and your roses suck," I mutter.

He doesn't respond, focusing on what is happening behind the makeshift wall between my head and my stomach. At this moment, I notice his bloody shirt and split lip for the first time. He grabs my hand and entwines his fingers with mine. It's not the right moment to pull my hand away from his and start another argument. So, I wait and stare at the ceiling, avoiding his bruised and battered face and my bruised and battered ego.

There's chatter, chaos, and anticipation around me. Time becomes fuzzy, and my eyes continue to watch the lights until the moment my heart jumps out my chest, singing a song of ecstasy. The moment the sound of my baby's wail breaks the silence, and officially, we welcome a son into the world.

There is joy throughout the room, and I stretch my neck to see the wrinkly little baby lifted into the air, covered in goo. I am besotted and smiling through my tears at the beautiful sight. Moving my head to the left, I watch as they take him away to clean him up, rubbing him vigorously with a towel. Then the nurse wraps him up and calls Haden over. She hands him our son, and with a slow and careful pace, he walks over to me with a gentle smile and brings the baby closer, so I can study him properly.

I am in awe.

He is the epitome of beauty, and everything else in my life becomes insignificant because this little baby has completely stolen my heart.

"Say hello to Mommy," Haden whispers, bringing the baby close to my face. I stare at him in astonishment, and I am desperate to touch him. I rub my nose along his cheek and smell his soft skin.

He has broken me but in a good way.

My ill feelings toward Haden wash away at this very moment because of my gratitude.

If it weren't for him, I wouldn't be experiencing a love so great. A love that has consumed me whole.

I love him more than life itself.

The baby, that is.

And maybe, somewhere very deep inside, the Jerk as well.

TWENTY-ONE

I yearn for peace, silence, and a moment to take it all in. I yearn for life to stop, even if just for a minute, so I can stare at my son's face and absorb the miracle that is this beautiful baby boy.

From the moment they wheeled me out of recovery and into my room, an endless stream of visitors armed with flowers, balloons, and blue, stuffed toys arrive. It is like a nonstop circus. If it weren't for the adrenaline running through my veins, the circus would have gone on around a sleeping Presley.

It isn't just the visitors, but the nurses as well. They bustle around me, doing their rounds and checking on the baby and me. Haden, being the stubborn jerk he is, refuses to leave the room, wanting to make sure everything is okay. But I put my foot down during the breastfeeding tutorial. My boobs out for show and a baby who has difficulty latching on due to his size is something I don't want Haden seeing. Of course, my wishes aren't respected.

Afterward, I found out he went to the nurses' station to

ask questions about my breasts, and the nurse happily went on and on about them.

Yeah, I'll just lay here and pretend I didn't hear any of that.

The baby is doing great, considering how early he arrived. The doctor is happy with his growth and breathing, recommending I stay in the hospital for only a week as long as he sees progress and no complications. It is a giant—and I mean *giant*—learning curve for the both of us, and I am surprised Haden's caught on to the whole bath, nappy, burping, swaddling routine so quickly.

He visited after work every day, armed with something new for the baby each time and a little something for me. We had the routine down pat—I texted him what I wanted for dinner, and he snuck it in every night. I figured if I was going to die of a heart attack by eating the greasiest burgers that existed, I might as well do it while I'm already in a hospital.

Okay, stupid guilt attacked me afterward when I remembered that everything I shoved in my mouth went straight to the baby. Then it was all rabbit food from that moment onward.

It's a couple of days after the birth that I meet Haden's mother for the first time and am officially introduced to Mr. Sadler as his stepfather, David. Mrs. Sadler—Liz—seems nice enough, and just like Haden said, she's a lot like my mother. I can see where he got some of his looks from, but according to her, Haden is the spitting image of his late father.

Like any proud grandparent, Liz refuses to put the baby down and gives me endless advice on how to swaddle. Who would have thought that my whole life would one day revolve around swaddling? Half the time, I'm worried she'll swaddle him to death with how tight she wraps his little body. But I soon find out why she does—my kid is a wriggler. He wriggles his way out of every swaddle unless you wrap him like he's in a cocoon.

Mrs. Sadler picks up the baby, rocking him back and forth in her arms.

"Presley, I can't thank you enough for bringing our beautiful grandson into the world. Look, David, doesn't he have Haden's eyes?"

"He looks just like him." Mr. Sadler smiles.

In all fairness, the Jerk *is* beautiful, so I guess it's not a bad thing. When I first laid eyes on my son, he looked like a wrinkly old man, but as the days pass, certain features start to form, and he looks more and more like Haden each day. Except for the hair. It's curly, and we all know where that comes from.

"When Haden was born, he cried for days on end. Nothing would settle him."

"What was wrong with him?" I ask.

"He had terrible wind."

"Gee, Mom, thanks for telling everyone that," Haden complains, sulking in his chair like a spoiled child.

The nurse, who is taking my blood pressure, snickers as she writes down my results. Mr. Sadler appears amused but doesn't want to anger Haden. Ignoring his mother, he takes out his phone and busily types away. He mentions something to Mr. Sadler about an email that was sent through.

"Please, enough of the business talk. Can the two of you please enjoy this moment?" Mrs. Sadler pleads with Haden and Mr. Sadler. "Now, as I was saying earlier, it's perfectly natural for a baby to experience wind."

"Yeah, I know that," he grunts. "Just lay off all the Baby Haden talk."

It's late afternoon, and with many visitors already gone, I yawn as exhaustion creeps in. Haden leaves to get something from the cafeteria but walks back into the room not long after, carrying coffees. He hands them to Mr. and Mrs. Sadler, then asks me if I want something. I shake my head, and as much as I would kill for that coffee, the last thing I need is a baby who's wired up and awake all night long.

"So, do we have a name yet?" Mrs. Sadler coos, rocking the baby gently.

And then we're back to the problem with the baby's name. I had some thoughts on boys' names, but Haden was quick to shut them down. Annoyed at his input, he would mention names that would make my eyes roll at the lack of thought put into them.

"Are you just naming superheroes now? What's next, Bruce Wayne?"

"He'd be the coolest kid in school."

"No." I put my foot down.

The argument continues on for days, and even after my parents, Gemma, and Melissa arrive, they too end up leaving without knowing the baby's name.

The nurses are amused that six days in, Baby Boy Cooper is still nameless, which prompts another argument. I want the baby to be Malone, and Haden, of course, argues for it to be Cooper.

"The baby will be with me all the time. I don't want people calling me Mrs. Cooper."

"Well, I don't want people calling me Mr. Malone."

I growl in frustration. How can someone so good-looking be so damn stubborn?

He takes the baby from my arms and sits in the armchair beside me. "I've got a name." He smiles, hopeful.

I roll my eyes again at this back and forth debate. "Clark Kent?"

"No, this is... it's my dad's name."

"Your dad?" I raise my eyebrows at him.

I have learned one thing about Haden—he doesn't like to talk too much about his dad. It's a sensitive subject and one which I never pushed. When he does talk about him, I simply listen. He admires him so much and only ever speaks fondly about him. I get it. He misses his dad terribly, and it was so tragic to have lost him that way.

"Masen."

I stare at our little boy's face as he's nestled in Haden's arms. I say it out loud, and the moment I do, I know it's our baby's name. Everything about it fits perfectly from the way it rolls off Haden's tongue when he says it to the look on his face when he calls him that for that first time.

"Masen. I like that. Masen Malone Cooper," I agree.

And just like that, our beautiful baby boy has a name. It's the only thing we have ever agreed on, but that doesn't matter.

It's *the* most important decision, and for once, we've made it together.

"Your phone has been beeping like fifty million times," I tell him.

Haden fell asleep on the lounge chair midway through his routine visit with me. Honestly, he looks completely worn out. From what Vicky told me, he has been returning to the office every night to wrap up all the work I didn't get a chance to hand over and to finalize details on *Fallen Baby* before it goes to print.

"Huh, what?" Dazed, he removes his glasses and rubs his eyes.

"Your phone," I speak slowly. "It beeped a million times."

He pulls it out and looks at the screen, then immediately places it back in his pocket.

I fix my blanket and find the courage to ask the question that's been eating at me.

"So, Eloise. Is there a reason she hasn't visited the baby yet?"

He turns to face me. "She sent you flowers."

"I know. I'm asking why she hasn't visited because according to her, you two are getting married this coming weekend."

He diverts his attention back to his phone, removing it again from his pocket. He doesn't say anything for a while, and I'm left wondering what the hell happened. The last thing I want is another argument, and just as I'm about to drop it altogether, he says, "The wedding has been postponed for another month. She wasn't sure we should go ahead with it yet, given the added stress right now."

"What stress? You're not lying in a hospital bed with stitches," I remind him.

"I mean for her."

"Right. It's always about Eloise," I mumble, resenting him for thinking about her well-being over mine.

"What's that supposed to mean?"

"It means that you still never denied what she told me the day my water broke. Is it true you want joint custody? Is it true you're trying to have a baby with her?" I question, raising the pitch of my voice as I plead for answers.

Standing up, he moves toward the window and glances outside, his back facing me. He is still dressed in his gray pants and a white shirt, abandoning his tie as he does every night.

In front of the window, his body stands tall, and for a moment, I wonder what it's like to lean my head against his back and wrap my arms around him. I snap back to reality as soon as he opens his mouth.

"It's true about the joint custody. I'm scared, okay? I have no idea what to expect. I don't want to be a dad who visits his kid every other weekend. I want to see him every day," he stammers, unable to control the emotion behind his admission.

"And the baby stuff? About you trying?"

"I was drunk and off my face on some shit Marcus gave me after we go into an argument over you. I'd have told the homeless guy around the corner I wanted to have babies with him."

This changes everything, but it shouldn't. He provides an explanation to my questions that have haunted me ever since my lunch with Eloise. But the big question, the one still yet to be answered properly, is why is he still marrying her? I'm in the mood to ask again, and frankly, I'm sick and tired of lying in this bed. I miss my real bed. I miss being a normal, functioning human who can shower without the assistance of a nurse. And most of all, I miss everything about the former Presley, the one who had her whole life planned out.

"I'm tired," I yawn, turning my back to him.

"I should probably go."

I cover the rest of myself with a blanket and nestle my head into the pillow. With Masen fast asleep, I'm hoping to catch a few extra hours of sleep tonight myself.

Haden walks over to Masen and kisses him gently on the forehead. With a placid smile, he walks around the bed, ready to leave the room, but just before he does, I blurt out to him, "You can see Masen every day, I promise you that. We'll make this work, Haden."

He stops just shy of the door and turns back to face me. Not saying a word, his lips curve upward, and he gives me the most genuine heartfelt smile—the Haden smile that always melts my insides, triggering those butterflies to spread their wings and flutter in delight. I smile in return, and without any more words left to say, our actions speak the loudest.

It's the biggest commitment we can make, the commitment to raise our child *together*.

TWENTY-TWO

Motherhood.
No amount of textbooks and advice can prepare you for it. And those damn diaper commercials, what a load of crap. Guess what? A baby cries nonstop and for no apparent reason. I have a mental checklist.

Hungry.

Wet.

Gassy.

Tick, tick, tick! But when I've ticked it all off, what then?

We are forced to stay in the hospital for a couple more days, just as a precaution. This is not the news I want to hear, and it makes me sob like a baby. The nurse said it is normal to feel emotional after giving birth due to my hormones being all over the place. Argh! I am so sick of these damn hormones and crying at the drop of a hat.

My parents returned for another week before Dad had to go back to work. It is great having them around, but sometimes my mom drives me insane. Every time someone walks through the door, she makes them sanitize their hands.

Yeah, trust me, I'm all for a germ-free environment, but she is over the top. She also drives the young nurses insane, talking about the way hospitals were back in her day. I think they were glad to see me go just so they wouldn't have to deal with her ever again.

Haden continued with his visits, but still no Eloise. Apparently, she's got the flu and didn't want the baby to catch it. Fair enough. I don't pry further, but we both know it is a load of shit.

The day the doctors give the all-clear, I am beyond ecstatic to finally leave the hospital. Talk about paranoia, Haden hires some car with an extra special car seat fitted by some expert, but I let him do whatever keeps him happy, considering the stress he is under. It is evident, and he's dropped a lot of weight, not to mention that ridiculous beard has made a comeback. Every time I ask him if he is okay, he grunts and walks away.

Settling at home with Masen is harder than I thought it'd be. During the day, he sleeps like an angel, but at night, boy, does he have a set of lungs on him. It isn't until the end of the first week that I've establish a routine and get him to settle down for a couple of hours at night. Kate is a godsend, and even though I feel like I'm imposing on her personal space, she's always quick to shut me down.

"For the millionth time, I love having you here. Do you know what I'd be doing right now if you weren't here? Buying some sort of wonder mop from an infomercial I got stuck watching while shoving spoons of ice cream in my mouth."

"But I feel bad. You can't exactly bring somebody home to a crying baby."

"Trust me, doll, the last time I brought somebody home was when Justin Timberlake was still dating Britney.

Besides, the men I get involved with like to keep personal space exactly that—personal. I swear I pick the wrong men."

"You and Vicky both."

"Uh, no. Vicky has dated some gorgeous creatures. She just won't settle down with one instead of pining for that married loser, Patrick."

The door opens, and Vicky appears with a shopping bag and Haden behind her.

So, here's the thing. Since I've been back home—all seven days—Haden has come over every day. When I tell him he doesn't have to, mainly because I know how exhausted he is, he gets offended and rants about parental rights. And so, he's now formed his own groove on the couch, and I might have even seen an extra toothbrush hanging around in the bathroom. It's like a goddamn zoo in here sometimes, but secretly, I wouldn't want it any other way.

Standing behind Vicky, he is armed with what looks like pizza boxes. *Oh, the smell.* I know I should start to get rid of this baby weight, but who can resist the smell of melted cheese.

"I got pizza, and yes, it's that fatty cheese you girls want."

"What a gentleman," Kate roars.

"Eloise would kill me for getting anything but low-fat sheep cheese."

"You mean goat cheese." I laugh.

"Yeah, whatever."

The four of us dig in while Kate turns on the television. We get stuck watching some game show, and we argue over the answers. If not for them bringing me down with their silly answers, I would have won a million dollars and a new car by now.

On cue, upon finishing my slice, Masen begins to squirm in the rocker beside me. I go to pick him up, placing him over my shoulder and patting his back gently. Last night, he was extremely unsettled and didn't want to feed, so, of course, I've barely slept.

"No offense, Pres, but you look like hell," Vicky says, taking Masen off me only to have Haden immediately take him out of her arms.

"Baby won't sleep, and Mommy would love a shower."

"Go shower," Haden commands.

I'm not going to say no to that. I'm desperate to feel like myself again. I stand up, sore in all the wrong places, and begin to make my way to the bathroom.

"Oh, wait! So, you know how you were talking to me about how your nipples were bleeding from feeding?" Vicky rummages through her purse, unaware that she just embarrassed me in front of everyone.

"Um... yes, but you didn't really need to broadcast it."

Haden snickers, his head down with a grin on his face.

"Ta-da! The Mexican nipple hat!" She produces this small box, and lo and behold, it does look like a Mexican hat for my nipples.

"Where on earth..."

"I googled your problem, spoke to some moms at my Pilates class, and found them at the drugstore."

"I'm not sure whether to laugh at you or hug you."

"You'll be hugging me when your nipples aren't tugged like a milked cow."

I head to the shower, shaking my head at her. Inside the bathroom, I carefully take off my clothes. My breasts are sore, veins popping. I decide I'll feed him and release the pressure after a quick shower. With my incision on the mend, I wash as instructed. I wrap a towel around myself after briefly drying my hair, leaving it damp. When I head back to the room, Haden is sitting on my bed with Masen.

"You feel better?"

He doesn't look my way when he asks, and I feel practically naked standing here in a towel. He has no concept of personal space and hangs out in my room every time he comes here.

"Yes, a million times better. Probably better if I get some clothes on... in private."

"Get dressed, then. I won't look."

I can't be bothered to argue, and head to the closet to get changed in there. I emerge moments later and stop at the vanity to quickly tie my hair up into a bun. I settle for wearing a loose, white button-down shirt and khaki shorts, hoping to take Masen out for a walk later. Not getting out of the house during the day has made me extremely restless. For someone who is accustomed to being at work all day, this whole stay-at-home-mom gig is a huge shock to the system. If you ask me who guest-starred on *Ellen* this week, I can sadly give you every name.

"I think he's hungry."

"He is always hungry, hence, why these things keep getting bigger and bigger."

"I've noticed."

I shoot him a sarcastic smile, then settle into my chair. Haden is watching me like he always does, and I manage to get the baby to latch on without breast exposure. I yelp at the slight sting, then remember the Mexican hat. I use it, and instantly, I feel less pain. Seems like I owe Vicky big time.

"That bad?"

"That bad. I mean, I've had them tugged before, but shit... this is painful."

His mood instantly shifts, and he begins to fidget with the fray of his jeans.

Too much nipple and breast talk.

Forgive him. He's a guy, after all.

"I really need to get out of here." I sigh, switching subjects.

He lifts his head, making eye contact. "How about we go for a walk? It's a warm night out."

"Sounds perfect."

The walk is just what I need. The night air is warm with a slight breeze that picks up as we turn the corner. The streets are still bustling with people heading out to restaurants and clubs. It's a Friday night, and it feels so different pushing a baby around the streets.

An old lady is sitting alone at the bus stop. Clutching onto her purse, she peers down the street, looking out for the bus. She stops, noticing us, and smiles. I smile in return, and when it's time to walk past her, she greets us.

"What a beautiful baby." She peeks into the stroller admiring Masen. "I've got eight children and thirty-four grandkids."

"Wow, you must have been really busy." Haden chuckles

I jab him with my elbow, reading his dirty mind. He grins in return as I shake my head at him, smiling. She pulls back and something about her changes, almost as if we had touched on a sore subject. Haden and I look at each other, confused by what's just happened, then turn back to face her.

"None of them are in the city. In fact, my George lives

in Japan. Imagine that? Living all the way in Japan. My youngest, Maggie, visits every Christmas."

"I'm sorry. That must be hard for you," I tell her.

"It is. But then I see a couple like the two of you, and it reminds me of when my husband, Frank and I, used to walk down this exact street with baby George. It was before he went to the war. I remember it like it was yesterday," she says wistfully, clutching onto a gold necklace draped around her neck.

"We're not actually a couple," I correct her.

Haden glares at me for clarifying that point.

"Well, you certainly look happy, both of you. Enjoy these moments because before you know it, you're catching the bus to go home alone."

The bus pulls up to the curb, and the old lady waves goodbye. She has a point, one that kind of sticks with me. Thirty-two years of my life have passed, and now Masen is here, and all I want to do is freeze time, so I can cherish this moment. Life is short, and as I look over at Haden tucking Masen into his blanket, I wonder what life is all about. Love, laughter, happiness? And how does Haden fit into that equation? I have to admit since the raging hormones died down, we get along much better.

We are friends.

We are partners for the sake of raising our son.

But then my focus moves on to Masen. My goal each day is to try to stay awake and feed my son. Talking with this woman about her life causes loneliness to wash over me. I want everything she just said—babies, a husband, and a lifetime full of happy memories. Watching the man who helped create our son pushing his stroller, it triggers the emotions I keep pushing away.

"You okay?" He stops just a few steps away from a busy restaurant blaring loud Spanish music.

"Who would have thought that you of all people would be spending your Friday night pushing a stroller?" I say, ignoring my emotions and motioning for him to continue walking.

With a sly smirk, he continues to push our son, stopping only to wait for the lights to change. "Who would have thought that Miss OCD would have forgotten the baby bag at home? Because someone's definitely dumped his load."

I scowl as the whiff of his soiled nappy hits my nose. Haden turns the stroller back around as we begin our journey home again. *How silly of me to think Masen could go ten minutes without pooping his pants.*

"Sometimes I don't know what's happened to me, you know? It's like my focus has shifted, and I can't think ahead. Take, for example, apartment hunting. I have no idea what I'm after or where I'm even looking. Old Presley would have found a place by now, moved in, and already repainted the walls."

"You've gone through a lot. It's expected."

"Maybe. The only place I'm even semi-excited about is this cute bungalow a street away from Gemma's."

He stops, prompting a couple behind us to swerve in annoyance. I swear they curse under their breaths, but Haden is oblivious.

"As in California?"

"Uh, yeah." I take the stroller from him and continue pushing, hoping this argument can be avoided. *What was I thinking?* It's merely an idea I've been toying with because Gemma and Melissa would be able to help me out. Nothing is concrete, though.

"Were you going to tell me about it?"

"No, because I was only looking. If I felt it was more serious, then yes, I would."

"You didn't even tell me you were thinking about it. What about Masen? I live here... how can I see him every night?"

We reach the door to my building, and I stop in front of it. He is standing against the railing with his arms folded, nostrils flaring like a bull ready to attack. Apparently, I'm holding the red flag. Surprise, surprise. Mr. Irrational is acting like a petulant child.

"Would you keep your panties on? Nothing, and I mean nothing, is set in stone. I'm keeping all my options open. I'd have consulted with you first. I realize it's not just my decision."

His trademark move of running his hands through his hair begins. "Bullshit. You don't care what I think. I'm going home." He doesn't say another word, turning his back on me and walking out of sight.

I told him I was looking at all of my options. Of course, I can't just up and go, but the more I think about it, the more it makes sense to move. With the money I have from the sale of the apartment, I'll have a healthy down payment on a house in California. Masen will have a backyard and warm weather almost year-round. I can afford to work part-time, and most importantly, Gemma and Melissa will be close by. Charlie and I have been emailing back and forth about California. She is extremely helpful, giving me tips on the best schools and places to take Masen.

Well, it's a thought.

Just that.

For now, the Jerk has nothing to worry about.

By now, I'm used to his little temper tantrums.

I move on and push the stroller into the building,

quickly making my way to the elevator. Upon arriving at my floor, I take out my keys and notice a man standing beside my door. He looks familiar, but I'm on guard just in case. I wrap my hand around the mace in my purse. He tilts his head sideways, and I catch a glimpse of his jawline.

I would recognize that jawline anywhere.

"Jason?" I ask, in awe.

"Presley... wow..."

He moves his focus to the stroller and appears to be in shock. "I was told you had a baby and thought it was a joke, but I had to see for myself. You have a baby."

"Yes, I know I should have told you, but it's complicated."

We both stand there at a loss for words.

Jason, seeing me with a baby.

And myself, having forgotten how handsome he is.

He reaches his arms out, and I move forward and hug him. My body instantly relaxes in his embrace. But I don't want to complicate things, so I pull away, unable to control my happiness at seeing him again.

"Jase, I can't believe you're here."

His smile remains fixed as he ruffles his hair before asking, "Is it mine?"

I laugh softly. "No, it isn't. As I said, it's complicated."

"Indeed. Are you free now for dinner or something?"

I look at my phone and notice the time. Masen needs to be changed and fed so I can tuck him in for the night despite how much I want to have dinner with Jason.

"I really need to get Masen down. How about next weekend? I can ask my roommate to babysit."

"Sounds like a plan. I'll text you during the week?"

"Sure."

He begins to walk away but stops, leaning into my ear. "I honestly forgot how beautiful you are, Presley."

My body reacts instantly. I melt at his words, missing the familiarity.

I close my eyes for a brief moment as he walks away, his lingering scent invading my senses.

I miss him, and now all I can think about is next weekend.

My dinner date with my ex-fiancé.

The once love of my life. *Jason Hart.*

TWENTY-THREE

I toss and turn all night thinking about Jason and questioning whether or not I've made the right decision. Well, truth be told, if I hadn't parted ways with him then, I wouldn't have had my son. But now, after seeing Jason turn up at my doorstep, I wonder if it's too late for us. Being in the company of Jason Hart was easy, carefree, and relaxing. He's not the type of man to create unnecessary drama unlike some other jerk I know.

Haden, as predicted, hasn't texted or called me after storming off in a huff. This game of his is getting old, and his short temper only causes more friction between us. Yet, when we get along, I really enjoy being around him.

Is there such a thing as male PMS? I swear, Haden Cooper could be the frontrunner for a nationwide campaign for it.

My mind refuses to shut down, and just when I begin to fall asleep, Masen wakes up demanding to be fed. Half asleep, I nestle him into a feeding position and try to keep my eyes open. For some unknown reason, he refuses to latch on, squirming uncomfortably and crying. Following the normal routine, I check his diaper, attempt to burp him, then try again to feed him. He still refuses to latch on, and an hour later, I am out of my mind.

"What do you want, Masen?" I cry, rocking him back and forth.

Nothing appears to work, and I've already deemed myself a horrible mother.

I grab my phone and dial Haden's number, not expecting him to pick up after our argument earlier tonight. After several rings, he answers. The background is loud, and no surprise, he's probably at a club getting wasted.

"Malone, are you okay?" he yells over the noise.

"No, I'm not. Masen won't settle, and I don't know what to do." I hold back my tears and, of course, Masen continues to wail over me.

"I'll be there in twenty minutes."

That twenty minutes feel like forever, and the second my door buzzes, I scramble to answer it. Haden enters immediately, throwing his helmet, keys, and phone onto the sofa and grabbing Masen from me. He's dressed in a pair of black dress pants and a dark gray shirt rolled up at the sleeves—it's different from his normal casual attire of jeans and a tee on the weekends. He looks good, real good. But hey, what do I know? I'm sleep and sex-deprived, and neither one of those problems will be solved anytime soon.

He moves toward my bedroom, and I follow behind him. It only takes a couple of minutes of Haden rubbing his back in a circular motion for Masen to finally settle. When ten minutes pass without a single sound, my emotions and tired state get the better of me, and I begin to cry.

"I can't do this... alone."

"You're not alone. It's just one bad night," he reassures me.

He moves to sit on the bed, keeping Masen comfortable and quiet while I continue to stand there like a sobbing mess. I'm a wreck, dressed in my old baseball tee and boxers with my hair a wild mess. Heavy bags have formed under my eyes, and my skin appears dry and pale.

"This is hard. Look at me... I haven't slept. My hair hasn't had a proper shampoo in forever. I've been wearing the same shirt for the past two weeks because I can't get to the laundromat. I have no clue what I'm doing."

"Presley, just calm down. It's not that bad. Why don't I get my mom to help you for a few hours? She's dying to spend time with Masen."

"Not that bad?" I raise my voice slightly. "I'm a mess... and... I feel like the worst mother in the world. I bet Eloise won't look like that when you guys have babies. She'll probably just push that baby out and—"

"Presley..."

I continue to ramble on, ignoring him. "And I bet she has the type of hair that's silky and smooth all the time like those shampoo commercials where the chick just flicks her hair, and she looks like she just stepped out of the salon."

"Malone," he raises his tone.

"What?" I say, exasperated from my rant.

He doesn't say anything further but nods his head, motioning for me to look at my chest. I look down and through my shirt that my milk has leaked and left two patches. Just fucking great, and here come the waterworks.

"See? I can't even feed my child, and then this happens," I cry.

He lays Masen down beside the pillow and covers him with a blanket. Haden moves toward me, and in my pathetic state, he wraps his arms around me and pulls me closer into him. I don't care what's happening right now and continue to cry into his chest. Holding me tight, he gives me time to release my frustrations until my sobs slow down.

"Thank you," I whisper.

He kisses my forehead and slowly pushes me away, still keeping our bodies in close range. Cupping my face, he gives me a sympathetic smile before speaking quietly so as not to stir Masen. "You've got to learn to ask for help. I'm here, Presley. I'll always be here when you need me. Just don't drop bullshit bombs on me like earlier."

"You've got a life, Haden. You can't stop living it. Like tonight, where were you?"

"It was a stupid party for Eloise's friend. Trust me, I didn't want to go."

His deep stare and bewitching smile only reiterate what I'm terrified of feeling. How could the man standing here in front of me, the father to my son, not be the person I'm supposed to fall in love with? Yet every time we fight, it somehow brings us closer together, and I fall into the trap of thinking I really am in love with him.

How can I be in love with Haden Cooper?

I want to pull away from him, create the distance my heart needs right now, but he moves his hands down my arms until they're sitting on the base of my shirt. Without saying a word, he grips the hem of my shirt and motions for me to lift my arms. I have no idea what he's doing, but in my tired state, I let him take my soaked shirt off. I stand there in only my bra as he wraps his arms back around me, kissing my shoulder. As much as I want to stay like this, Masen begins to squirm.

"I think he's hungry. Why don't you take your bra off and feed him? I promise I won't look."

I laugh softly. "Have you seen them? They're impossible to hide."

"How can I not notice them?" He smirks. "But seriously, our son is hungry. I can turn around."

My bra is wet and uncomfortable, and I know I need to release the milk. I ask him to turn around for a brief moment as I unclasp my bra. It's a relief to take it off, and I feel the pressure subside immediately. Making myself comfortable on the bed, I move to lay on my side and pull the sheets to cover part of my skin. I pull Masen closer to me, and he latches on with ease, gently sucking away. Haden turns around and lays beside me on the bed. Stroking Masen's hair, he hums a tune I don't recognize.

"You're doing a great job," he whispers. "You're a natural even though you don't see it."

"I have no idea what I'm doing."

"No first-time mom does."

"Yeah, but first-time moms have husbands who help them."

"I told you, I'm here."

"You won't be here forever. You'll be doing the same thing with your wife soon."

"I don't want to talk about that."

I keep my voice down so as not to sir Masen. "You never want to address it, Haden. If you love her, then marry her. But these moments we have, they need to stop."

"What if I don't want them to stop?"

"You can't have your cake and eat it, too. Sometimes you've got to make decisions and deal with the consequences, whether it be good or bad. I'm a realist. I stepped away from a relationship even though it wasn't easy."

"But you don't think with your heart."

"Of course, I do. I loved Jason—"

"But you wanted more," he interrupts. "Tell me, what's your heart telling you now?"

He is asking me a question I dare not answer truthfully because if I do, there's a huge possibility my heart will be exposed and shatter if he walks down that aisle with her. But on the flip side, I'm sick of this emotional rollercoaster and walking on eggshells.

"It's telling me that love is a constant battle. The man who steals my heart... I want him to fight for *me*. I want to be the only woman he thinks about, the only woman his heart beats for. I want to be the object of his desire, the body he worships every day. I want to feel like nothing in this world exists if he doesn't feel all those things for me."

Behind his glasses, his beautiful eyes are consumed by my words. I know he feels something, but how much? I have no idea. My fingers ache to reach out and caress his face, but I'm terrified. The tiny human lying between us is at stake. One wrong move and his life changes forever.

"You deserve all that and a man who will give you that."

On cue, my heart sinks, confirming what I've known all along. He cares. Just not enough. And maybe these thoughts in my head need to stop, just like my relationship with Jason. I pulled the plug when things weren't as they should have been. If I did it once, I can do it again.

Masen's gentle snores start as he falls asleep peacefully at my breast. Haden lifts him slowly and pats him, prompting a loud burp before moving him to his crib and wrapping him tight. Lying here, semi-naked, I'm vulnerable both physically and emotionally. Haden removes his shoes and climbs back into the bed with me, this time moving under the sheets. My body appears flushed, and the way his eyes are laced with desire can only mean one thing.

"Presley, I can't hold this back anymore."

His luscious lips have found their way to mine, and with his tight grip around my waist, it's impossible to pull away, especially with my body betraying me. His tongue circles mine as we both moan into each other's mouths.

Out of breath, I pull away for a brief moment. "Haden, we can't."

His lips have already moved to the base of my neck as he mumbles. "I need you."

The rush he gives me shoots straight down below and between my legs. I'm soaking wet. I'm struggling to hold onto my morals as my physical side demands he give me all of him.

Just one more minute, *then I'll stop.*

He knows I'll stop him, and with a desperate rush, he has made his way down to my breasts, licking circles around my nipples and causing my back to arch in pleasure. It's difficult to keep my moans to a silent plea, and sensing my desperation, he moves his right hand toward my mouth and covers it with his palm.

"Just let me have a taste... just one taste."

I don't have to let him. He takes what he wants, and the moment he sucks on my nipples, an impending orgasm is on the verge of breaking loose. *No, no.*

"Haden, we have to stop!"

I manage to push him away just as the orgasm is about to hit. Guiding his head back toward my face, I watch his eyes and the fire burning within them.

"We can't do this. Not while you're in a relationship. I'm not that person."

His chest is pumping hard, and trying to catch his breath, he finally speaks, "I know it's wrong, but I want you, Presley."

"I want you, too, Haden. But we can't, not unless you end things with her."

He pulls back. "Is that an ultimatum?"

"No," I correct him. "It's called having morals. I'm not a mistress, nor do I want to have an affair. I can't deny what I feel for you, but I'm not the one engaged here."

I see the turmoil in his expression and pull him closer one more time, for one last kiss.

"I should probably go," he whispers, disappointed.

"You probably should."

Reluctantly, he climbs out of bed and slides his shoes back on. He adjusts his crotch, and I ignore how hard he looks beneath the fabric.

Why, oh why was I raised to be a good, moral woman?

Walking toward the door, he stops and turns back to face me. "Give me time to sort out my life, Presley. I want you in it. I just need to fix the mess I've created."

Those are his final words, and for me, tonight, it's exactly what I need to hear—a promise of a future.

TWENTY-FOUR

The next day, I get a surprise visit from Haden's mom. Armed with a bag of wool and knitting needles, she insists I take a couple of hours off to do whatever the hell I want to do. At first, I'm reluctant. Masen is almost four weeks old, and I haven't been away from him at all.

"I understand you feel conflicted. The first time I left Haden with my mother-in-law, I was a blubbering mess. It didn't help that she was the wicked witch of the West. God rest her soul." She raises her head toward the ceiling and makes the sign of the cross.

"How about I just go for an hour?"

"Whatever you're comfortable with. If you need longer, please take longer. I just want to spend time with my grandson."

I opt to feed him before heading out. It gives me the peace of mind I need, plus chatting with Mrs. Sadler keeps me entertained.

"Please, call me Liz."

"Okay, Liz," I hesitate, not sure why. "So, Haden tells me he has twin sisters. That must have been a handful."

She continues to knit what appears to be booties, all the while managing to hold a conversation. "The girls weren't as much of a handful as Haden. He was and still is strong-headed. Takes after his dad."

"You're telling me. I've met mules less stubborn than him."

"He's a good boy, it's just..." she trails off for a moment before continuing, "His father's death was hard on all of us, but it was Haden who took it the hardest."

"Of course," I mumble. "Boys need their dads."

Looking down at Masen's angelic face, I can't imagine bestowing any pain on him. If I had my way, I would wrap him up in bubble wrap and protect him forever.

"Liz, I don't know how you do it. The thought of my son going through any pain kills me."

"Over time, you learn to let go, but only slightly. Haden shuts down and doesn't allow anyone in. For a couple of years, I was a wreck, worried for his life. He was erratic and had no regard for his well-being. David kept telling me that he needed to grieve in his own way as well as grow up. He was young when the accident occurred."

My heart breaks for Haden. It was too much for him to experience at such a young age, and so unfair that he was dealt that card. I love my dad so much and can't even begin to understand the grief of losing a parent.

"You know, Presley, you've done wonders for my son."

"For Haden? You must be mistaken. It's not like that between us," I stammer nervously.

She places her knitting needles on her lap. When she smiles, she looks exactly like Haden.

"Liz, both of us have had a lot of growing to do to be able to co-parent Masen, and even then, it's only been four weeks."

"Sweetheart, you don't see what I do. My son adores you."

With my eyes fixated on Masen, I speak solemnly, "He's marrying Eloise. Things between us are far too complicated. Whatever happens, happens."

"You know..." she adds, "... one thing I've learned about Haden is that he'll never listen to anyone. Every decision he makes, he feels he has to own it, whether it be good or bad. Just be patient, Presley. Let him do what he needs to do, but in the end, I have faith that he'll make the right decision."

The decision he made to marry Eloise is still the million-dollar question with no answer. But just like Liz said, he owns his decisions, good or bad. When he was in London, we were practically strangers—if you ignore our midnight rendezvous. I didn't know where his head was at or what his intentions were. Now, he seems completely different. He's matured with the birth of his son, and deep down inside, I know he is a good man. He's everything Liz said he is.

Our conversation leaves me with a lot to think about, so with a settled Masen, I grab my purse and kiss him goodbye. The second the door closes behind me, I burst into tears, overwhelmed by leaving him behind.

There are so many moments over the past four weeks when I just wanted a break, and now that I've finally got some time alone, I'm a blubbering mess. All I want to do is open that door, pull on my sweats, and never leave him again.

Reality check. I have to do this eventually, so I make my way out of the apartment and promise myself I'll be back in exactly an hour.

It turns out that I enjoy my freedom way more than I should. I stop at a local café and devour a meal in peace and quiet, followed by a trip to the salon. In the space of two hours, my regular stylist, Chantelle, works magic on my hair and eyebrows. She even manages to get the forest down below back to normal. By the time she's finished, I feel like my old self again. My hair is trimmed, and because I'm in the mood for something different, she dyes it a honey-brown color. My body is hair-free, and I can't believe how such a simple thing could lift my spirits so much.

As Chantelle wraps up, I quickly grab my phone and send Haden a text.

Me: *Thank you for sending your mommy over. I'm feeling much better and nicely trimmed.*

The chime of my phone goes off before I even have a chance to place it back in my purse.

Haden: *Poodle got a trim? Dare I ask where?*

Laughing out loud at his text, I hand my credit card over to Chantelle and finalize my bill. After saying goodbye, I stroll leisurely back home and respond to his text.

Me: *Mind out of gutter Jerk! My fro...*

Me: *On my head!*

It's in our best interest not to mention the *entire* makeover. That, and I'm still trying to adjust to being bare. I wait for what feels like forever until my phone chimes yet again.

Haden: *Always playing hard to get. Can't wait to see the trimmed poodle tonight.*

Every night this week, Haden comes over after work. This time, however, it's different between us. He stays for hours on end and lies beside me, just talking. Both of us share stories of our past, laughing at random memories from our childhoods to our awkward teenage moments. We share our dreams and hopes for the future, and every night I learn a little bit more about Haden Cooper. Tonight is no different, and Haden finally begins to open up about his dad.

"The night we got that call, we were all sitting at the dinner table waiting for him." He closes his eyes and continues to lie on his back recalling the tragic memory. "I was angry at my parents that night, especially Dad, for not letting me go to baseball camp. Mom had made his favorite soup, and I remember the skin on the soup forming over because it was cold. He didn't have a phone back then, so we just waited."

I lace my fingers through his, ignoring his sweaty palms.

"The police knocked on the door, and I watched my mom fall to the ground screaming. My sisters were really young at the time, so I told them to go to their room. I didn't want them seeing Mom like that. It wasn't the police who told me, but my mother. He had been driving home on a winding part of the road, and another driver swerved to avoid hitting a drunk hitchhiker and hit Dad's car head-on. The man driving lost his wife and young son in the accident."

Haden takes a deep breath and opens his bloodshot eyes, turning to face me. "The man driving that other car was David."

My mouth gapes open as the blood rushes from my face. "Mr. Sadler?"

He nods. "After the deaths and funerals, Mom and David became friends, both having to deal with similar grief. Romantically, nothing happened until years later, but it didn't surprise me when it did. I wasn't dealing well with anything, and everything just went downhill from there."

"You were fifteen, right?"

"Yes. Fifteen with a massive chip on my shoulder. The rest of high school I kept to myself, losing any interest in baseball or girls. Kids would tease and bully me, but I ignored them. When college rolled around, I was desperate to move, and David convinced Mom to allow me some freedom. I don't know if it's what I needed. It was a time in my life where I experimented with everything I could to forget the pain, and I also got a taste for sex." He chuckles lightly, unable to hide the wicked grin on his beautiful face.

I laugh along with him. College is the time everyone gets a taste for sex. Yet somehow, through the generations, parents still allow their kids to attend and move into frat houses.

"Remember this conversation when Masen asks to move across the country."

He simply grins. "That seems so far away."

Still holding hands, he continues to tell his story, "After college, I had no idea what to do with my life. I traveled a bit and got into extreme sports abroad. There is such an adrenaline rush when you jump off the highest bridge in the world. I got really addicted to that feeling, but after a couple of years, Mom and David had had enough. Plus, I ran out of money."

"And then what?"

"I couldn't hold down a job in the city. I was bored with the usual political shit until David offered me a position I couldn't refuse. He wanted me to learn the ropes at Lantern Publishing, so he could commence his five-year retirement exit."

"You know," I say, "it explains so much. Like why half the time you just didn't give a shit about anything."

His smirk widens, and as he moves to his side, he runs his finger down my cheek. "Oh, I gave a shit all right. About *you.*"

"Whatever." I laugh. "You never once paid attention to me unless you needed something."

"The very first day I started, you were wearing a black tunic with a white collared shirt under and those red pumps I couldn't stop jerking off over."

"Haden!" I say in shock.

"True story. But then I overheard you rambling on about your wedding, so I lost interest. I wanted to fuck you, not break up your engagement and have you wanting a commitment from me. So, I occupied my time at work by playing the stock market. Actually, I got quite good at it and managed to make a fairly decent amount which I've reinvested into property."

"You're so crass. I can't believe you thought about me that way."

"Well, the day the office buzzed about your broken engagement, I wasn't going to let anyone get a hold of you. Sergio and Russ were the first to express their interest in you."

"Russ with the beer gut and Sergio with the unconfirmed toupee?"

He shakes his head, laughing quietly, not wanting to wake Masen. "I shut them down, saying the reason you broke up with what's his face was because you had baby fever."

"You did not say that. They must think I lured you in like a cougar," I profess, half embarrassed.

"They can think whatever they want. I had my eyes set on making your life hell, so you'd notice me. I just didn't expect this."

"So, the *Fallen Baby* project?"

"I coerced David into letting me work on that. Mind you, that was before I knew you were pregnant."

"What about London?"

"That's half my fault. David wanted me there, but I kept refusing. After that night in the club, I knew I couldn't be around you. You're like this magnetic force field, and no matter how much I told myself I could resist you, I just couldn't."

I let out a sigh and try to take all of this in. How different things could have been between us if he were honest about his feelings all along. There is still the issue of Eloise, though.

"And Eloise... why?"

"Presley," he chastises. "Please let me sort that out. I've made mistakes, one's I need to rectify."

I turn over onto my back. This Eloise thing is the only thing stopping us from being together. From being a family. Why can't he just admit why he was, still is, in my eyes, marrying her?

"I need time to take all of this in," I confess.

"Take what in?"

"You, not answering my questions about Eloise. Everything about the past. I'm just... overwhelmed."

No more words are said. And maybe it's for the best.

He moves his body to a sitting position, then leans in to kiss my cheek. "So, tomorrow, you're bringing Masen into the office?"

I simply nod, followed by the only smile I can muster. A confused one.

Entering the office building feels like visiting your home after a long vacation. I missed everything about it from the hustle and bustle of the corporate world, to the office attire, and even the politics. Vicky greets me downstairs in the lobby, running toward me in new Louis Vuitton pumps.

"Ahem, what's going on south of your kitty?"

She gladly lifts her feet, proudly showing off her new attire. "Oh, you mean these? Well, Patrick bought them for me. Kind of like an I-want-you-back present."

I shake my head at her willingness to accept extravagant gifts from a dickhead who can't keep his pants shut. I drop the subject, not wanting to get into an argument.

"So," she drags, taking the stroller off me and pushing it toward the elevator. "What's happening tonight? Are you still meeting Jason for dinner?"

The whole week I went back and forth about canceling my dinner with Jason. Things are going so well between Haden and me that I don't want to create any unnecessary drama. But last night, after his confession, I thought long and hard about what I want. Having dinner with Jason is just that—dinner. I'm not planning on having sex with him, but although we ended on friendly terms, there is a sense of closure that I need from him to be able to move forward.

"Right now, I'm still deciding. But if I do, you're still okay to babysit?"

"Of course! Can't wait to hang out with my gorgeous soon-to-be godson." She coos at Masen.

"And about that. Don't mention this to Haden yet. I don't think he's religious, at all."

Vicky slides her finger along her mouth, then flicks it to the side. "My lips are sealed."

Bringing Masen to the office is extremely overwhelming. Every woman and her overactive ovaries are fussing over him, all fighting to have a cuddle so they can smell his skin. It was only announced last week that Dee is expecting a baby with her sugar daddy. Four months along, according to Mr. National Inquirer himself, Clive. She seems happy, asking me questions about pregnancy and birth. I'm not here to judge her, despite her sugar daddy being old enough to be her grandfather.

Clive is doing his thing, making weird sounds at Masen trying to make him smile.

"Jesus, Pres, he looks exactly like the Jerk."

"I'd question her if he didn't." Haden is standing behind an embarrassed Clive.

Haden moves into the circle, and my eyes move up his body and land on his torso. He's wearing a fitted navy business shirt with a thin black tie, and he has rolled up the sleeves like he always does.

Kill. Me. Now.

His face has broken out into his trademark smile, and his glasses...

Why the hell does he look so irresistible today? Because you promised not to touch him while he is still engaged to Eloise.

"Motherhood agrees with you, Pres." Clive raises his eyebrows and cups his chest, motioning to my huge breasts. "So, Masen drinks breast milk only?"

I nod. "Haven't had the need to start the formula yet."

"Have you tasted it?" Clive attempts to whisper.

"Clive!" Vicky scolds, followed with, "Yeah, have you?"

I shake my head at them, trying to hold in my laughter. "No. But I heard it's supposed to taste like—"

"Cantaloupe juice," Haden interjects. "It was on an episode of *Friends*."

Mortified because he must have tasted it the other night, I lower my head so as not to reveal my flushed face. Vicky and Clive snicker as Haden continues to stand there with a wide smirk on his face, rubbing his chin with his stare fixated on me.

"Well, there you go," I say with a fixed smile. "Cantaloupe juice. Not that I know what that tastes like, but I imagine it's sweet. Anyways, look at the time."

Haden kisses Masen before telling me he has a meeting that is expected to turn into a dinner since it's one of our stakeholders from London. I say goodbye to him before he disappears.

"Okay, so let me know about tonight?" Vicky reminds me.

"Thanks, Vicky, I will. I probably won't go ahead with it, but I'll let you know either way."

Vicky and Clive head back to their cubicles as I make my way to the elevator. It opens, and Eloise exits.

Shit.

Stepping out of the elevator looking like a supermodel, she spots me and plasters on a fake smile. As usual, she is dressed to the nines in a perfectly pressed pantsuit with six-inch pumps. Her blonde hair is styled—yes, straight out of the salon—and her skin looks nicely tanned and extremely clear. She makes it impossible to hate anything about her. At least if she had a giant mole on her nose and a long chin, I could refer to her as a witch.

"I didn't expect to see you here... with the baby."

She peeks her head into the stroller and finally gets a glimpse of her soon-to-be stepson.

There, I've said it.

Pulling back instantly, her fake smile makes another appearance. "He's pretty."

Pretty? She called my son 'pretty'? No one calls my son pretty and gets away with it.

I may have been polite to her before, but this time she

has something I want, and I'm not in the mood to play nice. "Masen is a boy, so I'm not sure 'pretty' is the correct word."

"Oh, you know what I mean." She shrugs it off. "Since Haden postponed the wedding and all, my mind is all over the place. The caterer is booked for the next six months, so I've been running around trying to find a new one. It's been a mess."

"I'm sure you'll find one." This time it's my turn to bring the fake smile to the table.

"We'd better. The wedding is next Saturday."

"You're getting married next Saturday?" I almost choke.

"Uh-huh. This is it. I told Haden no more postponing and he agreed," she squeals. "I hope you're free?"

"I... uh... Masen will probably cry and stuff."

Did I just say that? Excuse me while my heart throws itself onto the ground so it can continue to be stomped on, along with any self-respect and dignity I have left.

"Well, that's another thing. We'd really like it if Haden's mom can push the baby down the aisle. Actually, I bought this little outfit for him, and my mom decorated my old carriage with lace and flowers."

She pulls out her phone and flicks through photographs while I continue to stand here, shell-shocked.

The wedding is still going to happen, and everything Haden said was nothing but empty promises.

Lies, to be exact.

And just at that moment, the realization that maybe I'm living in denial in this sick and twisted game is like a sword piercing my heart, continually stabbing me until I am out of breath. My hands have clasped onto the handle of the stroller, and all I can see is my knuckles turning stark white. My breaths are few and far between, and all the while, the echoes of Eloise's laugh taunt me, naming me a fool.

"Oh! Here it is!" She places the phone in front of me, and I push it away, unable to control the fueling rage inside of me.

"He's my son," I grit. "I don't care what you do. But don't you dare expect to have my son attend your wedding."

"Presley, I—"

"I don't want to hear it!" I raise my palm to block her from saying another word. "You don't care about Masen. You didn't even have the decency to come see him."

"I sent you flowers," she answers defensively.

"Oh!" I laugh sarcastically. "I didn't realize flowers were the same as meeting your future stepson."

She remains still, her face in complete and utter shock at my outburst. And I'm just getting started.

"I don't know why the two of you are getting married. But know this... my son will not be a part of your lives. If I have to move hell and earth to make that happen, I will!"

I push past her, and thankfully, the elevator opens on cue. The second I'm inside, I repeatedly tap the close button until her wretched face disappears, allowing my tears to fall freely. With clouded vision, I take out my phone and send two texts—one to Vicky confirming that tonight is still on and one to Jason, letting him know I'm excited about dinner.

I have no clue what I'm doing. And that's the thing about broken hearts—they open up a dark abyss, and all you can do is try to stop yourself from falling into that deep hole, even if that means spending the night with your ex to get over the man who never intended to steal your heart.

TWENTY-FIVE

Vicky arrives to babysit Masen while I get ready for my dinner with Jason. It's no coincidence that I choose to wear my short black dress that fits even nicer than before with my new, full bust. I accessorize it with a ruby-red necklace, my hoop earrings, and those red pumps that the Jerk drooled over. They also happen to be Jason's favorite piece on me.

"You look too hot. MILF type of hot. The girls are totally out for show. Unless, of course, they're out on purpose."

"It's nice to dress up."

"Pres, what's going on?"

I grab my purse off the nightstand and kiss Masen on the forehead.

"Nothing. I'm having dinner with a friend. That's it."

"Okay, but we need some sort of code in case you want to come back and get laid."

"It's not like that. I'm going. Please call me if Masen won't settle," I gently remind her.

She simply smiles, and I also kiss her on the forehead before heading out to my dinner date with Jason.

Sitting close to Jason makes me realize how much I've missed him. Everything about him is so familiar and comfortable. Everything about him is drama-free.

He takes a sip of his red wine, and I can't help but stare at him. He has aged just a bit, and his hair is now a salt and pepper color that reflects his maturity. His eyes still do that thing to me, calming the storm brewing in my head. With his hands resting on the edge of the table, I remember how many times I've kissed his fingertips, how many times his fingers have trailed my body—all the things I haven't experienced with the Jerk.

"So, tell me, how did this happen?" he asks.

I swirl the glass of wine, taking small sips so as not to get too intoxicated. I cleverly pumped enough milk to last a lifetime, so I know I can have a glass and express my alcohol-infused milk down the drain. I start from the beginning, leaving out the whole 'it happened in the alleyway' part. No need for graphic details.

"Why didn't you tell me?"

"Honestly? At the time, I was ashamed. I was so careless. You know me, I'm one to stick to a plan. This was a shock to me. I had no choice but to accept the reality of the situation."

"And now?"

"It's the best thing that ever happened to me. Masen is my life," I answer honestly, smiling at him.

Behind the glass he is holding to his lips, he hides his sly smile.

"Why are you smiling that way?"

He takes another drink and motions for the waiter to bring him another. "Because motherhood suits you."

"I seem to be hearing that a lot."

"So, you're not with the guy... Henry..."

"Haden," I correct him.

"Whatever."

"No, Haden is engaged, and it's really complicated."

I desperately want to tell him the full story, but I'm scared he will convince me never to speak to the Jerk again. It's not such a bad idea after what happened with Eloise, but it's not just about my feelings anymore. It's about Masen and what he deserves.

"Well, he sounds like a jerk."

I laugh, shaking my head. "Yeah, what can you do?"

"You find yourself a real man, Pres. A man who's willing to give you everything." His eyes twinkle as they stare directly into mine. Moving his hand toward my side of the table, he plays with the ring sitting on my middle finger. My chest is pumping, but it's not all because of this intimate moment. It's the guilt I feel for sitting here with Jason when my heart belongs elsewhere.

And I *hate* admitting that.

The food arrives, and we eat in silence. My appetite is nonexistent, and with each bite, I'm swallowing a tablespoon of guilt.

"What did we do, Pres? We had it all, you know?"

"Did we, Jase? We were happy, but I don't know... it's like we got cold feet way too early."

"This could have been us. We could have had a child together," he says in a low voice.

"I guess so."

The question makes me think. Even if I could go back

in time, would I make Jason the father of my child? It would've been so easy and a stroll in the park. But everything that Masen is lies in his DNA. He has Haden's blood running through his veins, and truth be told, I wouldn't change that for the world.

"There's always the future, Pres. It's not a closed book between us."

"I miss you," I blurt out, not intending for it to come out the way it does.

"I miss you, too."

"It was so easy, what we had," I confess. "Life is so complicated now. I just don't know what I'm doing anymore."

"But is easy wrong?"

"No, it's drama-free, and all I've been doing for nine months is living in a world of drama."

Jason presses his palm against mine and leans forward. With only the glow of the candlelight between us, my body moves in, bringing us close together.

"We both were searching for something else, Presley. But we already had it all," he concedes. "Now we've had that time apart, I've realized no woman can compare to you. Sure, you have your quirks, but Presley, I want my life with *you*."

He said all the words I wanted a certain someone else to express. He's offering me everything we had on a silver platter with a nice red bow to complete the package—an easy life filled with love and happy memories.

"Jason, I have a son. My life is about him now, and he's not yours."

"I know that, but you know I was raised by Jeff, and he was a great stepfather. I'm not here to replace his father. I'm offering you a life, Presley. A life with me."

I lower my head and stare at the tablecloth. With his hands still touching mine, his offer appears too good to pass up. But I'm angry at the Jerk. Livid, in fact, and to make an important decision like this, I need a clear head.

I tell him I need time to think, and on cue, the alarm goes off, warning me that I have to return to Masen. I kindly tell Jason I need to go, and being the true gentleman he is, he offers to walk me back to my apartment.

It's a cool night with a heavy breeze, and just as my body shivers, he removes his jacket and places it over my shoulders. We talk about our families as we walk back home, reminiscing about the good old days and our joint family vacations.

"It was really good seeing you, Jase."

He leans in closer and kisses me on the lips. Suddenly, the guilt washes over me and I pull away, wiping my lips without even thinking. He looks taken aback by my ability to pull away, let alone wipe his kiss from my lips, but he doesn't comment on it.

With trepidation, he asks, "Can I come in?"

I open the door and notice the apartment is quiet. With only the hall lamp turned on, I assume Vicky is with Masen in my room. I motion for Jason to follow me, and he does until we reach the bedroom door. When I open the door, I almost fall back into Jason's body at the sight of Haden sitting on my bed, shirtless and holding Masen.

"I... uh... where's Vicky?"

"Nice to see you, Presley. Vicky had an emergency, and since Masen is my son, I thought I'd stay over and spend some time with him." His voice is dripping with sarcasm, and behind his frames, his eyes are fueled with fire and rage.

"Okay... Jason, this is Haden, Masen's dad," I introduce

slowly, preparing myself for the biggest shit-storm to rock this universe.

"Nice to meet you." Jason nods.

Haden is trying to hide his anger, but his outburst is imminent. "So, is there a reason why you went out and abandoned our son?"

Bingo. Typical Jerk saying his jerk-like things instead of communicating in a mature and adult way.

Another reminder of why Jason is a better fit for me than Haden could ever be.

"I'm going to walk Jason out," I grit.

I turn around and grab Jason's hand on purpose, guiding him to outside the apartment while I try to calm myself down.

Outside in the hall, he shakes his head. "A young jerk."

"Jason..."

"You want a real man, Pres? You know where to find me. And I'm serious about what I'm offering."

"I know, Jason. It's just... I love him."

I said it, the words that have taunted me for the longest time. It's both a relief and a burden to finally say it out loud. My lip begins to tremble as Jason glances at me with a sympathetic smile. He wraps me in his arms for a final good-bye, and my body comfortably rests against his as I struggle to hold back the tears. This new, emotional Presley is getting on my nerves. I have never cried so much in my life as I have over the past year.

Cupping my face in his hands, he wipes the tears away with the tip of his thumb. "I'm always here, Pres. Even as a friend. No, I don't want just that, but we've got too much history to let go of everything we had, including our friendship. You know where I am... I'm always here."

And that's the thing about Jason. Once he steps into

your life, there is no turning back. He may not be the man I want to spend the rest of my life with, or the man my heart so desperately beats for, but he will forever be a friend I can count on. And good friends like him are hard to come by.

With Jason gone, I have no choice but to face the music, and with every step back toward my room, my anger intensifies. I walk in, and Masen is sound asleep in his cot. Haden is still sitting on my bed, half-dressed. He is fidgeting with his phone, and the second he senses I'm in the room, his eyes lock with mine and glower back at me. With his lips pursed and his nostrils flaring, he throws his phone to the side, crossing his arms as he waits for me to talk.

"Get some clothes on," I bark.

"Tell me why you went out with him!"

"None of your business. Now, will you just go?"

Why didn't Vicky warn me he was here? My phone is inside my purse. I pull it out and see that the screen is covered with a dozen messages, all from Vicky. I don't have time to read them now, and I storm off into my closet to take off my shoes. He is in there so fast, blocking the entrance by resting his body against the archway.

"Did he touch you?"

"I don't have to answer that."

"Did. He. Touch. You?" Haden yells, slamming his fist against the drywall.

I swiftly turn around. "Yes. Yes, he did. Get off your jealousy horse because I don't belong to you. You're full of shit, Haden. You don't care about me or else you wouldn't be marrying Eloise."

"And everything I said meant nothing to you? I told you no one was to touch you but me." He follows with a sinister laugh, shaking his head as he continues to block the exit.

His body is exposed, and it becomes an unnecessary distraction.

From the corner of my eye, I can see his knuckles are stark white from clenching his fist so tightly. I have never seen him this enraged, and it scares me a little. But then I remember my conversation with Eloise yesterday, and I quickly change back to infuriated and bitter Presley.

"See, Malone, all along this is what I was afraid of. You're running back to the love of your life."

"I didn't run, Haden. I was standing still. Waiting for *you.* You're the one who broke me."

"You want to know why I proposed to Eloise?"

"Enlighten me, Haden." I stand here, arms crossed, waiting for his pathetic excuse.

"Because I never felt good enough for you. I was never the man you wanted in your life. Eloise wanted me, but to you, I was nothing, and you went out of your way to constantly remind me of that. I'm a mistake, as you so often say. So, I'll tell you what. You want to move to California with Jason? Then fucking do it! We were never going to work anyway."

He moves away from the closet and back into the other room, grabbing his shirt.

There are no slamming doors.

No more sounds.

He is gone.

And I pushed him.

Or, maybe, he pushed himself.

It doesn't matter because his words cut deep, and just like he said, we are never going to work, anyway.

I grab my phone and make the call.

"Hey, it's me."

"What's wrong? Isn't it like midnight there?"

"Yes. I've decided to move to California. Is it still okay if I stay with you guys?"

"Of course," Gemma replies in a worried tone. "Pres, what happened? You sound... weird."

She's my sister. She knows me well, and nothing ever gets past her. She's seen me at my worst. I begin to sob into the phone, making no sense with my words.

"I can't be around him anymore, Gem. It's just too hard. I love him."

"I know," she soothes. "But he's Masen's dad. He's always going to be around. And you're just figuring out now that you love him?"

"No, Gemma. I knew all along. I just kept denying the truth. He can still see Masen. I know a lot of parents who meet at a shopping center and someone else does the handover."

"Is that what you really want?"

I know I'm not thinking straight. I'm hurt. And when you're hurt, rational decisions are hard to make. Instead, you follow the broken path, praying that it will lead to some magical rainbow with unicorns galloping around it and baskets of cupcakes and chocolate.

"Yes. I'll book the flights."

My mind is made up.

This time next week, I will be in California.

TWENTY-SIX

I t's funny how in life, we gravitate toward people who embody the phrase, 'You only live once.' Like when you're watching some documentary on a reporter who travels the world to show you exotic places, or a well-known chef exploring different cuisines and opening up your mind to things you had only dreamed about. Curled up on the couch, I would always watch with such enjoyment, wishing I had the guts just to let loose and live life as if there were no tomorrow.

I thought I had lived a colorful life, having traveled to a few places outside the country, yet in reality, I've played it safe. I love to be adventurous but always with caution. Yeah, so I'm that annoying person who will ask the attendant on any rollercoaster the stats on the seat belts and when the ride was last checked for malfunctions. In the end, I always enjoy myself, wondering why I just don't let loose and do these kinds of things more often.

Years ago, I created a bucket list. It grew and grew because there was always something preventing me from doing anything on that list. Looking back on it now, I'm partially to blame. I gave excuse after excuse, and before I knew it, time had passed by at lightning speed.

And that's the thing about time. If we could stop it, just for a moment, we would have enough time to experience all the things our hearts desire. I always imagine how different life would be if we could catalog our memories and experiences, and with just one click of a button, be transported in time to that memory. Like the first time a boy leans in and kisses your lips, or the moment when your parents buy you tickets to your first concert and you're in the crowd holding up a sign for Bon Jovi to marry you. *If only he read that sign.*

Then there's that moment when the man you love gets down on one knee and promises you a lifetime of memories beginning with the shining diamond that sits in that little velvet box. And at that moment, you're sitting on cloud nine about to embark on the most joyous journey with the man who wants to spend the rest of his life with you.

But out of all these moments, there is no greater moment than seeing the face of your child for the very first time. The first time they are placed in your arms, and the world officially stops as you are introduced to this tiny human being who grew inside you for nine months.

These memories, all of them, are moments to be cherished.

Then there are moments that you wish you could fast-forward, place in a vault, and throw into the deepest end of the ocean.

This is me, now.

The way Haden ended things between us left me deeply depressed and made me question everything I thought I knew about myself. In my life, I have never before experienced all the emotions I've had in the past forty-eight hours. At first, I was livid. How dare he think or say the things he said. If he listened, just for a second, he would have heard what I was trying to say and possibly understand my fears and trepidation. But the Jerk threw himself into another one of his immature tantrums, leaving me no choice but to let whatever it was between us go.

I love Masen, more than life itself, and Haden marrying Eloise has already turned me into this bitter, toxic, ugly person who I never wanted to be.

I don't want that person around my son.

And why? Because I love him, and it hurts like hell.

Knowing that someone you love doesn't love you back is one of the most painful things in life. It tears you into pieces, and you believe there is no way to recover. Your mind tells you that you must be damaged goods because if that one person you loved couldn't love you back, then no one else could possibly love you either.

The next journey on this painful ride is denial. After figuring out he is indeed the biggest jerk to walk this planet, I refuse to acknowledge he exists. Yeah, it's the good old sweep-it-under-the-rug scenario, which is what I should have done in the first place rather than fall in love with someone like him.

Another thing. Don't let your broken heart even *think* about the man you love, who doesn't love you back, in any sexual way or form. That's just a recipe for torture.

Kate, as always, proves to be a great distraction during what I call the I-wish-the-Jerk-never- existed phase.

"You don't have to go," she reminds me for the millionth time today.

I continue to pack my box of shoes, all the while

wondering how I accumulated so much. Geez, I don't want to throw the term 'shoe whore' around, but it's difficult not to. Especially when I realize I have the same pair of pumps in three different colors. *When did I really think I would wear the crimson pair?*

"Los Angeles is great, don't get me wrong, but aren't you going to miss the city?"

Closing the box, I pull the tape across the top and stick on a label marked, 'Shoes—FRAGILE.'

There, done.

"I'm done here. I miss my sister. The open spaces and sun will be a welcoming change. California has some great schools where Masen can attend," I state, matter of factly.

"I can't argue that. I'm from England, and anywhere there's sun, I'm there faster than you can say the word sunburn."

I shake my head, giggling at her comment. Kate is awfully pale, and I can only imagine what the California sun could do to her delicate skin. Nevertheless, she is gorgeous the way she is.

"You're beautiful," I add, smiling at her.

She places the tape aside and jumps up, almost knocking me down as we hug it out. For someone who has only been in my life for such a short time, she's had a big impact. She is that person you can always rely on, no matter what. She is a selfless human being who genuinely cares for the people who surround her. I consider myself lucky to have met her and hope the distance won't affect our friendship. But then again, why should it? A true friend doesn't need to see or talk to you every day. You know they'll be there whenever you need them. Kate is and will forever be a person I consider a good friend.

"I'm going to miss you. I've loved having you as a roomie. And lil' Mase..." she trails off, letting go of me and picking him up from his crib. She's visibly upset, having grown so fond of him during our short stay together. Kate isn't one to cry, but her eyes begin to well, and I swear I hear a slight sniffle.

"It's only a plane ride away. And you said you visit L.A. often," I remind her softy.

"I know... just gotta get used to not seeing this little chubber every day."

Smiling back at Kate, I watch as she gently sways Masen. It's sad to go, but it's all in Masen's best interest. I constantly have to drum that into my stubborn head.

It doesn't matter what I want.

But that all soon falls apart.

The next night, I wake up sweating profusely, my lungs feeling like they have been punctured, not allowing me to breathe. Panicky and dripping in cold sweat, I clutch my chest, certain I'm having a heart attack.

I'm thirty-two. The likelihood of that happening is slim. The panic subsides, and the reality of being alone in this big bed hits me like a ton of bricks.

I'm suffering from what they call a broken heart.

I have all the symptoms. The aching heart, the lack of appetite, and no song can play in the background without causing me a complete meltdown.

On day four, it officially hits. Physically my heart is aching, and the stream of tears flows evenly, escalating in loud sobs. Not wanting to wake up Masen or Kate, I grab the pillow and shove it onto my face. The pain is unbearable. Several times I have contemplated calling and telling him to come over. I miss him so much, and the thought of being on the other side of the country has left me torn in my decision.

I miss his smell. That masculine scent that drives my senses wild.

I miss the way his eyebrows do that thing every time his face breaks into a smile.

But most of all, I miss the way he watches over Masen with unconditional love. The adoration in that one stare makes me realize that no other man could love Masen as much as he does.

I am out of my mind, clearly not thinking straight.

Then I do that awful stalker thing. I check his Facebook and Twitter accounts, but he hasn't posted a thing. Immediately afterward, I regret looking at pictures of him. *How can one human being be so beautiful, yet tear every inch of your soul to pieces at the same time?*

In the light of day with the sun peeking through my curtains, the world seems entirely different. My eyes are puffy and sore from my cry-fest. Last night feels like a big blur now, yet the pain still lingers. It only reminds me that there are many sleepless nights to come.

After all, this is only the beginning.

Liz is coming over later to take Masen out for a couple of hours, so I can run some last-minute errands. Since Masen is still fast asleep, I shower quickly and dress in my jeans with a knitted gray sweater. Makeup is mandatory as I have to cover up the bags under my eyes. My hair never cooperates, so I settle for running some product through it and leaving it down. All dressed and ready for the day, I change Masen and feed him, then finish packing his bag.

On cue, the doorbell rings, and a happy Liz is waiting impatiently for her grandson.

"There he is!" She pulls him from my arms as I motion for her to come inside.

Liz is a very attractive woman. I'd peg her for being in her early fifties with her youthful skin yet classic style. She is wearing a long, natural-colored overcoat and black leather gloves.

"Okay, so the stroller's over there, and his bag has enough milk for the day, spare clothes, and a ton of diapers."

"Thanks, honey." She smiles. "We're going to have fun today. Daddy is going to take you to the zoo."

"Daddy?" I almost choke at her words.

She stops smiling and moves her attention back to me, looking slightly nervous. "Yes. Haden took the week off work because of the hectic wedding schedule."

I have two options—I can be the devil and take Masen away from him, or I can ignore the way my heart just fell to the floor when Liz mentioned the wedding and act okay with it.

"I better get going," I mumble, kissing Masen on the top of his head.

"Presley." She stops me, clutching my arm.

I reluctantly turn to face her, struggling to keep my emotions steady.

"Let fate run its course. In the end, it will all work out."

Fate? Fate hasn't stopped screwing with me since the moment I told Jason we needed to end things. I can't rely on fate. I can't rely on anything. Call me a pessimist, a cynic, whatever the hell you want. If I want something to happen, I need to do something about it. Right now, I just want to get out of here. I don't want to think about the Jerk and his stupid wedding.

As soon as Liz is gone, I muster up every part of me not to shed one more tear. He has made his decision, and I have made mine. Grabbing my purse, I head out, forcing myself to enjoy my child-free day.

"I'll have the grilled salmon, baked potatoes with ranch dressing, and a salad on the side. You know what, throw in some nachos while you're at it."

I stare at my friend, amused. "Throw in some nachos while you're at it? Please don't tell me you're pregnant, Vicky."

She rolls her eyes at me while shoving a breadstick into her mouth. "No. You'd be proud of me. I haven't touched Patrick whatsoever."

"Wow. I am proud of you."

"I'm happy to accept his lavish gifts while he pines so desperately for my kitty."

"New wallet?"

"Yep." Her mouth widens into a smile. "Chanel. Isn't it a beauty?"

"Yes. But you realize he wants sex, and you need sex?"

"Don't worry about me. I bought this super-duper vibrator with all the bells and whistles. I've gone through a whole pack of batteries... in a week!"

Vicky spends the next ten minutes reciting the stats of the vibrator. She wasn't kidding when she said it had all the bells and whistles. It has five-star reviews, and we have a good laugh reading what other women had to say about it.

"At the rate I'm going, I may need to buy one, too."

I take a sip of water as the waiter places the nachos in front of us. My weakness, and today, I ignore my attempt to get back in shape. I eat like it's my last meal on earth. The gym can wait. Again.

"I saw the Jerk yesterday. He came into the office in the morning to grab his laptop."

"That's nice," I say without any emotion.

"Well, what I saw wasn't nice. He looked like a wreck, Pres. I mean, a scruffy-looking hairy man who probably hasn't seen a mirror or a razor in a while. He rivaled Bigfoot."

"Maybe that's the look he wants at his wedding."

She sighs. "You're not helping me here."

"Helping you do what?"

"He looks like shit because he misses you, Presley. And he knows he's a jerk and said jerk-like things to you. I don't know why he is marrying her if he loves you. It doesn't make sense."

"He doesn't love me. End of story. Now can we please talk about something else?"

I bite down on a tortilla chip, avoiding Vicky's penetrating gaze. She knows me well enough to know this is a sore subject. She can tell, not only because I'm avoiding making eye contact, but also because I do that nervous twirl of my hair around my finger thing and constantly tap my foot against the floor.

I swiftly change subjects. "So, I've lined up a part-time job at Lantern Publishing in L.A. I'll be working four days a week. Three days in the office and one day from home. Luckily, Gemma works from home as a graphic designer, so she jumped at the chance to take care of Masen till he's old enough to go to daycare."

"Sounds like you have it all planned out. Just like the old Presley," Vicky counters with her eyebrows raised.

Taken aback by her tone and comment, I place my fork down and wipe my mouth. "What's that supposed to mean?"

"It means that nothing's changed. Yes, you've had a baby, but you've turned back into Miss Plan-My-Whole-Life-Out Presley. It was fun being around you when you stopped giving a shit and just lived for the moment. The Jerk changed you in ways you haven't bothered to notice."

"Well, not giving a shit and living for the moment ends up with a broken heart. I'm sick of this. I just want to go live my life without all the drama."

"What about me?" she pouts jokingly.

"What about you?"

"Will you miss my drama?"

I laugh and lean over to squeeze her perfectly mani-cured hand. "That's the only thing I'll miss. You and Kate with your constant man drama. I'm going to have to take up watching soap operas to get my fill."

"I love you, Pres. Thank you for being my best friend. I don't know what I'm going to do without you just around the corner."

"Ditto." I smile back. "Now stop moping because you're flying to visit me next weekend."

"I'm excited! I've never been to L.A., and there's so much I want to do." She pulls out a piece of paper from her bag and places it in front of me. "So, here is a list I made of things I want to do, time permitting."

I hold my palm in front of her face. "Stop the press. Vicky made a list?"

"Are you proud of me? Mama Presley taught me well."

"So, you *can* teach an old dog new tricks." I laugh.

We fall into a fit of laughter until the cute waiter returns with our lunch. Despite Vicky's attempt to be organized, I'm not the least bit surprised when she follows the cute waiter back to the bar and asks him for his number.

∼

I arrive back at the apartment and see that Liz hasn't returned just yet. It is almost dark, and I'm starting to worry about them. Not wanting to call Haden, I find Liz's number in my phone and dial it immediately. It rings for a while before going to voicemail, only adding to my concern. I scroll through the contacts and land on Haden's number. Just as I am about to hit the call button, a tap on the door startles me, and I scramble to open it, glad to see Liz and Masen on the other side. I unbuckle Masen from his stroller and lift him into my arms. Bringing him up to my face, I smell his hair, and my nerves are non-existent with my baby finally back in my arms.

"I'm sorry we're late, sweetie. Haden just wanted some extra time with him."

"He could have told me."

"I know. He has a lot on his mind right now," she defends him. "So, listen, he asked me to give this to you."

She hands me a piece of paper, and I open it up to find a calendar for the next three months. My eyes divert to the boxes marked in red. In print, it says, "Eloise and Haden."

"What's this?" I ask, confused.

"Haden thought it was best to put together a schedule of when they could see Masen."

"But... but... this is every other weekend... and it says New York?"

She puts the baby bag down and gracefully places her hand on mine. "Sweetie. It was bound to happen. If you're moving to L.A. and Haden stays here, both of you will need to make an effort for Masen's sake."

"I can't fly out to New York every other weekend," I respond anxiously.

"Maybe Masen stays here for a week, or Haden flies out. He didn't get into the details with me."

Masen apart from me for a week?

What the hell is running through his head? I'm angry, furious to be precise, and that whole thing about not letting my emotions get to me, well, fuck it! I tear the paper up in front of Liz, much to her shock.

"This is what I think of his stupid plan."

Liz knows well enough to leave at this point. Kissing Masen for the last time, she waves goodbye but not before telling me she'll visit in a couple of weeks.

After my normal nightly routine, I put Masen to bed and head back to the living room to distract myself with mindless television. It doesn't work. I've channel-surfed for the past hour without settling on anything to watch. Kate arrives home, and the second she does, I burst into tears. Not once does she tell me I'm wrong or making a mistake. She allows me to cry and let out my unresolved issues. Feeling bad that I soaked her shirt, I pull away, apologizing for being a wreck.

"You have every right to be. You love him, and the Jerk's marrying someone else. Plus, he puts together a stupid plan?"

"Why is he doing this? I don't understand why he wants to take Masen away from me," I sob.

"You need to talk to him, Presley. Clear the air and move on."

"No. I don't want to see him." I stand up and head to the kitchen as Kate follows me. "He's made his decision, Kate. He's marrying Eloise. He wants Eloise to be his wife. I'm taking Masen with me and moving to L.A. End of story."

"If that's what you want, Presley. Just remember that despite him marrying her, he's still Masen's dad."

Of course, I know that. Masen looks exactly like him, even at this age. Every time I look at him, I'm reminded of that. How can I cope with a lifetime of staring at my child's face and being reminded of the man who so carelessly broke me to pieces? I have no plan for how to avoid that. That's what makes it all the more difficult.

No matter what you do, there's no plan for curing a broken heart.

TWENTY-SEVEN

S aying goodbye isn't too hard because the girls will visit soon.

It's the taxi ride to the airport that *kills* me.

The radio is set on some '80s love song marathon. It's easy to say I can just ignore it, but when Barry Manilow is belting out a tune, you better believe your heart aches along with him. When I was growing up, these songs were so corny, yet Mom and Dad would put them on and stare lovingly into each other's eyes while singing out of key.

That's love. Married for almost forty years, and even with all their quirks, that love's never faded. Mom once told me she loved Dad more now than the day she married him. Forty fricken years, I still don't know how that is even possible.

Stuck in the usual traffic jam to the airport, the driver turns up the radio when Chicago's "Hard to Say I'm Sorry" comes on. Blinking my eyes to stop the tears, I force myself to think about my mascara and how I don't want panda eyes at the airport. But I'm not that strong.

The taxi driver asks me if everything is okay, and I make

up some lie about being homesick. Don't need to get into the whole the-man-I-love-got-married-today-and-I'm-a-pathetic-single-mom-running-away-from-all-my-problems story.

Song after song plays, and the more they sing about love, the more my mind wanders to today.

Haden and Eloise are officially husband and wife right now.

The vows to love each other for all eternity have been said and done. The shiny bands are sitting on their fingers, and right about now, they're having their first dance as a married couple to some sappy song that probably played only moments ago in my cab.

I have shed so many tears over him. I've spent countless nights waking up in a cold sweat. If I'm ever to move on with my life, I need to grab that glue and start mending my heart. He may have torn it apart, but I'll be damned if I'm the one suffering this lonely life all because of him. He can go ahead and be married, have a dozen babies for all I care. We both stood at that fork in the road, and he went the opposite way.

Fate—you've laid out all the cards, and I'll take mine so you can leave me the fuck alone.

When street signs indicate the airport is only a couple of minutes away, I breathe a huge sigh of relief. The driver pulls alongside the curb and hops out of the cab, opening the door for me. With Masen in his carrier, an attendant pushes a trolley my way, escorting me to the check-in desk with my suitcases.

The hustle and bustle of the airport distracts me—streams of people lining up all heading to different destinations. There are plenty of businessmen standing in the first-class line waiting impatiently to be checked in. The economy line is full of families and crying kids, all waiting to continue their journey. It takes longer than expected, and by the time I reach the head of the line, I don't have as much time as I originally set aside before having to board the flight.

Shit. I don't know how this happened.

I scheduled everything and allowed for extra time for any incidentals like traffic or queues.

You dropped the ball, Presley. It's what happens when you're suffering from a broken heart.

Oh, shut up, brain!

As I walk toward the gate, I see a line has already formed. Just great. I'm not sure if I have enough time to check Masen's diaper and grab a bag of potato chips. I have barely eaten all day. Scanning the gate area for a spare seat to change Masen, my eyes move toward a man sitting by his lonesome near the entrance. With his head bent down, dressed in a black tux, he nervously plays with his wedding ring.

How odd. As if someone would fly wearing a tux.

It takes a moment for my brain to catch on, but when it does, it's like a strike of lightning followed by thunder. It hits me all in that one moment—that signature move of running his hands through his hair, rubbing his eyes beneath his thick black frames.

It can't be.

You're seeing things.

You're tired and delusional from the lack of sleep and food. You also possibly need your eyes checked for old age. Yeah, that's it. Blame it on old age.

Yet I am drawn to this mysterious stranger. His behavior is odd, and I'm surprised that airport security hasn't detained him for being a suspicious weirdo. *Oh God, what if he has a bomb?*

I'm walking slowly toward this madman, frightened for Masen's and my lives. *What the hell am I doing.* The nervous rush running through my veins is making the blood in my heart pump so hard I'm certain everyone can see.

Then I halt.

A few steps away.

My heart stops, the beats barely existent as I stand on the spot, frozen. The blood drains from my face, and like I've seen a ghost, the noises around me fade into the distance. My stomach is nothing but a hollow pit, the walls caving in as the pain eats away at every part of me that has struggled to exist.

All because the man in the black tuxedo is my jerk.

The man who has so carelessly stolen my heart.

I'm walking toward him like a zombie and somehow manage to place Masen's carrier carefully on the floor beside me. With a dry throat, I'm unable to speak the words sitting on the tip of my tongue. The words that have run circles in my head, begging me to speak them out loud every second since he walked away that night. But my pride steps in and straightening my posture, I try to act calm and cool, not wanting him to see how much he broke me.

"What are you doing here?"

He doesn't say anything, and the announcement reminding everyone that final boarding is commencing sends everyone around us into a hurried pace. Yet Haden is sitting perfectly still. Head down, staring at the carpet, twisting his shining wedding ring around his finger.

He got married.

You saw the wedding ring.

Run now.

Board that plane and never turn back.

Don't wait for him to shatter your heart even further if that's even possible.

"Did you know Britney Spears was married for less than twenty-four hours?" His tone is even, controlled, not a single whisper of any remorse.

Where is he going with this?

"Uh, yes, I did."

He laughs at himself like it's a sick and twisted joke, shaking his head as his shoulders slump. "Who would have thought I'd beat that record? Three hours. I mean, who the fuck separates after three hours?"

My voice cracks, and with a nervous stutter, I ask, "H-Haden, what are you trying to say?"

His eyes move slowly up my body causing every part of me to ache in his presence. When his eyes eventually meet mine, his stare is so deep that I'm terrified he has climbed into my soul and buried himself even further. He looks dejected, tired, and worn out. There's no life in his eyes anymore, even when he stares back at me.

And why would there be?

He doesn't love me.

"You see, all along I was waiting for a sign. Just like in the movies. You know, when the priest asks if anyone objects, and the girl of your dreams runs into the church professing her undying love and then the couple run down the aisle and into a fancy car."

"It was a guy stopping the wedding, and I believe you mean bus," I chastise with a weak smile.

"In my fantasy, it's an Aston Martin."

"That's some fantasy you've got."

His eyes dance playfully. Behind the dark circles, the corners of his eyes wrinkle as a smile escapes him. "So, I'm sitting at the head table as everyone toasts the newlywed couple, and I think, wait. I'm the *Jerk* here. How could I expect that fantasy to come true when the woman I love avoids drama at all costs? She'd never do anything like that. And if I had opened my eyes, I'd have seen that she gave me an opportunity. An opportunity that I selfishly ignored and placed my own insecurities in front of."

Another announcement interrupts, but I ignore it, eager for him to finish his story.

"Then, it's time to dance with my wife, and like a giant wrecking ball that knocks the life out of me, I realize I've made the *biggest* mistake of my life. I married the wrong person because I didn't think I was good enough for the woman who has consumed me.

"All along, my woman said she wanted more. She wanted my heart to beat for only her. She wanted to be the only one I ever thought about. And she is. My heart beat for her the moment I first met her and purposely spilled that tea all over her desk. It beat so fucking hard that I had no idea what to do. I ran away to London and clutched onto anything I could to forget you. I have never experienced anything in my life like this. I just refused to believe you could ever feel the same way about me. So, I married the wrong person hoping that the Band-Aid would fix the giant hole in my heart."

"Haden..." I whisper, tears falling down my cheeks.

"It's always been you, Presley Malone. Even before you even noticed I existed. I just couldn't handle how intense my feelings were for you. I was g-going insane." His voice cracks with pain.

I drop to my knees until we are face to face. Caressing his cheek, I don't wait for any more signs. I lean in and kiss his beautiful lips. The second our lips meet, a warm electric current electrifies every inch of my body, and I know at this moment that I can never let him go again. I want to fight for him, for us, for our family.

I pull back momentarily, still close to him. "You said the woman you love..."

"I love you." He runs his fingers along the side of my cheek, moving them toward my hair. His grin takes my breath away, and with a gentle whisper, he says, "I love you so much I don't know how to exist without you. I'm sorry I put you through all that to get to this point. I should have ended things with Eloise months ago."

"I love you, Haden Cooper. I'm sorry I didn't have the guts to admit that earlier. I was terrified. I've never felt so in love with someone as I am with you."

There, in front of the entire crowd, he pulls me in and kisses me deeply as if no one is watching. His tongue desperately searches for mine, and the moment we connect, both of us moan. I don't care who's watching us. I never want to stop. This belongs in my catalog of memories. A moment I want to hold onto forever because this time, I'm not going to let go of him, and I trust he will never hurt me that way again.

The crowd around us breaks into a cheer and applauds as we pull away from each other, shocked that everyone is watching us. A few are even filming us with their phones.

"I want more. But I'm not sure if I'm ready to be a YouTube sensation," I whisper in his ear, laughing.

"I don't care if the whole world sees this moment." He lifts me into his arms easily like I'm a feather and screams, "I fucking love you, Malone!"

The whistles and cheers don't stop, and I'm waiting for airport security to break up the chaos. Instead, they are standing on the sidelines with amused looks on their faces.

Suddenly, it dawns on me that we still have a major problem. "There's just one thing," I remind him. "You're still technically married."

Haden moves his lips onto mine, not answering. He pulls back, and the corners of his lips rise slowly in a half-smile, partly showing his teeth. There's a gleam in his eyes, and I know he is holding something back. A secret that I'm not in on, *yet*. Slowly, he moves his hands inside his jacket and like a magician, pulls out two tickets.

"First-class tickets to the Dominican Republic. Flight leaves in two hours."

The Dominican Republic? How will that solve this problem?

My silly, lovesick brain needs a couple of moments to catch up as he waits ever so patiently for the ball to drop.

"Oh!" I exclaim. "But my bags and Masen's stuff are going to L.A. The car is picking us up and—"

Gently, he places his index finger on my mouth. "Sometimes, Presley, life doesn't go according to plan."

"You're telling me. I can't believe I'm going to get on a plane to fly to the Dominican Republic with a man who got married three hours ago. You're still a jerk, you know."

"You still love me for being one."

Unable to control my joy, I smile back at him. "I wouldn't change it for the entire world."

And there, in front of the crowd of strangers, Haden has followed his heart, and mine skips along right beside him.

The trip to the Dominican Republic opened my eyes to a whole new world and a new life I would embark on.

Haden's mission was to get that divorce. In fact, he

made sure it was the first thing on the agenda the moment we landed. Okay, maybe not the very *first* thing. Haden surprised me by flying Gemma and Melissa over. Seeing them at the airport was a huge shock, but it didn't take me long to figure this puzzle out. Masen needs a sitter because apparently, we aren't leaving the room unless absolutely necessary.

And Haden was insatiable when we were finally alone.

I could go on and on about that, but my Kitty is delirious and hasn't been about to talk or walk. In fact, for the first time in my life, she's blissfully enjoying life on cloud nine. I mean, how did I not know all the positions one could have sex? The former Presley was such a prude, and holy fuck, Haden has a nice way of bringing the kink out of me. I could go on about his piercing and how every orgasm tore through me like a tornado, but what happens in the Dominican Republic, stays in the Dominican Republic.

Of course, I knew Haden is far from perfect. Mr. Stubborn turned into some jealous alpha during our divorce getaway. He was adamant that every busboy was trying to hit on me, and he speculated that maybe I didn't look 'freshly fucked' enough by my man—his crass words, not mine. We scrapped the idea of having lunch by the pool because he needed his fix.

Let's face it, I won't complain, ever.

But I learned a valuable lesson. Life isn't about everyone or everything being perfect. It's about the misadventures, the unplanned madness of losing your luggage and being forced to spend travel insurance money and going on the best shopping spree ever.

It's about sitting at the fanciest restaurant and seeing a rat run past the table, only to end up at the closest McDonald's in your formal wear.

It's called life.

Perfection is open for interpretation. Society makes us believe that when you find the perfect man, it's love at first sight, and you say "I do" and buy that dream house. Then you have your two or three kids and live happily ever after.

And guess what? We did the opposite.

Screw a stranger in the alley of a club, fall pregnant, run away with a newly-divorced man to live in a rundown bungalow out of wedlock.

This is our perfect.

And from the moment Haden promised to give me more, I finally understood the meaning of living life to the fullest. I now understand what it's like to have no plan and live for the moment. I don't have to become an adrenaline junkie like Haden. I just let fate do its thing. I savor every experience, good and bad, with the man who gives me more.

The man, Haden Cooper, otherwise known as my #Jerk.

EPILOGUE

Haden

He's got that stare.

Those dirty eyes.

Licking his lips in anticipation.

And he's watching *my* woman.

She's oblivious. She always is. Standing across the room, my gaze is steadily on her while she's talking animatedly with some friends. That dress isn't helping, and I'm so fucking torn between wanting to see her beautiful body showcased and wanting to belt every fucker who's looking at her. It's that fucking slit, the one that rides so far up her thigh, it doesn't leave much to the imagination.

And I know what every single fucker in here is thinking. I can read their minds. They are thinking exactly as I am by imagining how perfect her legs would be wrapped around their face. How her huge tits would bounce around as she rode them fast until they blew their load.

But she's mine.

My head starts to throb, slowly forming into a migraine

as I struggle to ignore the sadistic thoughts running through my mind. Blame the dress. This ridiculous dress caused a massive argument between us earlier. Stubborn woman wouldn't back down, calling me a caveman or some bullshit like that. I just knew what every jerk would be thinking. After all, that used to be me.

The room is dark and slowly morphing into a lions' den. The beasts are hungry, waiting for their prey to make a move—a wink, even a sly smile—a gesture that will have the beasts moving in leaps and bounds, thirsty for some meat. My eyes dart back and forth—one on the prey, the other watching the beasts. The one on my left I'm certain will be him. He's covering his mouth with a bottle, but his eyes have not left her. Then, he does the unthinkable. He moves his hand to his crotch and adjusts his cock.

Motherfucker has a hard-on already!

"You all right?"

Lex Edwards is beside me, having just stopped the waiter for a drink. I lose my focus, but only for a second. If it weren't for him buying a share in Lantern Publishing, this stupid party wouldn't be happening.

"Yeah... it's just... never mind."

He chuckles as if he's in on some joke. "You've got to let it go. Otherwise, you'll drive yourself insane. Trust me, I know. And you should know since you so eagerly tried the same move on my wife last year."

"Yeah, sorry about that, man," I apologize.

"So, the tables have turned, and you're about to smash every guy in this room for looking at your woman."

"I can take them out easily, especially that fucker on the left," I grit.

"You'll spend a lifetime fighting it off. You need to find a way to control the jealousy. It's a balancing act. Let her think you're cool but never, and I repeat never, take your eyes off the prize."

I don't know how Lex is so calm about all of this. His wife is standing next to Presley. The beasts are probably thinking of how to bag both of them in one go. The waiter returns but not quickly enough. I grab the scotch and down it in almost one gulp, burning my throat and following up with a numbing sensation, but it doesn't stop me from seeing red.

"If that's what I gotta do, then I'll spend my life fighting every fucker who thinks they can go near her."

She doesn't realize what she does to me, or every man in this room, except for Lex. He's fighting his own battles, despite being in denial.

It's been over a year since I made it my mission to crawl under her skin—the woman who drove me to the brink of insanity. And she had no clue either. Because beneath her mass of curls was a hardheaded, Miss Goody-Two-Shoes, feisty woman who rubbed me the wrong way. Boy, did that backfire. I thought fucking her in the alley and leaving her pussy wet with no happy ending would teach her a fucking lesson. It taught me a lesson. You play with fire, you get burned. The amount of shit I did to forget her was all a waste a time.

But I wouldn't change it.

My son is my fucking life.

And running through his veins is the blood of this woman who consumes me. It's not just her wild hair that cascades down her back and covers her body like a Greek goddess. It's everything about her—the way her big brown eyes stare back at me, drawing me in enough that I could climb into her soul and bury myself there and how her body begs me to take her, whenever and wherever.

Whenever. Wherever.

I've got it. Why didn't I think of this earlier?

You did, moron. You're always thinking about it. This is what happens when you're in love with a beautiful woman.

I finish the drink in my hand and place it on a table, abandoning Lex without another word. Walking straight to her, I don't break my gaze until she stops mid-sentence as my body presses against her back. My hands move around her hips, and I pull her closer until my cock is nestled in her ass.

Yeah, I'm hard. What's fucking new?

"Look who's here. What, aren't we allowed to talk to your girlfriend?" Kate teases, laughing along with Lex's wife, Charlie.

"Stop teasing him, Kate. It's this man thing they all have to do," Charlie chastises.

Kate rolls her eyes at Charlie. "Yeah, you should know. Your man is over there practically eye-fucking you."

Charlie scans the room and spots Lex. "Oh... the joys of being eye-fucked. I'll see you ladies later."

I don't give Presley an opportunity to say anything as I excuse us from Kate.

"Haden, what's wrong? Where are we going?"

Pulling her along, I weave my way in and out of the crowd until we are outside in the lobby. I look to my left, then to my right. There it is, my savior for tonight.

"Come with me."

Puzzled, she follows me until we are at the lobby desk. There is a bench located in front, and I tell her to take a seat.

"Wait here," I instruct.

At the counter, I pull the young busboy aside and whisper in his ear, "Key to the cloakroom."

I'm hoping he is smart enough to read between the lines since I'm holding out a hundred-dollar bill. At first, he watches the people behind me, then takes the cash. "All right. But you've got fifteen minutes, then my boss is back."

Fifteen minutes? I'll be done in five.

I make my way back to where she is sitting and grab her hand forcefully.

"Haden, for the love of God, what are you doing?" She scowls, trying to release her grip from mine.

With the key in my hand, we make our way to the cloakroom. I open the door and switch on the light, pushing her inside. Closing the door behind us, I don't give her time to ask any more ridiculous questions. I slam my mouth onto hers as I push her against the wall. She clutches onto my shirt and manages to pull away for just a split second.

"We can't do it in here. What about all the coats?" She panics.

"Fuck the coats. You gonna tease me all night in this white dress?"

"I wasn't teasing you, I—"

My mouth's back on hers. Our tongues are in a battle, feverishly fighting until she lets out a deep moan, the one that makes me rock hard, wanting to explode. I don't have much time, so I quickly flip her around, pushing her against the wall again, this time with her back to me until all I can see is that sweet ass of hers. I lift the corner of her dress, exposing one cheek. She's wearing those French laced panties that made me blow in my pants last time. Fuck. With her skin in full view, I grab my palm and slap her ass hard enough for her to let out a squeal.

"Guess you can't be quiet, huh?" I mock.

There are fancy coats hanging beside me, designer labels, probably. I grab the white one closest to me and pull the belt off the coat. It's soft and will do the job. I take the belt and place it over her head, then cover her mouth. Pulling it back around her head, I tie a knot, so it's firm but not too tight.

Moving her hair away from her ear, I lean in to whisper, "I'm going to fuck you now. It's going to be hard, and you're going to scream."

Her body is waiting, the goosebumps forming along her precious skin. I don't want to waste any more time, so I unzip my pants until my cock is free. I slide my fingers on her panties and feel how soaking wet she is. Fuck me. My woman is ready for me. No more waiting. Just fuck her hard and make her come.

I grab my cock, and just the slight touch causes me to moan. Pushing her panties aside, I slide myself in nice and hard, watching my girl arch her back as her knees begin to shake. I fucking love when her knees shake.

The tightness of her pussy feels like heaven. This is fucking torture. C'mon, your cock should be able to hold out for a couple more minutes.

Placing my hands on her shoulders, I push her against the wall, gripping tight as I continue to thrust into her. Sweat is dripping off my forehead and unable to control my thirst, I slam harder while I lower my hand against her beautiful clit. It's perfect, just the way I like it—pink and swollen.

I want it in my mouth.

I want everything right now.

But time is running out.

I can't be a complete jerk.

I loosen the belt enough for her to talk and let her dictate our happy ending by asking her how she wants me to make her come.

"My ass."

When your woman tells you to make her come by fucking her in the ass, you better pull your cock out of her pussy fast before she changes her mind. My cock is dripping with her juices. I rub the tip and shaft against her hole. Her moans escape, and I swiftly tighten the knot on the belt.

I always worried about how she would cope with my piercing, but I soon found out that it gave her mind-blowing orgasms. So anal, yeah, that's my favorite fucking style.

I slide my cock into her ass slowly. As soon as I'm fully in, her body gives me the green light. Her skin against mine is making this delicious sound, and as I lean in to rub her swollen clit again, my cock goes in deeper, and her body shakes instantly. Her wild screams are muffled, but hey, I'm not Superman. I don't have any superpower to stop what's about to happen.

I'm fucking seeing stars, exploding inside her as the sensations ravage every part of me. I let out a deep, rumbling groan, tightening my grip on her shoulders. I don't want to hurt her but the marks I've left, they are red.

Our heavy pants echo through the confined room, and with a gentle kiss on her shoulder, I ease my way out, slowly causing her to flinch. Untying the belt around her mouth, I throw it somewhere into the pile of coats as she turns around and adjusts her dress.

"You okay?" I ask while helping her with her dress.

With a wicked smile, she fixes my shirt and straightens my tie. "If that's the reaction I get out of you for wearing this dress, then I picked the right one for tonight."

I stare into her eyes with a stern face. "No, that's what happens when other men are trying to take what's mine."

"We talked about this. You've got to control your jealousy," she reminds me gently.

"No, you talked, and I refused to listen."

"And I told you there's nothing I can do to stop that from happening."

Oh, there is something she can do. I just need to get her home.

"Let's go home," I tell her, shutting down our disagreement.

On the taxi ride home, she quietly leans her head against my shoulder, trying to stay awake. Her eyes begin to droop. I've learned that when you make Presley orgasm, she gets knocked out quickly. It is cute, and many times I just have to go for round two with her half asleep.

The lights are off as we walk up the garden path and onto the porch. I fumble for my keys, nervously taking longer than usual.

"You want my keys?" She yawns.

I shake my head, finally getting the door open. She kicks off her shoes at the front door and bends to pick them up. God forbid you leave a pair of shoes at the front door. Miss OCD would have a heart attack.

"Come outside with me."

"Now?" She yawns again. "I love you, babe, but you took it out of me in the cloakroom. How about you wake me up in a couple of hours, and we'll go again?"

"I don't want you outside for that. I want to show you something," I answer, slightly anxious. "And I'll take you up on that offer of waking you up."

She lets out a tired laugh and follows me to the back porch. I flick the back switch that lights up the entire garden. I'm proud of this fucking garden. Who would have thought that Haden Cooper had a green thumb? This backyard was a complete dump when we moved in, and I turned it into something amazing. It isn't huge. Enough to have a small grass area for Masen and our dogs to run around in. The trees are trimmed, and because California has warm nights, I decorated with fairy lights so we could enjoy being outside longer.

"Have I told you how much I love what you've done with our yard?" She beams.

I lean across to kiss the side of her neck. "Yes. But you can tell me again."

She gently swats my arm as I walk her along the pebbled path to Masen's swing set.

"Stay right here. Actually, close your eyes."

"Okay," she says with a curious smile, sitting down on the swing.

Around the back corner, I have hidden the two surprises that terrify me to the point that I'm going to have an anxiety attack. I grab the small one first and walk back toward her, placing the box in her hands.

"What's this?"

"Open it."

She cautiously unties the pink bow and lifts the lid of the box. With a loud gasp, she says, "It's my Peaches 'n Cream Barbie! How did you get this?"

Her beautiful eyes light up as she admires this precious childhood memory.

"Your mom sent it to me. Now that you have a proper home, she thought you needed something that means a lot to you."

"It does mean a lot. My God... she was everything I wanted to be." She hugs the box and closes her eyes for a moment. Seeing how happy she is gives me the confidence to move forward with the next part of my plan.

"I was more of a GI Joe dude, but I'll take your word for

it." I smirk. "I've got one more surprise for you if you sit here and behave. Eyes closed."

"I'm on my best behavior." She salutes.

This time, I nervously walk behind the large oak tree. Taking deep breaths, I bend down, lift the surprise, and walk back toward the swing. Placing it on the ground before her, I position it carefully and then ask her to open her eyes.

The look on her face is priceless.

Shocked, she falls to her knees.

"How on earth did you get this here?"

"I have my ways." I grin.

Barely able to speak, she places her hand inside and touches all the small furniture. "This was my dream house. I played with this every day when I was a kid," she tells me. "I spent hours in my room pretending that when I grew up, I'd live happily ever after in this house. With my Ken."

I'm beginning to sweat. I don't fucking look like Ken? Who the hell is Ken anyway? Shit, it'll only take a few seconds until—

"What's this?" She leans into the bedroom of the house and pulls out a tiny black box. Even in the dark, I can see her hands shaking. Her eyes move toward mine, and all I can see is the woman I love, the woman I want to spend the rest of my life with.

"I love you, Presley Malone. I know I'm not perfect, and I know I can be a jerk sometimes... okay, a *lot* of the time. I may not be able to give you a dream house exactly like this, but I can give you all of this." I wave my hand around to show our house. "It's not pink, nor is it grand like your perfect home. But it's ours. And it will forever be the house where all our memories with our son began."

My beautiful Presley has tears streaming down her face.

I choke back my emotions, never expecting this moment to be so intense.

"I've never imagined it would be you that I wanted this life with. But I do. I want this rundown bungalow with the crazy ghost lingering in the spare room. I want to work alongside you, building our business and following our dreams. I want our family to be complete. I want everything I never knew I wanted. I can't promise you any more than to love you and Masen for the rest of my life."

I take the box from her hand and get down on one knee. She is at my level now, and with my heart thumping loud and my voice cracking under the pressure, I open the box and say the words I've been aching to say since the moment I realized I was in love with her.

"You said you wanted more..." I say, barely above a whisper. "I want our crazy life, and I want it with you by my side as my wife. Presley Malone, would you do me the honor of giving me more and marrying me?"

Her panda eyes are clouded with tears, and choking back her sobs, she nods her head as her face beams with happiness. "Yes," she says with exuberance. "I want everything you just offered me. But most importantly, I want you, Haden."

Now I'm shaking. This is the moment I've waited for, that I've doubted for so long and for no absolute fucking reason. She loves me. *Me!* End of fucking story.

I slide the ring onto her finger. It's perfect. After all, it belonged to my mom. My dad had this made for her. I barely made any changes. I want the ring on her finger to be something that represents eternal love.

"Haden... this ring is... I have no words." She continues to stare at it in awe.

"My dad gave it to my mom," I say quietly.

She looks back up at me and wraps her arms around me, playing with my hair as she plants a soft kiss on my lips.

"You've made me so happy, Mr. Cooper." She grins, then continues, "But 'more' doesn't mean skydiving naked, does it?"

I shake my head and laugh at her. This is why I fucking love her.

"And when you said crazy ghost in the spare room, you were joking, right?"

"Will you just shut up for a moment so I can kiss my soon-to-be wife?"

I kiss her deeply, not wanting to stop until the sun rises in the morning. But we're talking about Miss—soon to be *Mrs.*—Chatterbox. "You're still a jerk. You know that, right?"

I take her in my arms and lift her into the air, both of us laughing hysterically. She promised to be mine, sealed it with a fucking kiss. And it's right at this moment that it finally hits me. I never had anything to worry about. She was always going to be mine.

It has been a long journey, but fate just had a fucked-up way of getting us to our destination.

NEXT IN THE SERIES

THE MARRIAGE RIVAL

I entered his office asking about a new author we were about to offer a publishing deal, who wants to expand on their manuscript which would then move the book into another genre.

"I don't see what the problem is," I point out, pushing the manuscript toward him. "Yes, it's erotic romance, but we discussed this and how we would market it to the right audience."

His annoyingly chiseled jaw was resting in his palm, barely making eye contact with me, appearing completely uninterested. I know he's paying me back because I ignored him during *The Bachelor* finale last night.

"And I told you I don't think erotic romance can generate the interest we need to make this year's budget."

Haden's patronizing tone does nothing to curb the debate between us. How can a man so sexy be equally as frustrating at the same time? *You should be able to answer this in a heartbeat since you married him.*

"Is this about last night?"

His eyebrow twitches, a trait he does when he's about to lie. He thinks I can't read him, but I'm his wife—I have studied this man every day, countless hours lying in bed, just staring at his face while he sleeps. A beautiful face attached to multiple personalities depending on how many times he got blown during the week.

"Don't know what you're talking about. You were *busy* watching some program."

"I'm sorry." Apologizing, I lean forward and touch his hand only for him to retract—the stubborn ass wants to prove a point. Pulling back, I fold my arms to meet his stance. "I'm not having this argument again with you. So back to this author—"

"Fine. You show me numbers first, and I mean it. Don't offer a publishing deal until I see those figures on my desk. I don't care that we're married. I'm the boss here, and I make the final decision."

"Wow." Laughing, while shaking my head, I cross my arms in disbelief, again. "I thought we were partners in this?"

He raises his eyes to meet mine—a cold stare without a single blink and lips tight, no smile in sight. *Be strong, ignore the hazel spell he puts you under even in his jerky moments. Don't remember the words he whispered to you on your wedding day about being the air he needs to survive.*

"Yeah, well, partners also let them stick their dick inside them and get them off so..."

I knew it.

Fucking asshole.

"You know what?" I point my finger right at him, the anger raising my body temperature and changing my tone.

"You're a fucking jerk, Haden Cooper. Nothing, and I mean nothing, has changed about you. Sometimes, I wonder why I even married you."

"Well, honey, I knocked you up. You kinda had no choice."

OTHER BOOKS BY KAT T.MASEN

ABOUT THE AUTHOR

Born and bred in Sydney, Australia, **Kat T. Masen** is a mother to four crazy boys and wife to one sane husband. Growing up in a generation where social media and fancy gadgets didn't exist, she enjoyed reading from an early age and found herself immersed in these stories. After meeting friends on Twitter who loved to read as much as she did, her passion for writing began, and the friendships continued on despite the distance.

"I'm known to be crazy and humorous. Show me the most random picture of a dog in a wig, and I'll be laughing for days."

Printed in Great Britain
by Amazon